Susquehanna Legends

Collected in Central Pennsylvania

By Henry W. Shoemaker

"The world is but a great story book, containing myriads
of stories" – *Ivan Vronsky*

Published by Pantianos Classics

ISBN-13: 978-1-78987-639-0

First published in 1913

There is no grander view

Photo by H. W. Swope, Lock Haven, Penn

Contents

Introduction .... *v*

I. Teedyuscung's Face 8

II. The Man Who Loved a Fairy 13

III. In the Foothills 20

IV. Killy, Killy, Killy. 26

V. Eleve. 32

VI. Spiritually Dead 40

VII. One Hour of Happiness 45

VIII. The Play-Girl 52

IX. A Frontiersman's Diary 59

X. The Escape 64

XI. The Water Witch 69

XII. The Lonely Ghost 73

XIII. The Horse Beater 79

XIV. Queen Elizabeth 84

XV. The Headless Man 97

XVI. His Rival's Ghost 103

XVII. Canoe Place 109

XVIII. Golden Hour in the Camp 118

XIX. The Weathervanes 124

XX. Elphe Soden 129

XXI. The White Deer 137

Appendix A. **144**

Introduction

Although four volumes of Pennsylvania mountain legends collected by the undersigned have previously appeared, the compiler feels that unless he publishes all which seem to him to possess some intrinsic merit, his work is not ended. While as literary efforts they leave much to be desired, as pictures of the times old and new, and a glimpse of the folk-lore of the region they have some right of existence. The folk-lore of many foreign lands is a part of their literature and ideals, the history of the countries cannot be reckoned without it. In some countries it is collected under governmental patronage. England and Ireland are devoting much time to it of late, Scotland has always made it a part of her national story, France, Germany, Russia, Japan and India would lose much of the picturesqueness of their literature did it not exist.

To a certain extent the old legends of New England, of the South, and those springing up around the conquest of the West, have given a firm beginning to the folk-lore of the United States. In Pennsylvania a magnificent effort was made by the late Judge D. C. Henning, of Pottsville, but death claimed him before he had half completed the task for which, through deep human sympathy and literary skill, he was preeminently fitted.

In a comparatively small district, the Blue Mountain country in the Eastern part of the Commonwealth he acquired many beautiful and valuable legends. Some of these were identified by masters of folk-lore as survivals of myths old in the world's history. They showed the unchangeableness of human aspirations and belief.

In the Central part of Pennsylvania, where the present writer has confined his efforts, he has found a wide range of legendary lore. In fact so many stories have been told him that he has been at a loss to know which to try to preserve, which to discard.

By collecting in book form *most* of the ones which seemed best to him, he has hoped to carry out the responsibility in satisfactory manner.

It may be noted that there is a slight similarity between some of the tales. This shows their common origin. Out of a dozen which were brought to the Pennsylvania wilderness by the first settlers have grown a hundred versions, each distinctive to the locality where it is handed down. Even the legends which belong to the present generation have some subconscious tie with the past. The actors in them felt the welling of ancient emotions in their breasts and suited their lives and sorrows to the pathways of their ancestors.

Viewing the legends deeper, and selecting those which have no association with earlier traditions, they may point to some link with the infinite, with the unseen, towards which all thoughtful persons are struggling. To some primitive souls a peep behind the curtains of eternity may have been revealed, when denied to abler seekers.

It is in the forest that voices were first heard, linking us to the beyond. There is always a thrill in the mysterious, the inexplicable.

There are some of us who wish that every ghost story was true. These stories have the advantage of having been told to the writer as *truth;* they are not inventions, which while being read one can say "It is all made up." Their verification or the mental states which produced them can only be obtained by putting oneself into the place — and times — of the participants in these sombre episodes. Their gloom is their worst defect — as legends — if they could end happily like Post Wheeler's fascinating "Russian Wonder Tales," a much pleasanter impression would linger.

But the compiler has had no choice, he has had to set them forth exactly as he heard them, else they would cease to be legends and become mere hybrids between the facts and his imagination. He has, in every case, transcribed the stories as he heard them, except that, as stated in the introduction to his preceding volume, "Tales of the Bald Eagle Mountains," they have lost in native charm and weirdness in passing through his hands,

Some of the stories in this volume relate to the passions of every day life, and differ widely from those relating to ghosts or Indians. It is for that reason they are inserted, to vary the trend of the book, to prevent if possible its reading like a monograph.

A word regarding Central Pennsylvania itself. There is no lovelier land that tradition or folk-lore could associate itself. The most beautiful streams and rivers rise in its midst; impressive peaked and castellated mountains, the grandest forests cover much of its area; its farms are fertile, its climate extraordinarily good, its people sprightly, clever, good-hearted, the best product of a mixed stock. Charming novels have already been woven about it from the facile pens of Prof. E. S. Pattee, Nelson Lloyd, and J. P. Mowbray. The region has produced one poet of the first magnitude in James H. Campbell, an able philosopher in the late Jacob K. Huff.

While the compiler of these old legends feels that he might have done better with the rich vein uncovered, yet he is content in the knowledge that others will finish the work more artistically, more analytically, more patiently. He expects much from Warren S. Taylor, a young man who is working along original lines, in the same broad field. He can only express his heartfelt thanks to the newspapers, and to the public, who have been so kind to him in the past. He has found encouragement and praise, has kept at the work because of it. He feels certain that this beloved region will have a permanent place in "song and story," from all that has been written about it by so many capable hands, and hopes that his part will be to help incline other writers to delve deeply into these fields Elysian. He wishes to extend grateful appreciation to Mr. John H. Chatham, of McElhattan, Pa., his genial companion and dear friend on many trips into the wilds in search of the ancient traditions, who has given his time and sympathy so cheerfully to the subject.

HENRY W. SHOEMAKER.

At Sea,
March 9, 1913.

I. Teedyuscung's Face

(Story of Mahantango Mountain.)

When it was announced that Teedyuscung, the last great chief of the Lenni-Lenape, had been burned to death in his fishing-shanty at Nescopeck, by Mingoes, there was considerable difference of opinion concerning the motives prompting this cruel deed. Though Schela, a young squaw who was said to be deeply enamored of the aged chieftain, rushed through the flames and rescued the body, at the cost of frightful disfigurement to herself, there was not much left of what was once mortal of this high-minded redman. His exact sense of justice had shown him that no matter how altruistic had been the motives of William Penn, his disciples and descendants were decidedly harsh and grasping in their dealings with the Indian race. In public speeches he had pointed to the unfairness of many of the land purchases, especially the one known as the walking purchase.

In it there was stipulated that the proprietaries were to buy a strip of land bounded by as far as a man could walk between sunrise and sunset. Teedyuscung demonstrated that instead of this, fleet runners were engaged, one of them running so fast and so far that he dropped dead on the way. These speeches aroused the Indians, and also incited the jealousies of the Germans and Scotch-Irish who hated the Quakers for their oppressive real estate tactics.

The outspoken chieftain was considered a dangerous man by those high in the councils of the Proprietary party. He was first advised to move into the interior; he asked if his fishing camp at the foot of Mahantango Mountain, which looked out on that broad sweep of dead water which the colonists called the Irish Sea, would be satisfactory. He had actually arrived there pending an answer to his intimation, when orders came that he must move further on. The desire seemed to be to get him where his unanswerable allegations could not be heard or carried.

Or maybe there were more sinister motives. At any rate the old man gathered together his belongings and followed by a few faithful retainers, crossed the mountains to Nescopeck. The shallows there were a noted spawning-ground for shad, and salmon were abundant. He could fish the remainder of his days, even if he was denied the right to voice his people's wrongs.

His wife was dead, his sons and daughters dead or scattered; he would have been spiritually isolated but for the love of the beautiful Indian girl.

Her father Quiquingus had been one of the aged chief's most faithful henchmen, but like so many others had been murdered through the treachery of supposed friends among the whites. "I am too old to take another wife," the old chief remarked on numerous occasions, "but not too old to admire a fair young face." In this happy philosophy he whiled away a few autumn days, repairing his nets for the spring fishing, trapping wild pigeons in their southerly flight, and being loved by Schela. But this blissful retirement was short-lived.

A band of Mingo hunters, who professed the friendliest sentiments, appeared at the camp. They echoed Teedyuscung's plaint that the redmen were being forced further and further west, that they had been cheated out of their possessions. The Mingoes explained that they were on their way to the North Mountains to stalk a herd of elk; there were at least five hundred animals in it, they averred. There would be winter's meat for all, hides and the precious elks' teeth a-plenty. They extended a cordial invitation to Teedyuscung and his party to accompany them on the hunt. The old chief's eyes sparkled, "Twenty years ago I should have gone gladly, but now I am too old, too old for everything except to express my indignation at the wrongs done my race." But seeing the disappointed expression in the faces of several of his tribesmen he pointed to them, saying "Let my brave bodyguard go with you, they will acquit themselves well in the chase."

Ten stalwart braves were permitted to depart with the Mingoes. Two captains of unexcelled fidelity remained with their chief. They always slept with him in his lodge-house, a neatly constructed little building of red-birch logs. There were seven squaws, including the fair Schela, who of course remained. They occupied another, and similarly built lodge-house a few hundred yards from the royal structure. There was a partially completed stockade, eight feet high, which was to enclose the two houses, and continue down to the water's edge. The other braves who had gone with the Mingoes usually slept in tents made from buffalo or elk hides, or under lean-to's of boughs.

All went well until one windy night, less than a week after the departure of the elk hunters, when the giant pines shuddered and shook and moaned in the chilling blast. It was as if their misery almost assumed articulate form perhaps to warn the sleeping Indians of some presentiment of danger in their sylvan souls. In the distant forest depths came the boom of giant trees falling, as if in running with their ill tidings, they had been tripped by forces in league with unkind destiny.

Schela woke several times, rising up in her couch, and muttering to herself that she did not like the way in which the pines were talking. "A thousand years ago," she murmured, "the king of the Lenni-Lenape an ancestor of my dearest Teedyuscung, found a giant cave-bear chawing down Strobus, the great chief of the white pines; he killed the monster, and the great tree vowed gratitude, that his kind would forever warn the Lenni-Lenape of danger." She looked about her, in the gloom lay the six other squaws, sleeping soundly. It seemed a mistake to act on hasty impulse. She lay down again and tried to sleep. She reassured herself, too, because she did not hear the bark of Teedyuscung's Indian watchdogs. Three times she committed the foolish act of resisting the only true source of knowledge, intuition. Once she fell into a doze; she dreamed she saw a sunset which turned into a flame, and burned up all the world, her world. She rose up with a little cry — as she did so she thought she heard the crack of burning wood, it seemed as if she smelled smoke, it was fresher than the last vapors of the evening's campfires. But it was not until she saw the smoke drifting through the chinks of the lodge-house that she clambered to her feet, and ran out into the clearing. To her horror she found Teedyuseung's lodge-house in flames; the bark roof had already fallen in; it was like a blazing caldron. She did not hesitate for an instant, but plunged boldly through the red-hot fire. Under the flaming debris from the roof lay three bodies, frightfully charred. Digging among it, she quickly recognized the regal profile of Teedyuseung; he had a nose like the Grand Monarch, and oblivious of the fact that the fringe of her fawnskin garment was already ablaze, she dragged the corpse towards the doorway. Just as she was emerging the whole structure fell and she was stunned by dropping timbers. Luckily she fell outside, pushing the corpse ahead of her, as she went down. She was unconscious for a minute, during which time all her hair was burned off; one side of her face, which lay in the hot coals, was frightfully disfigured. She afterwards lost the sight of one eye.

The other squaws slept soundly all through the entire horrible catastrophe. They did not wake until Schela boxed their ears, and rolled them about to rouse them.

Dazed and grief-stricken they did all they could to minister to her in her sufferings. The heroic girl thought nothing of herself, but kept crying out for Teedyuscung to come back to life. "The lodge-house was set on fire by those Mingoes" she shouted in her delirium. Bear grease was smeared over her liberally, and she managed to get about. She laid the charred body of her aged lover, all wrapped in the best deer skins, in a cool place, under laurels and hemlocks, kissing the blackened forehead with an inhuman frenzy. Outside the stockade she found the watchdogs with their throats cut; her suspicions were confirmed. She searched the ruins of the royal lodge-house but could find little else beside the teeth of the incinerated henchmen. These she gathered together and placed in a small box made of canoe-birch bark. In her wounded condition she dare not travel to seek help, but it would have been a useless quest at best. All but a few Germans and Scotch-Irish would have rejoiced at the news of Teedyuscung's death; she could have gotten little sympathy or comfort.

Luckily the weather was cool and the remains of the dead king were in no danger of purification. Every night when she retired she looked up at the lofty pines. "Oh, why did I disregard your warning" was her plaint to them. But in the long run her earlier appearance on the scene would have availed but little. If the murderous Indians had seen her, they would have strangled her instantly; Teedyuscung would have been overcome by superior numbers and tomahawked instead of roasted to death in his lodge-house.

On the eighth night after the tragedy the elk hunters returned empty-handed. They had found no traces of elks in the particular part of the North Mountains visited. After hunting with the Mingoes for several days, the latter suggested that they separate and hunt in different directions. The Lenni-Lenape thought this a good idea, they could cover a wider territory thereby. They encountered no elks, became discouraged, returned to Nescopeck. And what a change met their eyes.

In the twilight they beheld the ruins of Teedyuscung's lodge-house, while Schela, terribly disfigured, hobbled out of her hut to meet them. There was wailing and lamentation all that night, as sonorous and weird as the portent of the pines the evening of the butchery. There was vengeance vowed "long and deep," vengeance as impotent as that of an injured soul against the infinite. The heart-broken braves all knelt beside the hideous remnant of their king, and kissed the still inviolate ridge of his regal nose. Only a woman who was beloved by a deceased monarch could kiss his brow or lips.

The braves suggested that the chieftain be buried before the ground became frozen. Schela was at first loathe to part with the beloved remains, but consented to an interment, to be made at his favorite fishing-ground at the foot of Mahantango Mountain. Decked out in freshly made war regalia, with masses of eagle feathers, elks' teeth, fisher's fur and deerskins, with his favorite musket tucked under his right arm, the dead king was laid in state in a pirogue. A flotilla manned by the braves and squaws surrounded the funeral barge as guard of honor, and started down the stream. The settlers along the banks came out and gazed in speechless curiosity. At Fort Augusta a party of frontier guards, who were off duty and hunting swans, fired at the sombre-looking fleet. One squaw was killed; the survivors considered themselves fortunate that they got into the reaches of the Irish Sea without more serious casualties. It was a country where Indians were thoroughly hated; they must be constantly reminded that they were not wanted.

It was a beautiful afternoon in Indian Summer when the canoe flotilla came to anchor at the foot of Mahantango Mountain. The place of debarkation was on the precise spot where Liverpool station, on the Northern Central Railway, now stands. The craft, containing the body, was lifted out of the water, and reverently carried up on the bank. Then the braves proceeded to the spot where the great chief's fishing-lodge had stood for so many years. It was a hundred yards east of the spring, which has been transformed into a well, with a pump-stock in it, and to-day furnishes sweet water to thirsty travellers. The fishing house had been torn away to the last vestige by the emissaries of the Quaker government when they had ordered Teedyuscung to "move on" only two months before.

Where the structure had stood a grave was now dug, and corpse, pirogue, finery, lowered into it. The trench was filled with heavy rocks, and a mound of rocks several feet high erected over it, to serve as a protection against the rapacity of wolves and mountain cats, and as a marker of the sacred spot.

When the interment was completed, just at sundown, the Indians joined in a weird song; it was more like a requiem for their race rather than the lament for an individual. Then all withdrew to the bank where their canoes were beached, and lit the customary campfires.

The sun had set clear and cold, every indication pointed to a calm night. The Indians were so depressed and desolate that they said little and ate little. All wrapped themselves in their blankets, and tried to forget themselves in sleep, as soon as the scanty repast was finished. During the night a wind arose, and a cold, wet rain fell by spells. Gradually the wind grew into a tempest of unprecedented fierceness; it was a storm such as raged the night that Oliver Cromwell died. The Indians were roused by the terrific gusts of wind and rain, by the lapping of huge waves against the shore; the Irish Sea, usually so benign, was like midocean in its fury. The roar of falling trees was bad enough, but presently huge rocks began to roll from the far, distant topmost heights of Mahantango Mountain.

The Indians hopped to their feet, only to huddle in the lea of the canoes, as the huge boulders tumbled by on every side, toppling into the river with heavy splashes. To-day many of these stones, rearing their black heads, like sea lions, are apparent at low water. The number and size of the falling rocks increased; it was as if the entire mountain was crumbling down. There was a hideous, ripping sound, as landslides carrying with them rocks, and trees as well as earth, scarred the whole face of the gigantic mountain in their irresistible course.

It seemed providential that the little body of Indians, huddled at the water's edge, were not wiped out of existence. But they were to be spared to witness a morning, with a transformation the nature of which they would never forget. As long as it was dark the tornado and the avalanche continued. With the first faint glow of dawn, the miracle was revealed. High up on the mountain, silhouetted against the sky, in the pink eastern light, they saw the aquiline face of Teedyuscung, the murdered chief of the Lenni-Lenape. During the hurricane, the inscrutable forces of nature had carved it, distinct and photographically correct to the smallest haughty detail, in the black, flint-like rock. Some overhanging branches above created the appearance of the warbonnet. Forgotten would be the knaves who slew him, or the mercenary wretches who instigated the crime, but the features of this noble redman were to be preserved forever and forever. Whether the face had appeared to inspire the remnant of the Lenni-Lenape to put into effect their threats of vengeance, or merely to preserve to future ages the kingly profile of this mighty chief, can never be told. The funeral band, when they saw it became rigid with terror, or perhaps reverence; they could not stir for hours, until the sun was high in the heavens, and was sparkling like diamonds on the Irish Sea. Then they suddenly relaxed, and burst into pitiful weeping.

The loving Schela led the way back to the canoes, and the mourners clambered aboard, and were soon paddling up-stream. At the mouth of Penn's

Creek they changed their plans, and started out this picturesque little river. It is said that they were the progenitors of the small but hardy band of Indians who defied the whites so long in Little Sugar Valley, until they were finally wiped out through treachery, at their stronghold in Colby's Gap.

II. The Man Who Loved a Fairy

(Story of Mt. Pipsisseway.)

The tradition of a hot boiling spring, and more particularly of a crystal cavern, somewhere on Mt. Pipsisseway near Quinn's Run, had always possessed a strange fascination for the young antiquarian.

The grave old man who told him about the wonders was too feeble to accompany him, the younger men too skeptical or unsympathetic to make desirable companions. Unaccompanied the young man had made several unsuccessful trips all over the summits and the irregular face of the giant mountain, "the mountain that the sun sets back of," but he was far from discouraged. The old man would draw rude diagrams with pencil on the backs of envelopes and enter into lengthy explanations, but the secret was well hidden. To many persons with whom he discussed the subject came the unfavorable suggestion that if the lumbermen "who had been all over the mountain" had failed to observe any cavern, there was small chance it existed.

But believing in the old pioneer, he continued his search manfully. But at length it seemed he had been all over the mountain; he was wasting time which might be spent to better advantage elsewhere. There were scores of ghost stories to be unravelled in the Seven Mountains. He was making himself ridiculous crawling as would a fly over the surface of some huge cake.

Late one afternoon on one of his searches, when he returned to the tree where he had tied his riding horse, he found that the animal had been prancing about until he had broken through a sink hole. Had he not been a sagacious animal, as *entire* horses usually are, he would have broken his legs in his inextricable position. The young man got the horse out of the hole, but in doing so noticed that there was a deep opening which resembled the mouth of a fissure or cave. He peered into the mouth of the chasm, there seemed to be plenty of room inside. Securely tieing his horse after watering him, he returned with his lantern and entered the aperture.

Once inside he was overjoyed, he had re-discovered the cave so often described to him by the old mountaineer. There was a sheer descent of nearly a hundred feet, down a wall of soft clay, at the bottom of which began a series of large chambers and labyrinths. He traveled about a quarter of a mile, sometimes crawling on his hands and knees through mud, smiling to himself as he recollected the saying "a person who is afraid to get dirty will only see half the world," other times standing erect, to marvel at chambers jewelled with stalactites, with vaulted roofs twenty feet high. While gazing in rapt admiration at some particularly exquisite formations, he felt as if somebody was near him. He looked around, noticing nothing; he looked down and saw a tiny little golden-haired girl. She had the proportions of a grown person, yet she wasn't taller than the average child of two years. He noticed that her features, which inclined a trifle to the aquiline, were very good, her eyes were large and blue, her complexion pink and white and free from blemishes of any kind. She wore what seemed to be a deep bine pansy as a cap, and her costume, with rather short skirt, was also of blue, of a queer woolen-like material. A white knitted collar alone relieved the color scheme. He was not conscious that his lips were moving, but he seemed to be speaking to her. He noticed that her lips moved, and while he understood clearly what she was saying, he could not hear her. "Can it be," it flashed through his mind, "that there is a roar of some subterranean torrent in this cavern, maybe the hot, boiling spring, that drowns the sound of the human voice!"

Then he was conscious that the little girl by his side was telling him that while he was human, he had some of the stuff of the gods or the immortals in him, and that she was only partly human, a fairy.

A fairy she let it be understood, is the descendant of a union between a beautiful ghost and a living man, oh, so long, long ago. Fairies then are ghosts with corporeal forms, mortals who live for an indefinite period. "As long as God lets us" they phrase it.

It was rather awkward for the young antiquarian, although he was by no means a tall man, to keep looking down on the little girl, or fairy. He seated himself on a broad stalagmite, and she curled up her little legs and sat down beside him. He noticed what tiny little bits of feet she had, that instead of shoes, they were tucked into dun-colored curled flowers, some kind of underground orchids. Then he noticed that she snuggled up close beside him as a tired baby often does, and placed one of her little hands in his. He started to squeeze it, but it was like holding an Easter lily too tightly. At this hand pressure the little fairy looked up in his face, with her appealing deep blue eyes. "She must be an Irish fairy" to have such eyes, he thought. But the little fairy could read his thoughts, and he understood that while the beginning of all fairies is Celtic, her race lived so long in South Germany, that even transplanted to the Susquehanna country, they were of Teutonic predictions. Then as the little creature snuggled closer, she gave him to understand she could change him, temporarily, into a person of her own size, though she could not make herself the size of a human being. He let himself be changed gladly; it was incongruous for him, a big, healthy youth, to try to embrace a little girl no bigger than a two-year old baby, when the mere holding her hand was like crushing an Easter lily. When he found himself the same size, she looked to him the most beautiful being he had ever seen. Was it so, or merely because of point of view, or their isolated propinquity?

"Hermionie, Cleise, Sylvania, what are they compared to this fair girl now so closely held in his arms?" Never had embrace seemed more vibrant, or kisses more enchanting. The first kiss initiated him into a new world of rapture; there was nothing in the old days on the earth above that could equal this. They seemed to have much in common.

The young man while unable to show any fairy origin, could boast of an ancestor who was a Gipsy. "A Gipsy loved a beautiful ghost, he had loved her in her lifetime, but he lost her, only to regain her at a waterfall, long afterwards, a frail and shrinking spirit." That explained why the antiquarian could enter into kinship with his pretty comrade of fairyland. As he had never felt such love in the actual, living world, and oft times for weary months at a stretch had never known any love at all, he resolved to make the most out of this rapturous opportunity.

In love, time and space are as nothing — the rest of the world stands still when two persons love. If he ever thought of the gallant black horse tethered far above, he *knew* he was oblivious; literally turned to stone for the time being. The touch of the little creature, once he had become her size, was the most entrancing he had ever felt; he knew now what meant all this prating about Paradise. Surely someone who has been there has returned — else how would those who have experienced its sensations in this life, know what it was like at all.

In the anguish of love, we forget the most pressing obligations, or postpone them, but not so when in the arms of a scion of the otherworld, who divines our motives, our needs.

How long the antiquarian would have continued that one long, exquisite embrace, that reminded so much of a mortal peering into the infinitive — probably forever. What was there in this joy that knew no ending, to call him to an outside world, where his constant battle was to be understood. He had found that a rapture growing keener and stronger each instant was the supreme answer to the riddle of existence. His spiritual faculties being merged in the spirit of the little girl, she detected his duty to others from the mass of half recognized motives which poured into her soul from his. Had she not been a fairy, a being mainly spiritual, all duty would have been lost, like in the carnal loves of life, when a man buries his thought of parents, wife, or children, in some engulfing lust.

His presence with the little girl could only last as long as she deemed right; happy is he who enjoys a spiritual love. All this time he could not recollect that he had said a word to her, unless the sound of his voice was drowned by the roar of a subterranean boiling stream. Probably several days of happy mental intercourse passed, yet the young antiquarian experienced no desire to return to the outer world. It was the little fairy who pressed her cool cheek against his and told him of his duty to others, of how he could not always remain with her in the cavern. He asked her, or imagined he asked her if she had no ties, but she said that only mortals owned such things as responsibilities. While he was kissing her soft red lips she changed him back to his natural size. He could scarcely realize that his armful of a minute before stood by his side, a dwarf, a midget. It was as if he had suddenly climbed to the top of a mountain and was looking down at her. But small as she now appeared to him, he still felt the thrill which she had sent through his flesh, he hated to leave her. "Isn't there," he intimated to her, "some way in which you can acquire the power to become my equal in size and come with me into the big world?" The little fairy hung her head, and tears came in the corners of her violet eyes. "I know of no power such as you wish. It is an immutable law that a mortal can take on the shape of immortality, but an immortal can never become flesh and blood."

The young man protested his deep love, his admiration for her witching beauty, the necessity of her companionship, his sorrow at leaving her.

The little fairy sank down on the stalagmite, and sobbed piteously.

"I did not know that an immortal could weep," he said, getting down on his knees to comfort her. "Immortality is only eternal tears. We may live *almost* forever, yet we cannot be like the living people we love most."

"Oh, what can I do to assuage your grief" he implored. "You say I must fulfill my duty to others and return to the big world, and yet you cry when I start to go."

"If you must know the real cause of my tears, it is because I want you to take me with you into the big world; I was afraid to ask you."

At this the young man was silent. Sitting down, he put his great sinewy arm around the little mite. When he pressed her near to him, she felt soft and spongy as a cuttle-fish. She was not made of flesh and blood; she could not endure in his world.

"You could not go to the big world, you would be a lost soul.

"And I am a lost soul here without you," she replied, sobbing more piteously.

In his heart the young man knew he did not want to take her with him because she was so tiny, her very inconspicuousness would make her conspicuous. And worst of all, he was painfully aware that she knew these secret thoughts, and they were the cause of her great grief. "You would be unhappy in my world" he continued. "You, with your cosmic wisdom surely know that."

"Yes, yes, I do," she answered between sobs, "but even an immortal can have pride wounded, and be unreasonable."

The young man pondered a moment. "I have told you of my deep love, your vast wisdom tells you that it is correct, and that I would return often to see you, will not that suffice?"

"Of course it will" she faltered, "anything to be with you, but if you loved me as I wanted to be loved, you would take and make me a part of your own world."

"But you would feel out of place, and pine for your crystal caves. There is a vast difference between this sweet calm life of love, and the turmoil of the physical life."

"It is the curse put on every fairy, that sooner or later she must love a mortal, and he crushed by him, like you mash a rose in your hand. It is a part of destiny, I may as well submit to mine," she said, bracing herself, and pulling down the tails of her coat, very like a mortal woman.

"I will return often, and we can be happy together; this cave will know that joy we hear so much of, the joy that passeth all understanding. Mind you, dearest, I do not want to go now, I am only leaving because you have reminded me of duties in the outer world. I even realize I have been harsh with my poor horse, he must be frantic now for food and drink."

"Oh, no," said the little fairy, wiping her eyes with a bunch of white moss, "I thought of all that when we entered. I made a signal to some of my fairy comrades who have kept your noble steed fed and amused while we loved in this labyrinth."

"But is there a fairy lover in your life, too?" said the young man, his curiosity piqued.

"There was, but once a fairy has loved a mortal, she has neither eyes nor sex for one of her own kind. She is forever afterwards sexless to fairy lovers. By loving a mortal, paradoxically, she becomes adamant to immortal wooers."

The young man mused to himself why was there no way that the torture of former lovers could be thus effectively effaced in the real world. It was an added reason why he would like to remain in the cave. The big world had no charms for him except for his family ties, the art, literature, music, beauty it contained. The dark wilderness he always felt was his natural home, his logical home some day. It is in the wilderness that new impressions are being constantly created; in the cities men and women are kept going by artificial impressions, which in reality are old impressions rendered over and over again. The city is the phonograph of human experience. But the sense of love and duty, which he had forgotten in the crystal cave, was with him again, departure was inevitable. In this cave he had experienced pangs of emotion such as he never dreamed existed, he could imagine what had been the pleasures of the spiritual inhabitants of the woods and grottoes in the far distant "mythological times." He understood that a time would come when our humanity will be semi-intelligible, or myths, to the inhabitants of this earth in ages far in the measureless future. He resolved to return often to the cave, he had striven to discover it for several years, now it had been found, and contained a hidden joy far beyond his anticipations. There would now be an excuse for visiting the mountains more vital that the dream-sensations of the dim cloud-wreathed peaks, the haze above the waterfalls, the sunsets of cerise, the caverns and Indian burial grounds.

All the gamut of his existence, its whys and wherefores, was rising before him, as he bade goodbye to his celestial companion. When he kissed the tiny lips there was a bitterness, a difference about it, he could not quite grasp, but the memory of past joys atoned for the lessened emotion of the present. He pulled a bracelet from his pocket, he had intended it for another girl, he slipped

The Mouth of Moshannon

it over her hand, it fell off, it was much too large; it could almost have encircled her waist. He left the little fairy in the Gothic-domed chamber with its "bush-hammered" walls; she did not attempt to follow him to the entrance. For some unknown reason, he did not ask her. He merely waved goodbye.

Through the muddy labyrinths he crawled, he trod the mammoth apartments, he clambered up the steep face of the vault, slipping and sliding in the mucky clay. The air seemed oppressively warm when he got outside. It was early afternoon, he judged, just about the kind of a dull cloudy, wintry day he had entered the cave. Had this all been a dream, caused by some marasmus vapors, or subterranean gases, or had he been in the cavern for days or perhaps weeks! He examined the horse critically. It seemed to be in no need of food or drink. He recollected how the little fairy had told him of having given instructions to have the animal attended to in his absence. Could this be true? If he had been underground for several days or a week, how came it that he felt neither thirst nor hunger. Had he really met a fairy at all, and been changed to her size, and made love to her, or was the whole affair a product of a too acute imagination? He recollected how beautiful she was, and there were moments when he actually regretted his refusal to take her with him. He might keep her hidden in his home, and she could change him to her size; in the stillness of the night be his spiritual comrade to end his loneliness.

As he pondered over these perplexing fancies, the brave little horse was cantering along the mountain road, bringing him nearer and nearer to town. By the time he had reached the old closed bridge which spanned the river, he wished he was back in the cave, and blamed himself without measure.

When he reached the livery barn in the alley back of the court-house, a dwarf ran out to take his horse. He had seen this dwarf for several years, they called him "Jeff" after a comic artist's nightmare of broken-down respectability, but he had never noticed him closely before. How odd and incongruous the creature seemed on this occasion, with his huge head, the bald skull, the short "banty" legs. Why should a hideous dwarf take his horse just when he was thinking about a beautiful little midget who dwelt in a cave, whose ancestors had been brought in a woolsack from South Germany? The sight of the diminutive hostler suddenly upset his illusion; the horrible thought crossed his mind that if he had brought the dear little thing with him she would have appeared just as odd. And as quickly he blamed himself for the cowardice of his soul. Just as some persons shun being seen on the streets with the shabby or unattractive, he would leave the unhappy fairy in her cave, because her size would make her look odd in polite society. He pulled himself together, and asked the dwarf the date. The little man pointed to it on a huge calendar, sent to the livery boys by a popular newspaper. He looked at it, he had been in the cave for three days and nights! What had happened in the world since then, while he had been "out of space, out of time."

A feeling of terrible depression settled down on him, he did not care to look at the newspapers in the stable office. He hurried from the barn, without saying goodnight to the dwarf. At the end of the alley, he turned about, and returned, to give a liberal tip to him. Why was he so unjust to the little people this day! He reached the railroad station fifteen minutes ahead of train time. There was plenty of time to meditate.

The evening was dark and cloudy, and becoming bitterly cold. The clouds, vast and soot colored, relieved only by a heart-shaped patch of cerise light, hung heavy over the summits of Mt. Pipsisseway. Two dead white pines, girdled to prevent their shading a trackman's garden patch, at the side of the station, rattled and shook like skeletons in the night wind. Gaunt and lonely, the young man paced up and down the station platform. His thoughts, revealing the innate selfishness of his soul, were consuming him. Though he had loved the little fairy, and expected all her love far in the depths of the crystal cave, he could not permit her to come into his world where she could be seen. He wanted his own pleasure, his sense of the beautiful gratified secretly, but *her* wishes meant nothing. Should he conquer this worldly pride and go back to the mountain in a week and bring her away, to a world where if she could not be happy, at least he could try to make her happy. Pressing his lips tightly together, as was his wont when dismayed, he let meaner views prevail, and vowed he would never return to the cave. "I cannot see her unhappy by refusing to take her with me; I cannot ask her love, yet secretly feel ashamed for people to see her. I am giving up a spiritual joy the like I will never experience again, yet as a memory three days of bliss are as good as three years."

His thoughts and reasonings were brought to a stop by hearing the whistle of the approaching train. As the head-light, half veiled in yellow smoke, emerged from the gloom, he took one last look at the western sky. The heart-shaped patch of cerise light had descended, and spread like a mantle of brocade over the tree-dotted, expansive summits of Mt. Pipsisseway.

III. In the Foothills

(A Story of the Upper Mahantango.)

"A panther is harder to kill than a snake," said old man Rau. "A snake will die when the sun goes down, but not so with the panther, there are certain moonlight nights when he'll always come to life again."

We were sitting around the old hunter's stove, one cold November morning, listening to his varied reminiscences of three quarters of a century of wilderness life. His little cabin was situated on a picturesque neck of woods which jutted into the upper Mahantango Creek, not far from its headwaters, in the foothills of Firestone Mountains.

20

Old Rau was of the tall gaunt type of mountaineer; in the army his comrades had dubbed him Longstreet because of his resemblance to that famous Confederate general. He had, despite his eighty years, a fine head of white hair, as wiry as Andrew Jackson's, and a flowing white beard of patriarchal proportions. As he grew older, and he reverted to the habit of his childhood and spoke only the picturesque Pennsylvania German tongue, it was harder than formerly for a stranger to glean many of his interesting experiences. But on this occasion, stimulated by the presence of one of his old army friends, he was particularly communicative, especially about his favorite panther story.

"I guess you have heard lots of stories about spook panthers" he went on. "There was one over to the White Mountains back of Troxelville, about ten or eleven years ago; it was the last of a dozen such tales I have heard in my time. We old settlers thought we'd never rid this country of panthers; after tracking them and killing them, they always insisted in coming back in the form of ghosts. These ghosts were harder to get rid of than the live ones. From Joe Knepp, Johnny Swartzell and other old hunters I hear tell of panthers being seen in these mountains at the present time, but I strongly believe they are only the ghosts of the varmints we killed fifty years ago. But now as I grow older I realize that the panther wasn't so much of a varmint after all. He had his place in the order of nature. When we had plenty of panthers we had lots of deer, and wild turkeys, and pheasants, and wild pigeons. With no panthers all we have left is a lot of degenerate, half-tame game, not worth a real hunter's time to go out and shoot. Panthers ate all the sickly and weakly game, animals and birds; they left alive only the healthy active stock, there was no danger of a pestilence wiping out a whole species as there is now.

"In those days there was no pheasant disease. We old hunters didn't know this until too late, it took us over half a century to get through our heads what 'the survival of the fittest' meant. When we did, gone were the panthers, and everything else with them. Well, I mustn't get off my story of this one particular spook panther.

"Old Jake Sansom killed him the year I came back from the war, in '64; he caught him in the act of entering his chicken house, and shot him through the hind-quarters. The animal backed out as best he could, and then young Dave Sansom shot him in the head. Old Jake was an antic sort of chap; he liked fun and nonsense. He took the hide, which was a very fine one and very dark in color — it is an odd fact but the panthers got darker the further south they were found; the Adirondack panthers were yellow, the Potter County panthers almost red, a Florida panther was nearly black — and stuffed it with straw and leaves. We did not know of taxidermists or glass eyes in those days, so the completed job looked rather uncanny with the great gaping, empty eye sockets. It measured a good nine feet from nose to tip of tail, and you can picture a pretty good-sized brute from that. After stuffing the hide, the old man set it up on the ridge-pole of his wood-house, which fronted on

21

the public road leading to Centreville. You can be sure it was the nine days' wonder of the neighborhood. With the jaws propped open to show the enormous teeth, for it was a male specimen, and with the tail high in the air, it looked almost as natural as life, and a hundred times more ugly.

"Horses and even mules shied at it as they were driven past; dogs barked at it and tried to climb upon the shed. Children on their way to school would not go by it unless accompanied by grown persons. As a result the little folks forsook the highroad and made a path along Penn's Creek, but even there they complained of being scared by the playfulness of fish-otters.

"But one unfortunate feature of the case was that the dead panther had a mate. These animals are very devoted to one another, and if one is killed, the survivor rarely ever mates again. The female in this instance kept coming to the edge of the dense brush at the rear of old Jake's garden, and howling piti-fully on moonlight nights. Doubtless she was disturbed by the distorted effi-gy of her late lord and master so immovable on the ridge-pole. Some of the more timid neighbors when they met Jake at church urged him to take the carcass down. 'It keeps the mate in the neighborhood, and our women and children can't have any peace at nights.' But Jake would only shake his hairy head and grin. 'I'm going to get that mate some day, I'm only waiting for her to get real bold and show herself, then there will be two stuffed panthers on the roof of my woodshed.'

"He had killed the male about the first week in April, but summer was now on the wane, and he hadn't gotten a shot at the mate. A number of the boys who lived on adjoining farms were hoping she might elude him. If she did, they planned a big hunt with dogs, as soon as harvesting was over. As it was, the dogs, whenever they were loosed, would take up the panther's scent, and make the nights horrible with their yelping. This was another reason why old Jake was urged to dispense with his stuffed panther. But the old man was obdurate, he was going to clean out the whole panther tribe, if given his way.

"In August there was camp-meeting in Emerick's Woods, near New Berlin, and the number of rigs and travelers on horseback who passed the stuffed panther was well up in the hundreds. All stopped to look at it, for many of the younger people had never seen a panther, they were getting scarce outside the Seven Mountains. The night of the second Sunday of 'camp,' old Jake and his boys went off in their carryall, leaving his wife and their crippled daugh-ter to mind the house. The old lady wasn't afraid; she said she could shoot straighter than her husband any time. It was a weird sort of night. Across the face of the full moon flew clouds shaped like panthers with long tails. There were awful gusts of wind, which rattled the loose palings on the front yard fence, and sent the gate swinging to and fro. Bits of the garden, and the or-chard, and the creek were bathed in a peculiar silvery light, other places it was impenetrably dark.

"'It is the kind of night we always saw the ghost of the Indian chief at the spring, when I was a girl,' the old woman was telling her crippled daughter.

"'Don't tell me that, mother, it frightens me,' said the girl, who was lying on a black hair-cloth lounge, and she pulled the patchwork quilt over her head.

"'Don't be foolish,' said her mother, 'ghosts are as much a part of this life as our daily meals, we cannot reckon without them.'

"'But I don't like to hear about ghosts,' replied the girl, 'I've always felt sort of uneasy ever since daddy set up that ugly stuffed panther on the wood-shed.'

"'My lands, girl,' said the mother, 'that's what I call an ornament. There never were any folks stopped to admire our premises until your father put that critter up there! They never noticed our hollyhocks and judas-bushes.

As she was talking, the patter of dogs' feet was heard on the kitchen porch. On the conclusion of her speech, she opened the door. Outside she found six huge hounds running about wagging their heavy tails. Two were her husband's, which he had liberated before leaving for campmeeting, and four strangers. 'Shoo, there,' she shouted to them, striking at them with a broom handle. The animals ran off the porch, and across the yard, where they began barking at the stuffed panther on the woodshed. The old woman looked out the kitchen window, and watched them as they leaped wildly against the sides of the shed, in their efforts to get at the uncanny monster. Her eyes rested on the panther itself, and she recoiled in horror.

"'What ails you mother? I thought you never got afraid,' said the crippled girl sarcastically.

"'I never do, but I didn't like the way that panther looked. That queer moonlight we have to-night was shining in his eye-sockets, giving him an expression that would have scared the devil himself.' While she spoke the yelping of the hounds became fiercer than ever, it seemed as if they would demolish the shed in their fury.

"'No wonder the neighbors complain they can't sleep,' broke in the girl again, 'between that she panther in the brush and the infernal carrying-on of the hounds, they might as well cut up their beds for kindling.'

"'I guess if we can sleep through it, they can too,' said the old woman as she sank into her rocking chair by the window. The scene apparently had a fascination for her that she could not resist. For several moments she watched the frantic, howling dogs, without uttering a word. Then, as the noise increased, she gave forth a piercing scream, ran to the door, and turned the key in the lock. Peering out the window again, she called to her daughter, 'The hounds are up on the roof, they are pulling down the panther! My but your father will lick them when he gets back.' The poor crippled girl could stand the excitement no longer. Forgetting her fear and disabilities, she dragged herself to the window, holding on to her mother with a vice-like grip. Just as she reached the window, she saw panther and dogs come rolling off the shed-roof into the yard. In an instant the angry brutes were on top of the carcass, intent on tearing it to pieces.

"In the midst of their fury, something that seemed like a shadow cast by one of the long, panther-like clouds which sailed across the moon, swept across the smooth-kept yard from the garden fence. It was no shadow, it was the drab form of the stuffed panther's mate. Taking the hounds completely off their guard, she plunged in among them, throwing them right and left. Yells of anger were succeeded by miserable, treble catterwauls of pain. Torn, bleeding, and helpless, the dogs lay about like sheep at a barbecue. With the last enemy dispatched, the pantheress sprang lightly to the side of the stuffed effigy of her mate. Pausing, she turned her uplifted head, and ground her teeth in defiance at the terror-stricken women in the cottage window. A narrow streak of moonlight fell on her at that moment, setting out in bold relief the slim, lithe lines of her form. She began licking the eyeless sockets of the effigy, crying softly. She rolled it over from side to side, sometimes standing it on four feet, where it looked ready to take on life and speed with her to the pine forests. Suddenly she emitted a piercing yell, and fixing her fangs tightly in the nape of the neck of the carcass she started to drag it across the yard. When she reached the garden fence she had considerable difficulty lifting it over, every muscle and sinew of her frame twitching with nervous anxiety.

"Why the women remained at the window during all these gruesome transactions they could not tell themselves. It was a sight that try as they might, they would never be able to forget.

"It was just as the devoted pantheress, with her ghastly burden was disappearing across the palings on the far side of the garden that rifle in hand I appeared on the scene. At that time I was living about half a mile up the road from the Sansom farm, nearer Centreville. My wife wasn't feeling well, so I hadn't gone to campmeeting that night. I had gone to bed early, but could not sleep for the hellish yelping of the hounds. It got so loud, and kept up so long that I came to the conclusion that the female panther was abroad, and I meant to put a stop to her career if possible. I was on the highroad already when I heard the pantheress let out that awful yell, but hurrying my utmost, I reached the spot too late. I pushed through the gate, and across the yard, only to see the heap of dying hounds on the grass near the woodshed. Mammy Sansom saw me coming, and ran out in the yard to meet me. She told the story as well as she could, but I could see she was half dead with terror. We inspected the dogs, perceiving that every one was fatally torn. A couple died as we were examining them, and I put the remainder out of their misery with the butt end of by rifle. I turned to Mammy Sansom saying, 'I believe I can get that pantheress to-night.'

"I had purposely left my dogs at home, they were only little rabbit hounds, as I didn't want them to get mixed up in the melee. As I was going out the front gate, on my way home after them, I heard the sound of an approaching wagon. I waited a few minutes and was rewarded by the appearance of old Sansom and his boys. Quickly as I could I explained what had happened. They ran into the yard, to where the dead hounds were lying, while I jumped into the carryall and drove up the road. I put my little dogs on leash, and threw them into the wagon. When I returned to Sansom's house, I found the old man and the boys waiting for me with their rifles. I put the dogs on the scent, and soon there was a lively tongueing.

"The trail led us through the garden, across a pasture lot, and into the brushwood which stretched for half a mile to the beginning of the vast pine forest that covered the slopes of Jack's Mountains. At the edge of the original pines was a spring. For some reason it had always been called the 'panther spring,' now it was to become doubly entitled to the name. The moon, which had been temporarily obscured by long, slim clouds, like panthers, suddenly shed its rays upon the spring. What had seemed to us like a couple of old rotting, moss covered logs, turned out to be two huge crouching panthers, drinking. The smaller of the two raised its head at our approach, looked around, grinding its teeth at us. Then it quickly caught the other animal by the nape of the neck. When the larger brute wheeled, we noticed it had very imperfect eyes. We recognized it as the animated form of the stuffed carcass which for six months had ornamented the ridge-pole of old Jake's woodshed.

I have heard of 'buck-fever' hundreds of times, but I had never experienced it myself until I saw those two devilish panthers. I could not raise my rifle to my shoulder. My dogs, usually eager to attack anything big or little, cowered at my feet, shivering and shaking. Jake and his boys were rigid with fright. We stood there in the moonlight, as if transfixed by a spell. I who had faced death at Malvern Hill and Chancellorsville allowed the two brutes to get away from me, without turning a finger to prevent. The weak-eyed panther moved more slowly than his mate, he was evidently being re-animated gradually. With any amount of sense, we could have shot them both, but it wasn't to be. When they were safely out of reach we 'woke up.'

"All three of us commenced swearing at ourselves. Once I thought I'd whip my dogs, but I figured out if a thinking, reasoning human being like myself hadn't backbone enough to shoot, how could a pair of little rabbit hounds he expected to begin the attack. Sheepishly we all turned about and returned to our homes. It was the most unsatisfactory, cowardly night of our lives. After that experience we never discussed the subject, let alone went on another panther hunt.

"The story of the panther being torn off the shed roof, and the mate coming to its rescue and killing the hounds became widespread, but our part of the adventure we 'kept dark.' Many of the neighbors complained about two panthers being heard in the brush at night, when the moon was full, for they always wailed most mournfully when the silver orb was at its zenith. 'That cursed panther of Jake Sansom's has brought two around to avenge it, instead of one,' was their common talk. But Jake, his boys and myself knew that the second panther was none other than the revivified form of the stuffed effigy from the woodshed."

IV. Killy, Killy, Killy.

(Story of Peter's Mountain.)

High up among the crags of Peter's Mountain, crags as vivid and pink in color as his breast, circled the sparrow hawk, shrilly calling "Killy, killy, killy," that cloudless autumn morning. As he flew hither and thither uttering his mournful cries, the clear blue of his wings seemed a part of the sun enamelled sky.

Suddenly dropping into a field, close to the foot of the gigantic mountain, he began his day's task of ridding the arable soil of animal and insect pests. Never molesting a game bird, or a song bird, and disdaining poultry or pigeons, he seemed a model of propriety, the product of a long line of righteous ancestors, incapable of sin since the Unseen Power pressed them from a block of the blue ether.

But in reality the sparrow hawk is the descendant of an arch-criminal and his virtuous and industrious deeds are in the nature of expiation, atonement. He seems so happy in his life of doing good, that it might be best to leave unexplained the sad story of his ancestry. Intelligent to a degree, he is said like Horus, the hawk-god of the Egyptians, to be of human origin.

The story is a sad one, and dates to that period of the world before exact species were fully determined upon, when the Gods and even some men possessed the power to turn one creature into another. To-day some of us through evil influences take on the nature of beasts, but not the outward forms to any great extent; but in those days body and spirit could be changed without a moment's warning.

It was not long after the period when there were monsters, and giants, and dragons, when mountains were in the building, and trees and flowers changed color over night. Unhappy was he who received a heavy sentence in those days, for Nature was settling into an unalterable state, from which prayer, and penance, and rigid life could constitute no appeal from the fiat.

Among those in closest harmony with the eternal powers, was a young redman named Keow. He was wise beyond his years and generation, and as such was revered by all who knew him. Constant thought had probably retarded his physical development, as he was several inches shorter than the average of his race. His head was large, with a broad expansive brow which overhung his deep-set, dark grey eyes. His nose was sharp, and inclined to the aquiline, his lips full but always held tightly compressed. According to the standards already set up by the women of his time, he was not considered good looking. The fair sex preferred men closer adhering to the type of the race; they must be taller in the first place, their heads less strongly marked and not so "characteristic."

Keow, with all his worldly wisdom, became aware of these points of differentiation about the time when he first craved the society of the opposite sex.

He instinctively felt that he was not favored as were other young men of his age; perhaps he was clumsy or tactless in manner, perhaps worse. He looked at his reflected image in pools, critically, carefully. The story was revealed there; his countenance was not of the conventional type, and Nature dearly loves to perpetuate a type and not a lot of diverse individuals. This sense of difference made him shy and taciturn.

He admired women as much as before, but mostly from a distance. There were many he saw whom he might have loved, might possibly have made supremely happy, but he shrank from them, especially after the faintest sign of indifference. His physical desires and artistic nature, even though he was a savage, made him hunger for the company of women even more than any who conformed to the type of the race. There was always a burning longing in his soul, that no material triumphs might quench.

As a warrior he soon won renown, in the chase he was unequalled, in divination and healing he was the leader of his day. And yet the pain in his heart found no surcease.

There was a pestilence raging among the tribes who wintered about the foot of Peter's Mountain. Keow, whose home was far off among the headwaters of the Susquehanna, was sent for, and responded cheerfully. Over the snow and ice he came on primitive snow-shoes made of beech hark. It was an easy task for him to cure the disease; had he been sent for sooner there need not have been any deaths. As it was he cured all the survivors, and changed wholesale mourning into rejoicing. Keow was modest, and liked no demonstrations for what he considered a simple duty.

The grateful Indians wished to banquet him, and even hold animal drives in his honor, but he firmly declined all such suggestions.

There was only one reward he would liked to have had, and that could have been his for the asking. This reward was the noble maiden Killy, daughter of the chieftain Wulitehasu. If he had intimated his wish the maiden would have been his, but the wise man preferred to secure her love before desiring to possess her. He naturally became acquainted with her, and she seemed to delight in his society. She praised the great work he had done, and asked many questions concerning his past life, his aspirations, his ideals. She seemed to recognize in him a superior soul. She accompanied him on several strolls in the forest, and when he went out on days when the snow was crusted to slay the moose and elk. She was a beautiful picture, on her snow shoes, this princess of the primitive redmen. Hers was a slight, supple form, with all the straight lines and willowy grace that comes at eighteen. Her hair was inclined to curl, her grey eyes were full and sincere, her cheek-bones accentuated the broadness of her face. The nose was not too large, hut it was in perfect proportion with the broadness of her cheeks.

Never, thought Keow, had the unseen powers devised such a perfect being. If only by some chance she might take a deep liking to him! On one occasion in the depths of the forest she had allowed him to hold her in his arms; she had coyly nodded her head when he asked her if she cared for him. He dared not ask her if she loved him, he was too self-deprecatory for that.

That night, around the camp-fire, his temporary elation was chilled. There was a young Indian, tall and slim, of the conventional type named Pawal-lessit, one of the many who had been cured of the plague. He had not regained his strength and sat moodily before the fire. Killy had come and seated herself beside him, and was striving to entertain him, when Keow, after a final visit to his most backward patients, emerged into the fire-lit circle. From a respectful distance he eyed the pair, the girl displaying genuine interest, the convalescent passively interested. Keow hung his head, and leaned against a tree.

Back of the rest of the throng about the fire sat an old squaw named Nepe. Formerly she had been the doctoress of the tribe, but her failure to cope with the deadly pestilence had caused her to fall into disgrace. She had been rudely crowded away from the fire by many persons much younger than herself, but she made no complaint. She had noticed Keow when he came out of the forest, how he quailed when he saw the beautiful Killy entertaining the young convalescent. Despite the fact that the young doctor had supplanted her, she felt for him as one kindred big soul always does for another. She dragged herself to her feet and hobbled over to the tree where Keow was leaning. He bowed respectfully as she approached, which was more than most young redmen would do. "Brother wise man," she whispered, "I divine that you feel sad because somebody apparently shows interest in another. Mind it not, it is only her womanly sympathy towards an afflicted being."

Keow shook his head. "Mother wise woman," he answered, "I lack your years and experience, but something within the springs of my spirit tells me that all is not well, that she is fond of that sick man."

In her heart old Nepe knew that he was correct, and turned away without attempting to argue the question.

Keow cast a few more wistful glances at the young couple by the fireside, and then slunk back into the blackness of the forest, to his cold bed under a lean-to of hemlock boughs. He lay awake and tossed and shivered all night. He, who could literally bring folks back from the grave was powerless to alleviate the sickness of his own soul. The next morning he met Killy; she was just as fascinating, just as winsome as ever; there were no signs from her that there was anyone else in her life except the young wise man. She remarked that he was unusually quiet. "That is because my work ended, I must return to my home among the headwaters."

Killy urged him to remain longer, but if not, to return in the Spring.

"I will be back when the redbud is in blossom, if you will be true to me."

"I will be true to you," said Killy deliberately, looking at him squarely with her full grey eyes. He took her two plump hands in his, he reached over, they were soon in the elysium of a prolonged kiss. Yet amid the rapture of that kiss he felt the presence of Pawallessit, the convalescent. It made him feel sick to his stomach, else he could have continued the kiss longer.

Killy divining the continued sadness in his face, repeated voluntarily, "Rest assured I will be true to you."

"But do you really love me, Killy?" he entreated.

"I do, I do," she protested, and buried her curly head on his breast.

Were his fears of the night before unfounded? It surely looked that way. But at the same time his instinct had never been incorrect in the past, was he to have proof of fallibility now? His homeward journey was tedious and unhappy. There were thaws which made him discard his beech-bark shoes, and heavy, disheartening rains. When he reached the home encampment, in the mountains of what is now Clearfield County, he was sick at heart, morose, disgruntled.

He had a close friend, young Netami, who while not a wise man, had apperceptive powers. The youth questioned Keow about his apparent sorrow, at a time when he should be all elation at his wonderful cure of the plague victims at Peter's Mountain. Keow confided to him the story of his great love for Killy, of his doubts and fears. Netami put his arms around him saying, "Be brave, good friend, at this very moment she is eating her heart out for you."

Keow shook his head, just as he had to the old wise woman Nepe, when she tried to console him. It was a prehistoric version of the doubts and fears of the young Bonaparte in Egypt concerning his beloved Josephine back in France. A wise man is a barometer as to love, he can force himself to have faith outwardly, but the spirit never wrong, is in open rebellion.

"No, she is not true to me," said Keow sadly, "I know I failed to impress her as much as Pawallessit, the convalescent, for he was closer to the type of the race."

"Your distinctions are too fine," interposed Netami, "men of individuality win a deeper and more lasting love than the commoner sort." This Keow knew was correct, but the man of marked personality can only be appreciated by a woman of equal individuality, and this Killy was not, though he would not admit it.

"She is untrue to me; with all my boundless love I have failed; what good is it to try to excel in life when the appreciation of the one most desired is denied."

Netami concluded that the strain of treating so many sick persons had unnerved the young wise man; a little rest and he would look on life with a fresh eye. During the remaining months of winter, despite his intuitive misgivings, Keow still cherished the hope of returning to the Peter's Mountain country, and making the fair Killy his wife. He might have urged the ceremony to have occurred before he left for home, but he wanted her to have plenty of time to consider the matter; his love was too unselfish to be successful in this material world. His soul was continually telling him that something was amiss; this strengthened his reserve force for the final catastrophe.

"Peter's Steps," Lockport, Penn'a

At length when the condition of the twigs indicated that by the time he got into the vicinity of Peter's Mountain, the scarlet tints of the redbud would be apparent in the bare, bleak woodlands, Keow started on his love quest.

After several days' travel he camped near the mouth of the Scootac to lay in a stock of fresh meat. Elks were abundant, a few choice saddles of their delicious meat might not be out of place in his canoe. When returning from his first day's hunt, which had been successful, he was accosted by an Indian whose face seemed familiar. "I am named Eemhoanis," said the stranger, "one of the grateful warriors whom you cured of plague." Keow shook him warmly by the hand, and bade him take half of his pack of elk meat.

"I am out on a hunt myself," continued the stranger, "to revive myself after all the excitement and feasting incidental to the grand marriage of our princess Killy to Pawallessit."

Keow, on hearing this, gave way to a severe chill, his teeth chattered, his knees knocked together in nervous excitement. "A fine state of affairs while the redbud is getting ready to blossom," he muttered under his breath. He gave most of his provisions to Eemhoanis, with reckless generosity, and next morning resumed his journey down the river.

Near the Peter's Mountain settlements he ran across several Indians whom he knew, and from them learned the details of the duplicitous marriage. He was told that the newly-wedded pair were living in a commodious lodge-house at the base of the mountain, not far from the river. When he came to within a mile of this abode, he moored his canoe to the roots of a giant red-birch, and started to pay a visit to the pair. He was unarmed, but with his un-bounded courage could have faced Machtando the Evil One himself. Perhaps some charm or incantation was leading him along a preconceived course.

It was at the base of the big mountain that he suddenly came face to face with Pawallessit. The bridegroom's countenance glowed with an evil show of triumph when he saw Keow; evidently Killy, with a woman's boastfulness, had told the entire story of the wise man's love. Keow eyed him savagely, and raised his hands, with the fingers widespread above his head, making several passes in imitation of a bird flying. As he did so Pawallessit's face took on the visage of a bird, the skull sloped back, the nose grew sharper; the arms took on pinions, his whole back sprouted dark blue feathers, his breast a salmon pink down. His feet became claws, a great forked tail of stiff brown feathers developed. The transformation came so quickly, he seemed unable to grasp its meaning at first. It was only when he began to reduce in size, it was probably the shrivelling of his evil soul that pained him, he uttered a series of piercing cries of "Killy, Killy, Killy." With the last he rose up in the air, with a wheeling, unsteady flight which seemed involuntary. High in the air he repeated his plaintive shrieks of "Killy, Killy, Killy."

Keow laughed with satisfaction when he saw that his revenge was accomplished. As he laughed, far up among the dizzy heights of the mountain came the echoes of "Killy, Killy, Killy." Then the young wise man continued his walk to the bridal lodge-house. Killy was at home when he appeared, cooking supper on an open hearth, outside the hut. She jumped up quickly when she saw her old lover; some instinct told her trouble was nigh. "Where's Pawallessit, what have you done to him?" she shrieked.

Keow stood before her, silent, with arms folded, a little god of retribution. Above their heads, out of the silence came the weird cries of "Killy, Killy, Killy." The affrighted bride cast her eyes upwards, high in the blue dome circled a strange bird, with unsteady, ill-balanced flight. "I guess that is Pawallessit up there who is calling you," said Keow, grinding his teeth with cruel emphasis. "Killy, Killy, Killy," drifted the cries; this time nearer, the bird showed up more distinctly.

Killy looked at it more carefully; she seemed to identify it positively, for she dropped her earthen pot, and started to run pell mell for the river. "My lover, my lover, my Pawallessit," she wailed. She tripped several times on the wild grapevines, but Keow, close at her heels, stood her on her feet after each fall. Yet he did not attempt to impede her course. At the brink of the water, she ran out on the roots of a big over-hanging red-birch; it happened to be the one to which Keow's canoe was moored. Headlong she plunged into the deep current, disappeared, then rose to the surface. Already the wise man was in his canoe, and with strong arms dragged her limp, unconscious body into the craft. Then he quickly paddled into midstream, and started, with his frail burden, for the east. Aloft in the sky, a blue bird with a pink breast, was tumbling about on wings that did not seem to suit, crying out in treble fury, "Killy, Killy, Killy."

V. Eleve.

(Story of Old Jersey Shore.)

Eleye could not win at Guttenberg, though Lemon Shaaber worked harder over him than any horse he had ever trained. The best he was able to do was finish second twice to Inferno, owned by a fellow Berks Countian, Billy Stufflet. In the early spring Lemon moved Eleve to Gloucester, where there was less class to the fields. On one occasion the old horse ran third to Marty B., but thereafter always finished in the ruck. When the county fair circuit opened in Pennsylvania he decided to pocket his pride and try for smaller honors. He had the utmost faith in his horse, as he always ran true, and never sulked or acted badly at the post.

In his day Eleve was considered a handicap horse, when he was owned by a New York millionaire of international repute. But when he ceased to be a bread-winner, he was ruthlessly consigned to a weeding-out sale in the paddock at Morris Park, where Lemon Shaaber laid out his last dollar to get him. He had backed him place both times when he finished second to Inferno, which paid the oats bill, and the shipping charges to Gloucester. The move to the fair circuit was most fortuitous; it opened with a victory at Kutztown, over Fleetwood Boy, and continued in an unbroken sequence of an even dozen wins at half as many tracks.

Not a defeat marred the old campaigner's season, and in bets and purses his owner gathered in a goodly store. After his fifth or sixth victory, Eleve began to be noticed by the crowd, which made him prick up his ears, to take on a few peculiarities, as became a champion. He was a horse of striking individuality, which was accentuated by his being entire. To look at him it was no wonder that when he sold for five thousand dollars as a yearling, Billy Easton, the auctioneer at Tattersall's predicted that he had a brilliant career before him, remarking from the box "He has size and substance, and above all, that sure sign of a good and game racehorse, a Roman nose."

As an aged horse he stood sixteen-one hands, heavily boned, and high-shouldered, with a ponderous head like a camel. His rough coat, in color between a dark chestnut and a bay, further gave the impression of a "ship of the desert." He was bang-tailed, according to the custom of the day, and always ran with his mane and foretop tied up in ribbons.

At the close of the season, a Lancaster hotelkeeper offered Lemon a thousand dollars cash for him, it is said. But the shrewd Berks Countian replied in the slang of that time, "not for a mint, no sir-ee." There were some who suggested that Lemon try another winter at Guttenberg, that Eleve's form had improved; it was *that* and not the inferior fields which caused his successes on the fair circuit. Lemon didn't seem sure of this either, but wisely refrained from the lure of Guttenberg.

The old horse, his victories, his owner, created much talk in the country and even in the Philadelphia papers. This was in the good old days, over twenty years ago, when the horse was king, before he had to divide attention first with the bicycle, and later with the automobile.

Lemon Shaaber used to be in the milk business, so he turned the horse over to his former partner, who still maintained the route, and who was his neighbor in old Shillington.

Whether the horse had ever been put in harness before wasn't definitely known, but at any rate he took to his task like the proverbial duck to water. Above all, he would stand without hitching, even for an hour at a stretch, while his driver sat and warmed his hands before the stove and gossiped with some pretty housewife in her kitchen. In the spring he was put back into training, his muscles like iron, his courage and speed not having deteriorated like they would have if he had spent the winter ruminating in a box-stall.

During the previous season he had met only one real antagonist on the fair circuit. This animal was named Iceberg, but his name was always spelled on the programs "Iceburg." Like Eleve, he was an aged entire horse, and a former ornament of the Guttenberg merry-go-round. Iceberg was a big, fine looking horse, a very dark or mahogany bay, with two white hind feet. He was not as well bred an animal as Eleve, but he was more beautifully turned.

Six times he finished second to Lemon Shaaber's horse at the county fair races, hut he could not get his nose in front, trying might and main.

Eleve made the first start of his second season on the "little" tracks at Point Breeze, on Memorial Day. Iceberg was in the field of nine that opposed him. It was a half mile and repeat affair, the general form of running races those days. In both heats Eleve made a show of his field, except Iceberg, although he beat his old-time rival handily each brush by a length. This try-out stamped the last year's champion as invincible for the races to come.

Every four or five years such a horse appears out of the "nowhere" on the county fair tracks, sweeping everything, until he is raced to death.

But Lemon Shaaber was too shrewd a horseman to kill his bread-winner; his policy was to race him fewer times, and keep him on the turf longer.

There was an early race meet at Lancaster, some time in June, where Eleve won both running races in a gallop. He was in the Susquehanna country, at the mid-summer fair at Milton, on July 4th and 5th, and cleaned up a score of antagonists in two races, showing his heels twice to his persistent competitor, Iceberg. After this the fairs commenced in earnest, and there was a chance to race every week, if so desired. Eleve swept through the circuit with a chain of unbroken successes. His triumphal course, instead of scaring away opponents, brought them from every conceivable nook and corner. There were New England cracks, New York cracks, Western and Southern cracks. Fields of such size were never known before on the circuit. There was so much horse talk in those days that it is hard to say if Eleve's victories created the banner year of the county fairs, but for some reason the gate receipts were tremendous.

With each easy win the old horse became surer of himself, his idiosyncrasies aggrandized.

Chief among these was his hatred of unsexed horses. When he was lined up at the starting post between two entires, or two mares, he was as docile as a house-cat, but if between two geldings, or even to be near one gelding, was the signal for him to begin an outbreak of biting, kicking and rearing. Several times geldings were bumped into him at the start, in the hopes he would forget his paces, and break behind the bunch, but he was too old a bird to be caught by such a handful of chaff. He had one eye for his antipathies, another eye for a quick start. As he never lost a stride at the post, Lemon Shaaber rather indulged his likes than interfered with them. Since he had come on the fair circuit no horse had defeated him; by the last week in September he had won his twelfth race of his second season. This made a total of twenty-four wins out of a like number of starts in two years. He had run twenty times during the fall and winter previous to joining the fairs, being twice on two occasions, and once third.

His thirteenth start of the second season was to be made at the picturesque old course at Jersey Shore, which overlooked the "dreamy Susquehanna," and the "sleeping panther mountain" over by Antes Gap. It was the most characteristic, old fashioned fair on the entire circuit; it maintained its delicious flavor of a simpler and happier day to the last. In fact the fair where Eleve figured was the last ever held on the historic grounds. Racing had been held there almost uninterruptedly, even through the days early in the nineteenth century, when anti-racing associations were formed all through Central Pennsylvania. To those who have seen the old engraving of the course, with a swarm of trotters and runners in full cry swinging around the track, further explanation is unnecessary. It had been the abode of clean, healthful sport for two-thirds of a century, the inspiration to thousands of growing boys and girls. With grand old trees, its river view, its mountains in the distance, the richly cultivated hills behind, it was one of nature's paradises. In addition to the annual autumn fairs, political and patriotic meetings were held there, as well as barbecues and reunions.

Once a "tame" buffalo, which had become too vicious to suit his owner, who shipped him east from Kansas, a shivering little calf several years before, was slaughtered and roasted to the edification of a concourse of Democrats. There had been thrilling balloon ascensions, parachute exhibitions, shooting matches, coursing meets, every kind of amusement conceivable, at the old track. It was an early home of running racing, many of the old-time long distance races having ended by the horses going once around the course before finishing.

And here was to be the scene of another of Eleve's performances. Entries came in thick and fast, when it was given out he was to be on hand. There was a very showy gelding named Robert E. Lee, racing on the Southern chain of fairs which included Winchester, Frederick, Hagerstown, York and Bedford. He had won seventeen consecutive victories, principally in Virginia, that season. His greatest achievement had been his beating in straight heats, on July 4th of that year, the famous Neptune, afterwards bought for ten thousand dollars by Mr. Jack Barnard, of Long Island. It is claimed that twelve to fifteen thousand people witnessed that race, and there was a howl of disgust when the popular idol went down to defeat.

Robert E. Lee's owners, Kline and Gilroy, were gradually working him North, hut the dates did not suit for him to encounter old Eleve until fair-week at Jersey Shore. Those who had seen the two horses were loathe to express an opinion of their respective merits. "They are so different" was the explanation most commonly heard. Robert E. Lee was a small animal, standing little over fifteen hands, a blood bay. He was finely made, delicately coated. After a race his eyes became bloodshot, his veins stood out all over him like whipcord. Sensitive to a degree, it required great tact to handle him. Encouraged and patted, he would gladly do all that was expected of him. He was a son of old Bothwell, who became famous as the actual sire of Mr. William C. Hayes' great steeplechaser, The Rat, although in race programs he was given as by Wooster.

A few years ago The Rat, at an advanced age, was shot, and fed to a pack of fox-hounds, on a farm near Warrenton, Virginia. Such are the tragedies of even the most industrious of race horses.

In contrast to Robert E. Lee, Eleve was like some great ungainly camel. One succeeded by brute force and courage, the other by smartness and slickness. The heavy, ponderous Eleve could never be called smart or slick. The meeting of two horses with unbeaten records was the prevailing topic of conversation among the horsemen. "Robert E. Lee will win" said one man, "if Eleve doesn't maul him to pieces at the post."

"Too bad he's a gelding," said another sorrowfully. But Robert E. Lee was quick and spry, there was no danger that Eleve could hurt him, even if he felt so disposed.

It was all in the days of good sportmanship, when even Judges, bankers, priests and clergymen owned race horses, before there was such a thing as "crooked" starts, or "fixed" races, so the contest would go down to history on its merits solely. The distance was the usual half mile and repeat. Mile and a quarter "dashes" were unknown. It is well they were, for nothing is worse than to see three or four patched up cripples crawling two or three times around a half mile track.

All the jockeys and stable boys in those days were negroes which added another picturesque feature to the sport. Now there are said to be more colored stable hands at Maisons Laffitte than at Pimlico. And colored jockeys are a thing of the past. Gone are "Pike" Barnes, "Monk" Overton, Perkins, Clayton, Hamilton, Simms! There was a love of glory which the modern turf does not possess. This was due to the prevalence of gentlemen owners; when they withdrew their support, the bottom dropped out of the fair circuit, the sport was only preserved in the name.

Lemon Shaaber, though a poor man, had imbibed the prevailing spirit, and was a thorough sportsman. Likewise were the owners of Robert E. Lee. But an old farmer, with a long yellow chin-beard, who was discussing horse-racing outside the stables remarked, "To my notion the only true sportsmen are those who race entire horses. If I was rich enough to afford a racing stable I'd want the genuine article in horses, no poor, weakly, unsexed things for me."

One of the trainers nudged his companion, whispering, "Why old Jake McCloskey could buy the whole fairgrounds, and every horse on it, if he wanted." Nowadays it is any kind of horse that can win by fair means or foul, the glory of the turf has had its sunset, in this country.

There were so many visitors to the course, just to see the horses, that it seemed as if the crowd which assembled on the opening day of the fair could be no larger. It was a good old-fashioned fair, with plenty of big hogs and steers, and pumpkins, ears of corn, and apples, innocent side shows, good humor everywhere. There were no gambling games, no indecent catch-pennies, no rudeness, no disorder. It was typical of the country we live in "before the Gringo came." The chief attraction was the races, harness and running events being given every day.

Old Orange Chief was in his prime as a trotter, and when he won the 2:25 trot the opening day, in straight heats, the crowd went wild with enthusiasm. The weather was perfect, clear and crisp, so enticing that farmers drove in from Nauvoo, White Pine, New Bergen, Loganton, Wolf's Store, and Rebersburg, without their horses feeling the exertion. The trees on the mountain tops, and a few of the maples and gums in the lowlands near the track were already tinted red and orange, the autumn breezes swayed the woodbine which clustered about the pale, listless elms. It was weather when folks were thankful to be alive, when all the world seemed kind, and full of joy.

The first day's running race a big field was won by old Creole, who afterwards spent his declining days between the shafts of a traveling market wagon. Neither Eleve, Robert E. Lee, or Iceberg started. They were kept in their boxes for the two hundred dollar purse which was "hung up" for the second day. There was a big crowd which overflowed from the grandstands on the lawns and infields to witness the "real" contest. Even a few Indians from the North were present. The day was the finest of the season, Nature was continuing her wiles to make everybody happy.

When the horses came out of their stables, it was noticed that there were only three starters, Eleve, Robert E. Lee and Iceberg. The other five that had entered failed to appear. But they would have been superfluous. As they paraded to the post, Eleve marched very close to Robert E. Lee, hut did not make the slightest attempt to savage him. The old horse moved with majestic tread; several times he tossed his massive head at the applause of the spectators. "There's Eleve, there's Eleve, there's Eleve," came in a rippling chorus all along the rail. The old champion felt another triumph would be his, he regarded his foes as beneath notice.

Robert E. Lee was in fine form, carrying a trifle more flesh, he was less attenuated than usual.

Iceberg, superb horse that he was, brought up the rear of the procession, on conformation he was the winner in this trio. Soon they lined up at the starting post, and the starters with their red flags ran about the track as animated as hull-fighters. The three horses stood as closely together as if harnessed to an invisible vehicle. Eleve made no move to molest Robert E. Lee, but stood motionless, with his fine head held high. It was an easy task for the starter. A flash of the flag, and the three animals were "off."

Robert E. Lee was quickest in motion, his jockey, a coal-black lad styled "Young Isaac Murphy," being first to interpret the starter's signal. Past the stand they raced, with the gelding's nose showing in front. Shine, the black boy on Eleve, and Sailor, the rider of color on Iceberg, were playing their whips unnecessarily, it seemed. "Wait till they hit the back-stretch, we'll make Robert E. Lee surrender" yelled an old soldier on the stand, who was evidently one of Eleve's partisans. Around the first turn they swept, with

Robert E. Lee still having a shade the best of it. Those who had good eyes said that his nose was still in front all along the backstretch. Rounding the far turn it looked as if Eleve was not to make a runaway race of it after all. Shine was keeping up his whipping tactics, but his mount was racing for everything that was in him. Iceberg lost ground at this turn, and open daylight separated him from his two competitors. Coming down the stretch there were terrific yells to Eleve and Shine to come on and win. The jockey plied his whip like a demon, but he could not gain the inch which differentiated him from Robert E. Lee. Nearer and nearer the wire they came, "Young Isaac Murphy" bending far over his horse's neck, holding him straight, and whispering encouragement in his ears. Shine, on Eleve, plied his whip so fast that the whalebone was lost in a yellow cloud. A hush fell over the crowd so intense that the bang, bang, bang of the hoof-beats, and the panting of the breaths sounded clear and distinct in the autumnal air.

There was a wild look in Eleve's big agate eyes, a terrific tension to chest and quarters, he was running the race of his life. The wire was reached, the pair rushed under it. From various points of view it was difficult to tell which horse won, but the majority ruled, including the judges, that Robert E. Lee was victor.

The momentum of the straining horses was so great that they could not be eased until after they had run an eighth of a mile further. By the time they returned to the judges' box, the names were hoisted, "Robert E. Lee, 1; Eleve, 2; Iceberg, 3; time, 50 seconds." There wasn't much applause when the winning jockey dismounted. A big crowd congregated about Eleve, to see if anything was wrong with him, to hear if his rider had any excuses to offer. He had none; "Eleve's nebber run a better race" he faltered, tears running down his dusky cheeks.

The old horse seemed to take his defeat philosophically; he was led quietly back to his stable to be cooled off, with the victor trotting a couple of lengths in front of him. He made no outbreak, maybe he thought that he had won. Three or four harness heats were contested before the bugle blew to call out the runners for their next essay. "Eleve's going to win this time" came the gossip from the stables, "he's cooled out grand."

The sun was beginning to decline behind Mt. Pipsisseway, half hidden by its footstool of hills, and there was a decided chilliness to the atmosphere. A boy who peddled a few early roasted chestnuts sold out in five minutes; coffee and hot cakes were in great demand. The crowd was too cold to take any interest in the antics of Andy Waggoner, who was on hand to amuse young and old. Eliza Huntley was closing up her tintype tent for the night. But no one made a move to leave the track; they must see Eleve turn the tables on his Southern rival.

The old horse moved splendidly; perhaps the first heat had merely limbered him up. Robert E. Lee looked thin and drawn, yet full of "go;" Iceberg, magnificent embodiment of horseflesh, cantered along like a king's hunter in an old sporting print. At the post, the three horses behaved admirably. Like in the first heat, they were off at the first drop of the flag. To the dismay of Eleve's admirers, however, "Young Isaac Murphy" managed to get a shade the best of this start for Robert E. Lee. Shine, who had ridden Eleve in most of his races, could hardly be criticized, except on the ground that "Murphy" was a cleverer rider. But the advantage was so slight, it could be readily overcome. Past the stand they thundered, with Robert E. Lee's nose in front. Around the turn they swung; Iceberg was running stronger this heat, and was even with his competitors. As they turned into the backstretch a mighty shout went up from the spectators, for Eleve, with a dynamic effort had forged to the front. There was open space between him and Robert E. Lee and Iceberg, who were running abreast. Up to this time Shine had wisely refrained from using his whip; the old horse ran better on his own courage than when goaded. When the colored boy, looking over his shoulder, realized he was ahead, he forgot himself in a delirious desire to win, and began beating the old horse unmercifully. Despite this Eleve kept his lead until he turned into the homestretch, when Robert E. Lee and Iceberg crept upon him, and the three raced down the track, so close together that, to use a racing expression, "a blanket would have covered them." A hundred yards from the wire Robert E. Lee's nose showed in front; "Young Isaac Murphy" kept it in front, and he flashed under the wire, a winner by a head. There was no cheering when the result "Robert E. Lee, 1; Eleve, 2; Iceberg, 3; time, 50 seconds," was announced. The horses were wheeled about and brought to the judges' stand.

Eleve's big head was hanging; Shine holding on to the lines with both fists, his whip tucked under one arm, was trying to keep him from stumbling over himself. But he made no attempt to bite at Robert E. Lee, as side by side, they were unsaddled. Once, as they were being led into the stabling enclosure, he made a grab at his successful rival, but Shine, who was at his head, struck him with his elbow, and made him desist. "He's dead tired," remarked a score of onlookers as he was being cooled off. Never had he seemed so listless, as with head drooping, he was led around the improvised cooling ring. When he was put in his box, and locked in for the night, he showed no desire to eat. He lay down on the straw, and moaned audibly. If anyone had heard him it would have sounded like an attack of colic. When the old horse got up half an hour later, he began scanning the stall, as best he could in the gloom. Hanging from the rafters were two nooses of stout rope, used to swing the brooms and forks out of the horses' way. With a deep sigh the old campaigner raised himself on his hind feet and stuck his head through one of these. Then he let himself drop. It was high enough to allow his forefeet to dangle several inches above the floor. His weight drew the noose tight; he bore down on it with all his weight. The stall began to swirl in circles like myriad race courses; streaks of light as varied as jockey colors flashed before his eyes; there was a roar like the hoof-beats of a cavalcade, then all became darkness, silence.

Ernest Renan has said that animals are not automatons, that they have the intelligence of little children; there are many children who kill themselves after some bitter disappointment. Next morning when Lemon Shaaber and Shine opened the box they found the faithful horse dead. "Didn't I tell you, boss," said Shine, tearfully, "dat de ole feller 'ud nebber get over bein' beaten by a geldin'?"

VI. Spiritually Dead

(Story of Penn's Creek.)

So you're collecting the old legends of the Indians, and witches, and ghost stories" said the English miner, "how would you like to hear a real experience, one that happened to me right here in this town?"

"I told him that I would be more than delighted to have him tell his story." The Englishman, who had been standing near the bench where I was sitting at the stove in the Golden Swan, seated himself beside me, and commenced his narrative. All the others in the big room were so busy discussing the pros and cons of Col. Roosevelt, it was a night or two before election, that the ghost story might go unlistened to and undisturbed, as far as the rest were concerned.

"It was twenty years ago coming All Souls' night," he began, "and before I was married. I had been talking politics in the store-room here, just as I was to-night, it was during the Cleveland-Harrison campaign, until it got so late I decided to spend the night at the hotel rather than climb the ridge. It was a few minutes before midnight when I turned in, and as I had put through a busy day, was asleep the minute my head touched the pillow. My last thoughts on losing consciousness were about Grover Cleveland, so what happened came from none of my waking impressions.

"I never believed in ghosts, though I'd heard hundreds of ghost stories since moving into these mountains. My parents were good Christian people, they sometimes admitted there were such things as ghosts; yet I grew up a scoffer. The bed was comfortable, and I would have undoubtedly slept until daybreak had I not felt a cold draught blowing on my face. I awoke with a start, with the impulse to jump out and shut the window.

"As I rose up in bed I saw a dark figure standing between the bed and the window. There was a faint reflection of some kind in the room, where it came from I couldn't tell. By this I perceived that the dark figure was that of an Indian, dressed in full warrior's regalia. He had a fine aquiline face, it was turned so that I could watch the magnificent lines of the profile.

"For some reason I wasn't frightened the least bit; especially as the figure remained so rigid I ought to have no cause for alarm. I must have gazed on the motionless form for at least ten minutes; meanwhile its outlines were becoming more distinct. It seemed, in some way, to be drawing its vital forces out of me. The longer I looked the more it materialized, as the spiritualists say. At last, when it became the most solid looking Indian one could wish for, it turned towards me. Even then I did not become frightened; I actually liked the dark, melancholy countenance of the savage. It made no attempt to come nearer to me, but I could see the muscles of the mouth twitch as if it wanted to speak. It must have been a severe effort, for several minutes elapsed before I fancied I heard anything. In my dazed condition it seemed to me that the Indian spoke to me in English. If he didn't I don't see how I could have understood him, unless he talked Pennsylvania German, of which language I knew a few words, even before I had married a Dutch wife, and brought up eight German speaking children.

"At any rate the Indian spoke to me, calling me by my name, Jack Carter, to my great surprise. When he uttered my name, and I nodded my head as much as to say that I was the man, the Indian smiled on me like a long lost brother. 'My good friend' he said, as well as I can recollect, 'I have always heard that you are an honorable and accommodating young man.' At this compliment, I unconsciously nodded my head. 'I want you to do a great favor for me to-night, you will never regret it.' I nodded my head again, and began crawling out of the warm bed. 'That is right' said the Indian, 'I want you to go with me on the ridge.'

"Now as I had put up for the night at the Golden Swan to avoid the climb up the ridge, it seemed odd that this was the very thing that the Indian wanted me to do. I had gone to bed in my underclothes, so it did not take long to dress. I was in a hurry to put on my clothes for another reason, the room was terribly cold; it was zero weather in November. The unearthly light which enabled me to see the Indian, gave me the ability to dress without striking a match.

"When I had my overcoat on, the Indian, without saying another word, turned the key in my door, and opened it. He led the way into the hall, and down the creaking staircase, I following like a sheep. I was afraid I would wake the landlord, and he'd shoot me for a house-breaker, but I got downstairs unnoticed. In the entry, the Indian unlocked the front door, and we were out on the porch, in the frosty night air. I recall just as we stepped outside I saw a big rabbit scamper across the wide street in the direction of the old court-house. That was an unusual spectacle; but this was All Souls' night when rabbits are said to feast on the bodies in the grave-yards. 'Oh for a shotgun' I said to myself.

The Indian quietly took the key from the door, locked it on the outside, and handed it to me. I remember sticking it in one of the pockets of my overcoat. He led the way off the porch, around the corner, and up the street past the old Academy in the direction of the ridge. There was no moon, but the frosty night clarified the atmosphere almost to the extent of making it luminous. I fancied I even saw Jack's Mountain. The Indian was an excellent pathfinder; he seemed to know the smoothest paths, for never once did I stumble.

41

At a farmhouse just beyond the school, a couple of shepherd dogs ran along the inside of the fence barking at us. If it hadn't been for that incident I might have begun to fancy this was all a dream. When we began climbing the ridge I knew it was no dream; my heavy coat made me pant; I would have stopped for breath but I did not want to lag behind my guide. Once or twice he looked around to see how I was progressing. He seemed to notice my distress, as he remarked that we would soon come to a fine spring where we would stop and I could drink plenty of good water. His consideration made me begin to feel that he wasn't a ghost after all, but a belated masquerader from Halloween just a few nights past. I was amazed at my docility in his hands. Around the old town many called me behind my back "a bull-headed Englishman," which meant that I was stubborn and not tractable.

Finally we reached the spring; I had been there many times before when out huckleberrying or hunting. It was the biggest spring on the ridge. Someone years before had walled up the sides, there was a bowl of water three feet square, and of like depth, water deliciously sweet and cool. The reason it tasted so good was that a mammoth hemlock which grew directly above the spring had been left standing. It shaded the water; its roots, according to the old belief, sweetened it. There was a large gourd on one of the retaining walls, so I drank my fill.

Then I sat down cold as it was, on the wall, but did not seem to feel it. The Indian took a seat opposite and began eyeing me intently. "Kind friend," he said, "you have come this far without complaining. I know I have asked a great deal of you, but the real favor will now be explained." Then he sat silent for a moment or two, still gazing at me. I liked his big, strong, open face; there was something about him that would have made me lay down my life for him.

"Come with me," he resumed, rising to his feet. I obeyed mechanically, and he began climbing the ridge above the spring. We had gone about a hundred yards over the loose rocks, when he halted. "See there," he said, pointing to a circular mound of jagged lichen-covered rocks, overgrown with evergreen ferns, "under that hillock is buried all that is mortal of my sweetheart, who was the beautiful Pilurvi, a niece of Shickalemy. I am Nisuque, a chieftain of the Lenni-Lenape. The fair maid and I met, we loved, we became betrothed, and then alas, she suddenly died. I always believed she was poisoned by a maiden of our tribe, who was needlessly jealous. We buried her here; I was disconsolate. For protection against the wild beasts, I filled the grave with heavy rocks, but they may have also served to imprison her spirit. In all kinds of weather I visited her tomb nightly, hoping to hold communion with her *tschipey* or ghost. But naught but damp vapors from the crevices of the rocks met my straining eyes. I called in the wise men; they invoked all their mystic incantations, and songs, and entreaties, but absent was the fair Pilurvi.

Then I was ambushed along the Susquehanna one afternoon, while I was fishing peaceably. White men, Scotch-Irishmen did it, and my body stripped of its strings of elks' teeth and beads, was thrown in the river. My spirit emerged, full-blown, and completely conscious, I could move through the country with the velocity of the night wind. I visited my Pilurvi's grave; I penetrated its inmost depths, holding in my ghostly embrace her few remaining bones. But she seemed to be spiritually dead, there was no ghost. I became aware that there could be no further progress for me in the spiritual world unless I could assemble her wraith. In my flights through the living world through all the years I looked at many faces, but there was none but yours, that seemed to have the sympathy or the *power* to help me.

"I knew you were not given to spells or powwows, but from your old mother you had learned some of the English witchery, a thousand years old. I came to believe you could raise the dead, that is make the ghost of a departed person assemble itself. I tried to appear to you on many occasions in your own home, but could not. The reason was that you reside in a new house, there has never been a death in any of the rooms. I can only materialize in a room where someone has died; in such an apartment particles of the disembodied spirit cling to the woodwork, the furniture, the pictures. These stimulated materialization. At last my wait was to be rewarded. Tonight you became belated and decided to spend the night at the Golden Swan. To my infinite good fortune, the landlord assigned you to a room where there had been a death. A young woman, abandoned by her lover, cut an artery, and bled to death there, over sixty years ago. Ghost-fibre is more pregnant in the particles of a victim of a violent death. The fragments of her mutilated personality, lingering in the woodwork and old window sashes, helped me admirably. I appeared; I led you willingly from the room. Now will you not raise the spirit of my beloved Pilurvi, to make me happy until the great forces of oblivion forever disintegrate us?"

As he ceased talking, the Indian held out both his dark, brawny hands, in an appealing gesture. I was touched by his appeal, but for a moment could not recollect my mother's instructions for raising the dead. In my boyhood, we had often sat before the red light of the stove, having blown out the candle for economy's sake, talking of the ghosts and witches of Lancashire, while we waited for my good father's return from his lodge meeting.

The Indian and I were standing on either side of the mound; I could see, by the weird unearthly light which shone from its indefinite source, that he was deeply agitated. I would help him, if I could, even if I lost my soul in so doing. "Raise a body lose a soul," was an old expression my mother oft-times made to me. But here I wasn't asked to raise a dead body, it was only to bring back a prematurely disintegrated spirit. Suddenly, what I must do, dawned on me. The Indian detected the smile in my eyes.

"Oh, friend," he exclaimed, "you have found it, it is to come to pass, I am to see my beloved Pilurvi."

I motioned to him to follow me. We retraced our steps back to the spring, across the jagged rocks. I took the gourd from the wall, filling it with water. I breathed on the water, and returned to the mound, carrying it as carefully as I could. If I spilled a drop, the spell would be lost, for that night at least. Heavy on my feet as I was, I managed to get back to the mound, without spilling any of the water. Arriving there, I breathed on it again, then poured it slowly over the hillock. When it touched the rocks, a steam resembling what arises when water is poured over a hot stove, enveloped both the Indian and myself. It was a peculiar vapor, hot and oppressive, smelling sweet like the water had tasted. There was a tremendous amount of steam, considering the small quantity of water.

The Indian was less excited than I; it was the first test of powers conveyed to me years before; I felt like a bird caged a lifetime at length freed and given a chance to try his wings. But after a few minutes the volume of vapor began narrowing, to assume a spiral form. The odor gradually became that which we associate with newborn babies. Surely something was coming into entity. I was thrilled with a consciousness of my greatness. I, Jack Carter, a poor English miner, could actually be the genesis of a ghost. The spiral shortened, tapering itself into a human form; it began to take on natural tints, to solidify. It was not long now before there stood between the Indian and myself, tiptoeing on the rocks of the mound, the fragile figure of an Indian girl.

"Oh, Pilurvi, Pilurvi," the hysterical lover shouted, as he leaped forward, and clasped her shrinking in her loveliness, in his arms. It was an affecting love-scene, even to me, who had not read many love stories, nor seen much of lofty kinds of love in my sordid career. I could see her put her slender, graceful arms around his waist, and press her face against his neck, and begin kissing him.

How strange that my old mother's talk would come to pass like this; it was the necromancy of the Druids, nothing less. I recollected that my maternal grandmother had often boasted of being born in the shadow of Snowdon.

But even in the midst of his long-deferred rapture, the Indian was not forgetful of his finer traits, especially the one of gratitude. Softly taking his right arm from around his sweetheart's waist, he extended it to me. I clasped it; it felt *real*. It was like shaking hands across the gulf of infinity, the gulf of the unknowable. Even while holding my hand, I noticed the clasp grow less intense; it soon faded into emptiness; I saw the two figures waft themselves away together into the dense tanglewood of the ridge.

I was alone out there on that dismal mountain. Guided by the same unearthly light, I climbed back to the spring, and from there managed to retrace my steps to the mountain road. From that point on, I got along very well. When I re-passed the farmhouse above the old Academy, the two shepherd dogs ran along the inside of the paling fence, barking hideously while their long hair stood on end like the bristles of Irish terriers. I thought I saw a dark figure disappear around one corner of the Academy; I had heard that the grounds were haunted by the ghost of an old drawing teacher who was dismissed because of the infirmities of age, and who had died shortly afterwards of a broken heart in his desolate lodgings. Why shouldn't he be out on All Souls' Night? Perhaps he, too, wanted me to do a favor for him!

When I reached the broad main street with its double row of stately maples growing visible at the approach of dawn, I saw that big rabbit again, right in the middle of the avenue. At the sound of my approach he darted away into the gloom of the old court-house. I went up the steps of the hotel, instinctively turning the knob of the front door. Then I recalled that I had the key in my pocket. As I turned the key, I looked down the street; it was light enough to make out the frowning height of Jack's Mountain, with all its pent-up romance and tragedy. As I went up the stairs I encountered the landlord's wife coming down to build an early fire, for there was to be butchering that day. "Oh, you sly boots," she said, shaking her plump forefinger at me, "I heard you go down stairs and out, after midnight; can't you keep away from that girl of yours even for one night?" I said nothing, only smiled; if she could only have guessed my nocturnal doings!"

VII. One Hour of Happiness

(Story of the Lower Mahantango.)

The lower Mahantango has two branches which come together near Klingerstown. In the language of the Lenni-Lenape they were called Wilawans or horns. The north branch rises from the boiling springs, high up in the laurel thickets at Locustdale. The south branch heads at Zerby Springs, gushing out from under a huge flat conglomerate rock. Mahantango, in its ancient usage, meant dragon's stream, and the two forks were called wilawans, after his horns. The mystic origin of the stream has been stated as follows: A great demon or dragon persisted in annoying the good Indians who resided in the rich vales bordering on the Susquehanna. The Getchi-Manitto or Great Spirit ordered the monster to leave the locality. Upon its refusal, he turned it into a stream, its horns being represented by the two branches. With such a beginning the vales of the Mahantango have always been tinctured with mystery and romance. World wide is the faith of Astarte.

The soothsayers of the Lenni-Lenape claimed that they could produce more potent spells in this vicinity than anywhere else. It also grew the finest Indian corn, tobacco and potatoes. Its braves were the most warlike, its women the most beautiful. Majestic is the scenery every foot of the way from the twin sources to where, under the spreading shade of ancient, smooth-barked white-oaks, it bids farewell to its quiet meanderings and plunges into the big river.

The Mahantango Mountain, commonly called the "old camel-back," ends abruptly at the river, its castellated heights are on terms of intimacy with the morning; the stern profile of the murdered Teedyuscung, last great chief of the Lenni-Lenape, menaces the broad "Irish Sea," and brings on storms when his thoughts turn to the subject of his wrongs.

There have been certain seasons of certain years when the Mahantango was navigable for canoes, almost from the headwaters of both forks. Lucky was the traveller who launched his craft at the proper season; it was like a pilgrimage through a real garden of the gods. No matter what the mood on starting out, how black the future loomed, the genial sunshine, the fleecy white clouds, the rich green mountains, the tasseled foliage of the ancient oaks, all would woo back a love of life, a wish to live always. It was the ideal region in which to change a mood. It was a remote corner of the world, yet in reality removed but a few hours from the busy centres, where one could begin life anew. While to the thoughtful person, life can never be absolutely happy, the almost perfect state of content can be realized along the Malian-tongo. To float down this exquisite stream on an afternoon in early summer would be to make anyone an artist, a lover of the world beautiful. The songs of the birds, from the shrill calls of the jays, to the introspective notes of the rarest of the warblers, would make a person love music more, for having listened to nature's own rhapsodies. The sight and fragrance of the unnamed host of wild flowers massing on the banks, would be conducive of pure, delicate, ethereal thoughts. A lofty thought always begins with the recollection of some fair woman, and ends with memories of another. To float down the Mahantango would be to feel restored to the enchanted company of the women we loved, or should have loved. Each little streamlet, that with resolute effort to be heard, tumbles into the parent creek, on the way, is like a resolve growing stronger with experience. The grand old trees are landmarks of our strongest, and most worthy emotions, the eternal verities of our existence.

Happiness can be experienced along the Mahantango, but life being a cycle, we must return homeward with the point of view which began our journey. No joy approaching true happiness can last. It stands out so strong in our memories because it is followed by the inevitable letdown, like a drab asbestos curtain shuts out the stage after a brilliant play.

Once upon a time there was a young antiquarian who thought he felt the pain that lasts through life. That pain comes from an untoward ending of a romance, leaving one alone. Some can never understand why it was for the best that the beautiful image with her golden hair and drooping eyes should go elsewhere, after declaring her fealty. The more one ponders on the subject the more perplexing it grows; it is as great a whirlpool of misunderstanding as the riddle of existence. We know a loving God made the world, we know He made this fairest of its creatures; and why not for us — when we surely could have loved her better than anyone else.

The young antiquarian after the sudden upset of his ideals was often drawn back into the neighborhood of his great romance, just as Petrarch, wandering in many kingdoms always returned to the valley of the Rhone. But what solace could there be in reviving old associations; literally it was like visiting a graveyard of the soul. A great hope was buried there, alas with no resurrection. Do not ghosts revisit scenes of their greatest joys or their deepest wrongs? After each visit he vowed he would never return; it had done no good; he could not hear even the rustle of an angel's wing. Nobody ever mentioned her name; this was done to save his feelings, he suspected, the profound conspiracy of silence.

But this golden image haunted him everywhere, on the seas, in foreign lands, forever he kept asking himself why it was so, why couldn't it have been otherwise? Then with the inimitable defeat of understanding, he fell back to the centuries-old lament, what had he done to incur God's displeasure? He felt that in the future despair would succeed despair; conceived in disappointment disappointed always.

It was after all this painful and profitless spiritual countermarching that one evening he found himself at an old farmhouse, in a patch grubbed out from the laurel jungles of the boiling springs. The happy ferocity of the foam as it sprang from its cavernous beginnings, and soon became a torrent charmed him; he felt in its virile anxiety the sensations of the new life. He must follow this exuberant youngster, and in its course his exquisite pain would be drowned in laughing ripples. There was an old canoe, swung over rafters in the farmer's workshop, that might be requisitioned. The farmer himself had navigated the course eighteen years before, yet not since. Was he in love then? From his smiling blue eyes, and broad, ruddy face, he had picked up enough happiness on the way to obviate the necessity of another voyage. But his trip having begun in happiness ended in happiness j that encountered on the way was the same emotion, only experienced in a different stretch of country.

There is a certain crispness of the atmosphere that belongs peculiarly to the first days of June, especially after heavy rains. There is an invigoration in each breath of air we take in, that calls us to begin our most exalted tasks, our most sincere revelations. It was on one of the mornings, after a downpour of several days' duration, that the young antiquarian dragged the rehabilitated canoe to the banks of Mahantango. As he slid the prow into the eddying current, a halcyon darted down the stream. "You will have good weather all the way," said the farmer, pointing to the shrieking, laughing bird.

The boat was as quaint, and sprightly as the stream or the day; one could scarcely guess that it had rested unused for eighteen long years. It had been kept out of the bad weather, all it needed was a good dusting off, and here and there a little patching, to make it "seaworthy." The cheerful farmer got out his red paint, and brightened the color on the little pictures of Indian arrows which were painted on the sides, near the bow. The boat was called the Arrow, because he had found an arrowhead of jasper imbedded in the sassafras tree from which he peeled the bark used in its construction. What a legend must have underlaid this incident! He gave the antiquarian the arrow-head; like the halcyon it augured well. "Don't travel too far in one day, or it will be over too soon," was the farmer's parting injunction.

Old River Bridge at Lock Haven, Penn'a

If we could only act the same way in life we might tarry where the world used us best; if we could only say to the gods "this moment I am happy, here and like this I intend to stay!" The trip down the little river proved the panacea expected. Memories of past sorrows faded into a thin golden haze, only the sweetest quintessence of romance reflected itself in the shade of the oaks, by the marshy iris-lined shores.

In some places the stream coursed through woods, mostly of white oak, but here and there were a few venerable white pines. In other places it passed farmsteads, neat little cottages of stone plastered over, with red roofs of tiles or metal. In front of every cottage, with outstretched branches sometimes dipping in the current, stood mammoth buttonwood trees, trees akin to the planes of the ancients.

Then one or two villages were passed, as quaint, and semi-conscious as any in the old world. It was a region, should Vergil come to life, he would instinctively drift to, and immortalize. Some day a rustic Vergil or a Catullus, will be produced in these hidden-away bowers who will give it the voice which it now lacks in its long silences. And indeed they were long silences; the breezes whistling through the tree-tops, the jaunty morning breezes; the ceaseless ripple, rush, run of the current, an occasional cockcrow, a tinkling sheep-bell, the rattle of the halcyon, the frightened squawk of a duck, beyond this all was still, as mute as the bland, expansive blue dome.

Following the advice of the farmer who had been the earlier navigator, the antiquarian stopped frequently, and rested under the old buttonwoods and red-birches, to absorb some effect of light or shade, to listen to the whistling breezes, or catch the shy, reflective notes of a warbler. In this way the little river's length could be expanded immeasurably. It would be poison to the soul to quit such scenes hurriedly.

But sometimes when the sky was particularly blue, the foliage peculiarly like brocade, the yongs of the yellow-throats hidden in the laurel, and red-winged blackbirds more witching, and the iris grew in thicker clusters, with an occasional white flower among them, that the antiquarian longed for someone to enjoy these delights with him. His was the plaint of Omar. Tears almost came to his eyes at the thought that the only way this nature's wonderland could be conveyed to others, would be through his imperfect writings.

That afternoon the mood of nature changed. The fleecy white clouds turned pink ash, then royal purple, then black. The whistling breezes in the mazy tops of the high buttonwoods and beeches assumed a roar, the swift running water fumed itself from terra-marine to brown. Many of the iris flowers lost their heads in the killing wind, their floating petals racing the canoe. The halcyon darted to his hole, the yellow throats and nut-hatches were silent. The wading cattle forsook the water, and sought cover in the lea of the bank-barns, the sheep ran hither and thither, rattling their puny little bells. A rush of hot-air surcharged the atmosphere, then came an icy gust from the far-off Broad Mountain summit surely, followed by the rain, sharp, cold, slanting rain. With it came flashes of lightning and thunder peals. The antiquarian liked the sensation of floating down-stream in a storm. However, as he did not have a rain-coat, or change of clothing, it behooved him to find temporary shelter until the downpour abated. "There is a destiny that marks our ends."

On the southerly bank of the creek, well-obscured by a heavy fringe of old willows, stood a small frame one-story cottage. It had a broad verandah, or projecting roof, more like that of a blacksmith's shop than a dwelling. There was an old-fashioned brick chimney, almost as wide, and several feet higher than the house. Myrtle and honey-suckle grew profusely about the foundations. A pathway, hedged by well-grown crocuses led from the porch to the river edge, and easterly to the public road. The door was locked, windows barred; no one seemed to be about, but here was to be the young man's temporary haven. He paddled to shore, beached the craft, and ran along the path to the verandah.

There was only one chair on it, a very small, narrow rocker, with a patch of faded buckskin laid over the wooden seat. Evidently there was someone connected with that house given to solitary contemplation, to introspective reverie. He knocked on the door several times, there was no response. He boldly seated himself in the chair, to try to conjure up a mental picture of its owner. What a charming way to wait while the storm continued. He was sure she was a woman, she might be a very old, feeble, friendless woman, but in his soul he saw the picture of a beautiful young girl. In his imagination he saw her coming up the path, between the lines of crocus, in the slackening rain, dragging an umbrella, her eyes cast down in pensive indifference. As she drew near, she raised her eyes, enhanced by long black lashes and brows, they were the color of terra-marine, large, and true windows of the soul. What he could see of her face was oval, very pale, a whiteness most unusual. Masses of wavy, soft dark hair blew about her face, so well-shaded by a broad-brimmed black straw hat. Her straight, full nose was the most impressive, as well as aggressive feature; her mouth sensitive and thin. She wore a raincoat, the lines of which did not altogether conceal a certain pitiful meagreness of hips, which strangely enough was one of her chief charms. She was of medium height, with that slimness of the teens. She wore a low, broad collar, revealing the smooth, round outlines of her marble throat. She had on a simple white shirt-waist, with some sort of tie at the neck, a dark skirt, low shoes encased in rubbers. That was the impression she gave, as she wandered up the path, in his imagination, his dream world. She was the most beautiful person he had ever seen, she was far more lovely to look at than the porcelain statuette that a friend of his possessed, and which he considered his idea of feminine perfection. Apart from this he thought her like no other woman, except that she was a little like one in far distant Tien-tsin.

He arose from the wobbly little rocker, which he now knew was hers. When she drew near he took off his hat, explaining his intrusion, and trying to engage her in conversation. On close view he was appalled by the completeness of her beauty. Her voice was soft and pleasing, her manner gracious, who could she be in this far-off, hidden wilderness of the Mahantango! He tried to converse with her, he was in deadly earnest in his desire to try to impress her, but somehow he was not at his best. After some urging she sat down in the little rocker, which she admitted was hers; he leaned against one of the uprights of the porch. How he longed to be able to fathom her secret thoughts and aspirations! But he could devise no leading questions, no interesting lines of thought. His *soul*, as he afterwards wrote in his journal, was dumb, his shallow exterior personality did all the talking. But he was never so completely absorbed in an object in his whole life before. He saw someone in whom was realized the striving of all artists, one of God's masterpieces. When God intentionally or unintentionally produces so many grotesques, how difficult it is for those desirous of feeling the ideal in nature to find inspiration or models!

The conversation continued, all the while he felt himself laboring under a disadvantage. His inability to do himself justice proved that he was loving a phantom. The last rain-drop had fallen; the countryside was enveloping itself in the cloudy silence of dusk. And yet he prolonged his talk, why should he seek to resume the empty unsatisfactory life. Why couldn't he say "This moment I am happy, here and like this I intend to stay!" But if real surroundings like these are unstable, how much so a little one act drama in the recesses of the soul! He heard a hysterical cry of a cat-bird, settling down to sleep, among the wild grape vines back of the cottage. He heard the slow and measured "tang, tang, tang, tang, tang, tang, tang," seven o'clock, of a sedate, tall timepiece, in a corner of the room, which he could dimly see through the small panes of the window. He had tasted some unknown person's hospitality long enough. If he had failed to find words to charm a wraith of happiness, how clumsy he would be in the presence of the cottagers.

With the cat-bird's dozing cry, he had seen no more of the fair, blue eyed vision in the rickety little rocking-chair. She was gone. He was alone with the memory of a grand ideal, happiness was less real than ever before. As he left the verandah the crickets had begun to chorus, maybe they were welcoming the cottagers' return, if he waited longer he might meet the pretty little girl in flesh and blood. But experience taught him the limitations of bliss; he walked sadly down the path, between the clusters of crocus, the spreading myrtle.

At the river-brink the wavelets were lapping among the swaying stems of iris; the calamus and cat-tails, half submerged by the swollen torrent, waved their heavy heads. He climbed into the "Arrow," and started on his way; he would glide along in the darkness for another hour or two. A short distance below the mystic cottage, a suspension foot-bridge of loose boards and cables spanned the stream. As he neared it he looked up, an aged, tottering woman, hatless, and shabby, was wending her way across, holding on to the wire supports as best she could. Under her arm dragged a faded cotton umbrella. As she was moving in the direction of the cottage, surely she was the owner of the little rocking chair, with its cushion of buckskin. She was the reflective person, the introspective listener. Perhaps in a day gone by she had looked like the dream creation who had come to talk to him; that was why he felt ill at ease, it was reality abashed before the infinite. And in the gathering gloom his mind traveled back to the thoughts of a lost love, blonde and beautiful, who had stirred him when he embarked at the boiling spring.

VIII. The Play-Girl

(Story of Middle Creek Country).

When Curtin Pewterbaugh emerged from the private office of the sales' stable in West Philadelphia, he folded, and placed in his wallet, a check mounting up into the four figures, the proceeds of the disposal of his carload of Snyder County horses. He had only spent a small amount of the roll of bills he had brought with him for expenses, consequently was feeling "well-fixed." Evening was coming on; he would spend one night enjoying the sights of the Quaker metropolis, before returning to his farm at the base of the Shade Mountains.

There all was so silent nights, save when the hylodes, crickets or katydids were in season, or the whip-poor-wills; sometimes the foxes barked from their dens on the bare cliffs; once he heard what old settlers told him was a panther. In Philadelphia night seemed to accentuate every sound. The clang of the trolley bells was louder, the shriek of train whistles, as they crossed the Schuylkill bridge, the honk of automobile horns, the rumble of heavy drays. It all seemed so different, he liked the very loudness of it, his consciousness seemed to open wider under this medley of sounds.

He strolled along a half dozen squares before boarding a trolley car; the lights of even the smallest shops were magnified to his receptive vision. He finally boarded a car which carried him down Market Street, into the very heart of the city. The hurrying crowds pouring into Broad Street Station fascinated him; he craned his neck watching them from the car-window. The charm of so much life and motion overcame him; he signalled to the conductor and got out. He followed the human stream up the steps into the terminal. For an hour he wandered about watching the out-going and in-coming travelers, wondering what their hidden purposes might be. For Curtin Pewterbaugh, despite his backwoods bringing up, was an imaginative youth. The depot restaurant looked good to him; he sat on a stool at the counter eating, hemmed in by hurried, hungry beings.

Later in the evening he strolled under the arched portico, and into the open-court of the City Hall, and out again into the brilliantly lit Market Street. He strolled down that thoroughfare a few squares, gazing at the crowds moving theatre-wards. He turned into one of the side streets, which he followed until he came to Chestnut Street. Here were more bright lights, gay, smiling throngs. He caught their spirit admirably, it drove away incipient loneliness. He saw a thick stream of people crowding up some steep steps into a theatre. The flare of the white electric lamps attracted him. He gazed with amusement at the uniformed, epauletted, stalwart Negro carriage-man dexterously opening the doors of horse-vehicles and automobiles. One or two old Germantowns in the line were in curious contrast to the mammoth limousines.

Several gayly colored billboards told of the play; he couldn't quite grasp what it all meant. He went in determined to find out what kind of a play it was that could attract such crowds.

When he got in line to buy his ticket, he recollected he had plenty of money, a seat in the orchestra would suit his taste.

He got a fairly good seat; he hired a pair of opera glasses, he gave the usher a quarter who seated him. Settling himself, he felt the equal of any person in the playhouse. Several women glanced at him from under their head-dresses; he was good looking, of a ruddy semi-blonde type seldom seen in the city. In the subdued light before the curtain went up, his dark clothes blended into the shadows, he seemed as well dressed as anyone.

He admired the picture on the drop curtain. It represented a shepherdess driving a flock of sheep, presumably homeward, in the moonlight. In the background was a river bathed in silvery moon-rays, and distant hills. The prevailing tone of the picture was a pink-ash. He had seen the Susquehanna at night look just that way. How beautiful, how fresh and open, was life where he had come from. How narrow, artificial, hot it was, in the life typified by the theatre and its patrons! His bosom swelled with conscious pride that he came from a wild, bold region, where one could look over endless ranges of mountains and valleys until vision faltered, where above all the eagle drifted on the wind. He thought of the highly mettled colts he had broken; what a virile occupation compared to scraping a fiddle in an orchestra.

The overture was finished, the curtain rose. The play was English, the Company were supposed to be, but like most aggregations of English players, most of them were Irish. The play was partly unintelligible to Curtin Pewterbaugh. He heard persons laughing on every side of him; he stared at them in blank amazement. To him there was nothing especially funny in the lines, he waited eagerly for a real joke. He recalled he had heard some good jokes in the opera house at Sunbury, when, "The Brass Monkey," by the late Charles Hoyt, played there.

Vanquished in his effort to fathom the plot, or fully understand the humor, he began scanning the faces and figures of the actresses. Surely they were a pretty and stylish lot. The hired opera glasses drew them very close, though he had a good pair of eyes. There was one girl, a little red-head, whom he found himself noticing more closely than the others. He said to himself that he liked her best. She reminded him of a girl who came to visit at Paxtonville several years before. She had been betrothed to the Lutheran preacher, else he would have "paid attention to her." She was a tiny bit of a thing, with a laughing expression to her eyes, eyes the color of beer, as it is said were Chopin's. It seemed a pity, he had thought, to marry her to a sky-pilot. He used to drive by the parsonage with his pair of steel grey colts sired by Col. Sober's old favorite Wilkes Boy, out of a mare by Blue Boy; they were twins, and a dashing span they made. He wished he could have asked her to go driving with him, especially on the clear Sunday afternoons in August, but she was the affianced wife of another. He had later heard she married the preacher, and gone to some town in Huntingdon County. This girl on the stage was her living image. Could the little red-head of his secret romance have run off from her sepulchral mate, and become a play-girl? He looked at her minutely through the glasses.

The girl on the stage had more fully developed features; her soul was not so deeply imbedded in the flesh. It was a more interesting personality, let the preacher keep *his* red head. There was a Berks County twang to the preacher's girl's voice; she always said "hea-h" for hear, and so on. The play girl had a delightfully clear English intonation. But physically she sent the same shudder through him as the preacher's fiancée had done, even at a distance. She awakened a longing which had burned itself down to a dull flicker, ever since he had realized his love must be "a bride of the church." The play girl had the same even white teeth; why did God make two persons both out of his reach so very much alike! He watched her intently all through the three acts of the performance; he had never been so happy in all his life. Once he thought their eyes met, and she seemed in no hurry to remove her glance. He felt that he knew her when the curtain fell on the last act; he could hardly realize that they had come to a parting of the ways.

In the lobby his eyes rested on the big lettering of the billboards laying special emphasis on the fact that it was an "English Company." "That girl will cross the ocean and I'll never see her again." Then he pondered to himself, "perhaps she has a sweetheart like the girl who came to Paxtonville, or maybe she's got a husband."

The home-bent crowd jostled him out of the lobby and into the street. On the sidewalk he heard a great clock somewhere tolling "eleven." He had time to go to his hotel, get his satchel, and board the eleven-forty night express for Sunbury. He would arrive there in the morning, before dawn crimsoned the river. He was so busy thinking about the play-girl that he reached his hotel, and the station with wonderful alacrity. We do everything quicker and more effectively when in trances like these. He got in the day-coach, turned back a seat, and throwing his overcoat over his knees, stretched out for a nap. He couldn't feel drowsy, his mind was too keenly awake, living over the thrills produced by the little red-head at the show. At best his impression of the rest of the play had been hazy; now he had forgotten it all except his beautiful vision. The thought of never seeing her again tortured him. He turned and

54

twisted in the seat; he read and re-read the crumpled play bill. He wanted to sleep, to draw a curtain over his misery, temporarily. He pulled down his soft hat, thinking the lights kept him awake, he tied his handkerchief over his eyes; but to no avail. He was wide-awake until after the train left Harrisburg; then he dozed off.

He dreamed a glorious dream; the little red head and he had met, and she loved him as much as he loved her. Why couldn't this dream come true, he thought indignantly, when fully awake. Why should fate make his grandest aspiration a mockery, an impossibility? The conductor and brakemen were calling out for Sunbury; he straightened his hat, swung into his heavy ulster, and joined the procession towards the carexit. Out on the platform of the station, in the crisp morning air, he felt very much alone and disconsolate. He had never once thought of the money he had made on his shipment of "chunks;" it was dead ashes in his hand now; what he wanted was the little play-girl.

He walked up and down the platform nervously, carrying his satchel, until the local was made up which would carry him to his mountain home. Dazed and upset, he got off the train; his driver opined his business had turned out badly. All the way to the farm he sat with head hanging. He made no attempt to drive the spirited pair of red roans, one a stallion, the other a mare, which on ordinary occasions he loved so well. He felt like a different man, a grander soul was settling itself into place in the recesses of his nature. He did not neglect his business on account of the romance, on the contrary, he was a shrewder dealer than before. He had a spiritual awakening, he was living on a bigger plane.

The first night at home he dreamed about the play-girl, and the next, and the next. Every night for a month he awoke in the middle of the night, feeling that he had been talking to her, that she had been by his side, but had vanished. He thought it strange that much as he had admired the preacher's fiancée, he had never dreamed of her, even when he longed for her most. With the play-girl it was different. She was uppermost in his mind all day, she was the sole participant in his dreams. He must have her, but how, in this mocking world! What good would it do to return to Philadelphia and attend the show every night? Besides he recalled he had read that the play was going on tour, it might even now be in Scranton, Reading or Pittsburg.

He did not know how to flirt, he was no adept in love-letters. The romance must burn itself out, even if it consumed him in the process. He recalled an old wooden candlestick of his grandmother's which had ignited from a burnt-down wick, and blazed to a cinder.

It happened after his four weeks of dreaming, that Curtin had put up for the night at a hotel at Glen Iron, some ten miles across the mountains from his home. He was on a horse-buying expedition, and an unexpected snow-storm belated him. The bar-room was the only spot to spend the evening. It was diverting to be there, as all the local celebrities who could brave the squalls, came in for a little cheer. Sammy Denham, the genial colored land-lord, amused him by telling the names of the different characters. Most of them had very little claim to notoriety; a few were grizzled veterans of the Civil War, a couple were wolf or bear hunters of the long ago; one was Adam Straub, the witch doctor. Although the young horseman had never seen this old man before, he had often heard of him, his fame had spread across the mountains into the Middle Creek Valley, and further south and east.

Old Straub was a hermit, at least he lived alone, his cabin was situated in the gap of the mountains, back of the old furnace, from which the settlement had taken its name. The young man gazed intently at the witch doctor, strange thoughts were passing through his mind. "Would you like to meet the old codger?" said the landlord, noting his interest. "I surely would" answered the young man with emphasis. The inn-keeper called the old man away from the bar over which he was leaning, and soon horseman and soothsayer were in an animated conversation. Curtin offered the old man a drink and a cigar; he took a good jorum of Tolu, and selected a Pittsburg stogie from the box which the bartender held out to him.

Then the horseman and the old fellow pushed through the latticed swing-ing door, and took seats in the office, back of the big stove. They leaned their chairs against the wall, conversing with all the intimacy of long-lost friends. The gist of the talk was that Curtin wanted old Straub to devise some means to ease the sorrow occasioned by his frequent dreams of the playgirl. He could never see her again; he would prefer to dream of her less. As the talk was drawing to a close, the old man shot this startling statement at his sur-prised listener. "If you loved that girl I could get her for you dead easy."

"Love that girl" said the young man excitedly, "I'd lay down my life for her. I never loved anybody in my life, except perhaps my own mother, like I do her!"

"Oh, I didn't understand it that way" replied the old man dryly, pulling at his long goatee, "I thought it was a case of someone haunting your sleep, and you wanted it stopped."

"I am dying by inches thinking and dreaming about her, she's a play girl, I never thought I could win her, I only wanted to stop dreaming about her to give my soul some peace."

"That's the way I like to hear a boy talk," said the witch doctor, his clear, limestone-colored eyes twinkling sympathetically. He continued pulling his chin-beard, and pondered a minute. Then he resumed, his voice lowered to an almost inaudible whisper, "Now listen, son, and I will tell you how to get that girl. In the first place no man ever dreams steadily about a girl unless there is something about him that would suit her to perfection; there is no such thing as one-sided love in the dream world. That girl's soul has taken a liking to you, though physically she may not have any recollections of having seen you. You and she would be happy together, no matter if she is a play-girl from the big world and you only a mountain stockman — else I would never

56

help this along. When you go to bed to-night make the firm resolve that when she appears to you in the dream you will grab her and hold her. Catch her in your sleep and she can never leave. You will have her body and soul for keeps. You will find that she will be only too happy to remain with you; the past will be nothing to her.

But by the by; I think it would be a mistake if you put this into effect at this public house. In the morning folks would wonder where you got the girl; it might help her friends in tracing her. Now I live in a shanty in a remote spot; come and spend the night with me; I can give you a clean room. After you get the girl, I'll come over here for your team, and you can hide her in my old buffalo coat and get her through the gap unnoticed. You'll have a twenty-four hours start on any pursuers. If she's gone forty-eight hours without a clue, they'll give her up; she will seem so at home with you, no one will suspect she isn't a native mountain girl. The young man told the landlord he was going to spend the night with old Straub. "I knew you'd like him" said the big smiling Negro, as the bill was paid.

After the old man had his night-cap of "bitters" and selected another stogie, the pair went out, and tramped through the snow to the lonely cabin in the glen. Just as he had said, the old fellow kept a neat house. There was a spare room, with two pillows on the bed, with lace shams, and a pretty patchwork quilt of many colors. "It's close to midnight now, turn in as quickly as you can, no one who falls asleep after midnight ever had a visitation."

The room was icy cold, the air sweet from infrequent occupancy; it did not take the big healthy stockman, firmly gripping his consciousness long to fall asleep. Nor did it take him long to begin dreaming about the little play-girl. She came, attired in brown and orange, just as she was on the stage, her hat wobbling with yellow ostrich plumes; there were gilt pumps on her feet. She was smiling happily; a gladsome light shone from her big blue eyes. Sleeper though he was, the young man was ready for her. Raising up in bed with the alacrity of a panther, he seized her around the waist, and held her fast. She did not scream, she did not even lose her genial smile. She seemed a willing captive. He squeezed her tightly. At that moment he awoke, he knew that he was holding real flesh and blood. To make sure he kissed those red lips which he had adored across the footlights. "I've got you at last, you're mine for keeps" he cried out, quoting the witch-doctor.

"I knew you would get me somehow, ever since that night I saw you at the show, I've dreamed of you every night since."

"I've dreamed of you too" said the young man, "every night, all day long besides!"

"I am happy to be here; it's too good to be true" said the girl leaning her head against his breast.

"Isn't it frightfully cold in here, let's get out of this, into the next room, and sit before the fire." "If you let me kiss you again I'll do so."

"Agreed," said the girl, whose kisses were even more ardent than his.

"Go in the next room and talk to the old gentleman who owns this house, while I dress. I'll be with you in five minutes."

The girl rolled off the bed, went into the adjoining room, and closed the door. The next instant he heard her laughing and chatting with the witch doctor. Groping about he found a match, and soon had the candle lighted. He dressed, and pushed his way into the cozy kitchen. By the stove, in a huge old-fashioned settle sat old man Straub, smiling blandly, while the play-girl chatted with animation. "Well, you've got your girl at last," he said, getting up to give the young man the seat.

"Yes, and I'm the happiest person in the world."

"No, there is one who is happier, *myself*," said the play-girl.

The old man walked over to one corner of the room, where a buffalo coat hung on a peg. He put it on, and came back to where the lovers sat. "Well, it does an old hermit's heart good to see such a handsome couple together. It's like complimenting Nature to have helped make this romance come to pass. Now I'm going to leave for a while, and go over and get that rig at the hotel. I told the hostler I'd be there and wake him up some time before dawn."

The couple, left to their own devices, talked demurely for five minutes, and then gradually melted into one another's arms, as the lamp and the stove burned low. Their rapture may have lasted an hour, they did not notice the old brown clock hammering away on the dresser. They were aroused from their state of bliss by the sound of buggy wheels crunching on the snow. Then they heard a cheery "whoa!"

The old man tied the horses to a big white oak at his gate, and came in. "Hello, boys and girls" he said, "it's soon dawn, you'd better be going." He took off the buffalo coat and put it over the play-girl's graceful shoulders. "Let me give you some advice, friends, get married as soon as you can, and announce it, else the show people will spring another suitcase tragedy on the public."

"That we'll do, we'll plan it all out on the drive across the mountains" replied the young man.

"Many thanks for accelerating destiny" said the play-girl. "You are a wonder."

"You know how grateful I am," said the stockman.

"Happiness and long life to both of you" the old man called to the couple, as the mettlesome colts dug their hoofs into the snow-crust in their zest for motion.

"Is this all really true or are we both dreaming?" said the young man, gazing at the girl, in the crimsoning dawn.

"It is really true" answered the girl, her cheeks growing as pink as the reflection of the morning glow on the snow. "I did not follow you here, I was in the show last evening, I never heard of this place before I came here in a dream. You made it a reality."

"At last I know of one dream come true" said the young man, in a wild imaginative flight. On the drive they decided that they would get married at Middleburg and take the wedding breakfast at the Washington House. Curtin was well known there; he would have no trouble obtaining a license or a clergyman. They would then telegraph to the manager of the play in Pittsburg that she had married, and would not be back. That would give her understudy time to get into the part for that night. Then they would take the train for Sunbury, and begin their honeymoon with a tour to Niagara Falls. They worked out these plans admirably. The court house officials and the preacher were "delighted." They ate their wedding luncheon on the Buffalo express.

When the manager received the telegram, he took it to the lessee of the theatre. "Where's a place in this State called Middleburg?" he blurted out. "One of our girls has run off and got married there!"

The lessee looked at the address on the telegram carefully. "She was in the show last night, wasn't she?"

"She sure was," replied the manager.

"Then this telegram's *phony*, she couldn't have gotten there in one night from Pittsburg; there's no trains."

"I don't care about that, she's gone and left us" said the manager frowning.

"Oh forget it" said the lessee, "her ducking will give another girl a chance; she's found a role which suits her better." The manager walked away, muttering to himself the words of the old diplomatist in the "Merry Widow," "Women, Women, Women." But he sadly underestimated the psychic possibilities of the one who had flown.

IX. A Frontiersman's Diary

(Story of Fort Horn, 1776.) (Note: See Appendix A.)

July 4th. Great doings, a wonderful day. Fine, clear weather, with the river as blue as the sky above. We met this afternoon, at two o'clock, and signed ourselves free from the British tyrants. We, includes the three Clark brothers, Thomas, Francis and John, Alexander Donaldson, William Campbell, James Crawford, Alexander Hamilton, John Jackson, Jacob Pfouts, Adam Carson, Henry McCracken, Adam Dewitt, Robert Love, Simon Curts, Hugh Nichols of Nichols' Run, Peter Pentz, Peter Grove, Robert Covenhoven, Samuel Horn, and I, Philip Quiggle.

William Pine, a respectable young Indian, who married William McElhattan's daughter, wanted to sign, but we would not let him. These redmen have betrayed us on too many occasions. You could have heard the shout that went up when the last name was signed, clear to Monsey Town.

We signed our names in the Clark family Bible, where Alex. Hamilton had drawn up the declaration. We had been working on this plan for at least two years. Those of us whose fathers came from Ireland hated the English crowd from the start, but it took the Ulster Scotch and the Dutch a full generation to see that what we always preached was correct. Whenever we met on the war-path, or in the canoe, we haled one another with the cry "Let us cut loose." If a narrow-minded sympathizer of the British overheard us, and shouted "treason" we could answer that we meant the Indians. On *this* we were all agreed, it was the only thing that made us feel that the English were human like ourselves. But only a few of us had any real enthusiasm from the start. The Dutch would say "let well enough alone;" the Scotch from Ireland would say "England has been a good friend of ours." But we who came of the old-fashioned stock could only say "Let us cut loose from them."

When the dispatches were brought to us of the glorious movement in Philadelphia, we were beside ourselves with joy. We had many doubts that the colonies would sign themselves free, there were too many of the landed aristocracy among the delegates, we couldn't see how they could benefit by such a change. We were afraid at the last minute they would alter their minds and cringe before the crown. "Let us cut loose from them anyhow" said William Campbell. That word added to our old war-cry was enough to get us all together. Even the Dutchmen felt good over it. They hated all aristocrats, the idea of landed gentry representing them in Philadelphia galled them. "And not a Dutchman in the crowd" they would mutter.

"Old Adam Dewitt, a Low Dutchman from New Jersey, who had a big still-house across from the mouth of Tiadaghton, whose oldest son had been killed by an Indian in the British service, offered to supply the spirits. That made the gathering a reality. Everybody was a patriot now. We were all fair play men, even those of us who lived on this South bank of Susquehanah, and were a bit jealous of the greater prosperity of those across the stream.

As for me, I always for fair play; I left Cumberland County to escape the oppressions of the landed party. I am proud I have no parchment signed by any Penn for the land on which my home stands; it is mine by right of conquest from the rightful owners, the Indians. Simon Curts, and Samuel Horn, my neighbors, feel the same. William McElhattan had a patent from the Penns, that was a black mark against him in my eyes. I would rather kill an Indian every year as rental than pay the Penns a farthing. All the boys across the river had Penn warrants; they looked down on me as a squatter and I in turn, on them.

But when old Adam Dewitt, the Low Dutchman, said he would send a batteau of sprits to the fort, we forgot our chains of title, in the common cause of fair play. Injustice was going to be a dead issue west of Shamokin; let those east keep it if they so desired.

We could have had more at the gathering, had we given longer notice. There was some uncertainty whether the Philadelphia delegates would take their action of July 4th. At first we had wanted to act on the same day. Then when we heard rumors of the indecision of some of the members we decided to hold our convention on the 4th of July, irrespective of them. Ours was an independent meeting, we did not care what others would do.

On day before yesterday Peter Pentz and Peter Grove started up the river in canoes. Peter P. was to go up Bald Eagle to inform the settlers there, Peter G. to his old haunts on the Sinnemahoning, on a similar errand. It was allotted to me to invite all who dwelt within the horseshoe on this side of the river, and to the south slope of Bald Eagle Mountains. Hugh Nichols was to invite those who dwelt on the broad flats across from us. Alex. Hamilton would go up Pine Creek, a few brave men lived there who were in sympathy with us. Adam Carson went down stream, as far as the long reach.

I found my first disappointment quickly enough. My good friend William McElhattan declared he was too busy with his corn to join us. He said he believed we were right; he would send his Indian son-in-law, William Pine, or Choleesaw to sign. I feared Indian William would not be welcome, but I said nothing. My neighbors were very happy to be on hand.

Simon Curts, veteran of High German wars, declared it was the proudest moment of his life in the New World.

Samuel Horn, a German builder of the present fort, and arch-foe of Indians and English, had suggested that we meet within the friendly confines of his stockade, so he needed no invitation. So much of importance had happened within this enclosure of two acres, that it was fitting we renounce the foreign tyrants there. Israel Aughanbaugh from his stronghold at the far easterly tip of the horse-shoe, was glad to be on hand. Conrad Rosencranz from over on the Rock Oak mountain said he would be with us if he could. If the other committees had as good results, the gathering would be a great success numerically. We told everyone to come and bring their families, come good weather or bad. The real patriots, we knew, never minded rain or hail, it would only add to their enthusiasm. They were used to obstacles.

We have had an exceptional spell of good weather, ever since Whit-Monday, so we felt reasonably sure that July 4th would be fine. Sure enough no fairer day ever dawned than this. It was as if Providence smiled on our undertaking. There wasn't one of us but who felt twice as determined to make a success of the undertaking, since the day began so fair. We told all to assemble after the dinner hour; we hardly expected many before. Instead there were half a hundred men, and as many women and children within the stockade at high noon. A regular fleet of canoes and dugouts was out on the river at one time. One would have thought Fort Horn a seaport town like Belfast to see the line of craft moored under the shadow of Horn's hill. A lot of Indians were on hand as usual. They scented the spirits, they liked gossip and excitement, there was no keeping them away. Sam'l Horn ordered that no redman be allowed inside the stockade, except William Pine. This Indian having a white wife, formerly Vashti McElhattan, was exempt from the regulations. His old father Hyloshotkee was kept outside. He did some swearing, but nobody took it up.

Pastor Laughlin came early. I tried to get him to promise to sign, but he shook his head, said the Crown had been mighty kind to his people in the old country. This I do not believe, they were not considerate to my folks at Kildarry in Donegal, and why should they have been to his at Swatragh in Derry? When it became noised about that Pastor Laughlin disapproved, I fancied he was coldly treated. If he had not been an expounder of the Word, he would have been driven out of the stockade to consort with the Indians and their dogs. We wanted no spies or traitors hanging about to mar a grand patriotic celebration.

I do not know who wrote the actual words of this Declaration of Independence. Some say Alex Hamilton was the author, hut it was in Thomas Clark's handwriting, in the Clark Bible. It was kept carefully guarded until Hamilton called us to order at two o'clock. There were two hundred souls within the palisade, the biggest assemblage ever held in the Valley of the Otzinachson. Outside were half as many Indians and their families. Some of the young bucks climbed into the tops of pine trees so they could look into the stockade, and see what we were doing.

Hamilton's speech was very good; it seemed we cheered him every time he closed a sentence. He *gave* it to the Crown, and all the aristocratic crowd in the colonies who favored it. By this time even Pastor Laughlin felt enthusiastic, and offered to say a prayer. We had not asked him to do so before as we feared he might say some unkind words about our project. He prayed ten minutes, and asked Goodness to smile on us. He paid us many a fine compliment, which as lovers of fair play, I do believe we deserved.

Then Alex Hamilton spoke again. He said in Philadelphia at this very moment a declaration similar to ours might be in process of signing; he hoped so; if not, ours would blaze the way for freedom. He said we are the real people; the aristocrats are mere parasites on our ideas and our prosperity.

He called on Thomas Clark to bring forth the Bible. He held it close up, his eyesight is very poor, and read the brave words of our declaration. There was a wonderful lot of cheering; one old man, Mike Snook, shot off his rifle, almost hitting an Indian boy in a tree. Then Alex asked those who wished to sign to step forward. He laid the open book on an oak stump, so it could be read and signed easily. Vashti Pine had made some fresh ink from oakballs, it was black and clear. She also furnished some nice quills made from the feathers of an eagle her husband had shot the day before. She looked prettier and happier than she ever did in my memory. "Wish I was a man so I could sign" she said when she handed me the quill for my signature.

We all signed that could, all but Pastor Laughlin. Alex. Hamilton gave him the quill, but after making a flourish, he backed away saying "I cannot show my ingratitude to the Crown."

Peter Pentz said he was mad enough to have knifed the old hypocrite. Just when Peter P. was signing his name a golden eagle was seen soaring high above the stockade. One of Aughanbaugh's boys was for shooting at him, but we all called him to put up his rifle. We signed the Declaration of Independence with eagle's quills, we could not kill the bird just then. The eagle is surely the bird of freedom. When the last name was signed there was a terrible shout of joy from all, old and young. The Indians outside the fence took it up, yelling "Jo-hoh, Johoh, Jo-hoh." The old hunters embraced one another, and Sam'l Horn danced a German jig. Robert Love got out his pipes, and played music, I do not know whether it was Irish or Scotch. There was an uproar for half an hour at least.

Old Adam Dewitt said it was about time to sample the spirits, for all hands to come into the fort, "to liquor up," as he styled it. There was a rush to be sure. The Indians in the trees moaned with jealousy. Pastor Laughlin went inside, and took a jorum, even if he hadn't signed. We let William Pine get pretty full, until he began to say he wanted to fight the English. "If anybody English is here to-day he dies on the spot" he kept repeating. There were none among us of English blood so there were no lives in jeopardy. We should have found a Britisher to offer up as a bloody sacrifice to this grand historic occasion. I believe the colonies are going to win their rights to be free. If they are not, we borderers must know why. It would not take much for me to fight, even though I am a family man. If I go down to my old home in Cumberland County in the fall I will study the situation; if we must fight, I will gladly volunteer.

It was sundown when some of the brave lads started for their homes. Pastor Laughlin, considerably befuddled, had to be helped into his pirogue. There was more handshaking, more cheering, more dancing before we could decide to part. We believe we have done something that will help the cause of fair play, of human liberty.

Only a few of the most enthusiastic remained, and the discussion came up as to the disposition of the book, with its precious declaration. Alex. Hamilton said it should be kept by the Clark brothers, as they owned it, but they feared to accept the responsibility. Old Adam Dewitt, the Low Dutchman, listened during most of the talk; he looked as if he was thinking deeply. "Brothers" he said, when everybody was quiet, "I have an old copper box at home, which my grandfather brought from Rotterdam. It has three locks; it is over a hundred years old now, it will last a thousand more. I suggest that we put our Declaration of Independence in this box, and bury it in the centre of this stockade. We can do it tomorrow morning, in the presence of those of us who have remained here to-night."

"Very good, very good" answered Alex. Hamilton. "But let us bury it to-night, it is a good two hours until dark, and we have full moon."

"Very well, I'll get the box," said the Low Dutchman, and he hobbled out of the palisade, and went down the steep bank to a canoe. He was back within an hour, during which time some of those who remained became more than necessarily hilarious.

Sam'l Horn got out his old German pick-axe and spade, and he and I dug the pit. It was in the exact centre of the stockade, on the top of Horn's hill. Alex. Hamilton placed the precious Bible in the box. He locked its three locks, keeping one key himself and giving the others to Thomas Clark and Dewitt. In this way the box could not be lawfully opened unless these three men or their heirs were present.

I lowered the box into the pit, and Horn and myself threw the rocks and earth on top. We carefully sodded the spot; one could hardly tell there had been any digging. "My cows will make it look all right, they'll trample it smooth by morning," said Horn. Alex. Hamilton spoke a few words when *we had finished, of a patriotic nature, and asked us to join him in a prayer. He never used such fine speech before, it was a prayer to liberty. My memory is not as good as it might be, but I think I can reproduce what he said, only in not such good language. We were standing about in a circle, and when he began we all took off our caps. The light of the full moon was streaming down upon us, it seemed a happy token.

"Providence," the prayer began, "that has given us this beautiful mountain home, perfect in every way, except for the baleful hand of the tyrant reaching over us, grant that after to-day, its shadow will quickly recede. We are truly grateful for the chance Thou hast given us, one and all, and we do not wish to seem presumptuous to ask for more. To keep what we have, and in a way that we can do the most for the Great Giver we need absolute liberty, fair play. We have taken steps to secure it. We promise from to-day we will never abuse our freedom. We will send it down to our descendants growing stronger with the years. We ask Thy blessing to-night as free men, workers for human betterment. Amen."

Without much leave taking, we silently dispersed in different directions. As I walked homeward along the river bluff I could hear the slap of paddles of the canoes through the still night air. As I neared my garden gate a lone wolf began his lamentations far up near the summit of the Round Top.

X. The Escape

(Story of Fisher's Ferry.)

Black Jack Swartz, the "wild hunter of the Juniata" was one of the most picturesque figures in the pioneer history of Central Pennsylvania. His name will live in Jack's Mountains, which were named for him. In these vast, rugged heights he ranged in all his glory, the foe of Indian and wild beast. But very little is definitely known concerning his personality and antecedents. He has been characterized as cruel and revengeful. He has been described as of Indian, Negro and German descent. While it is true that his skin was extremely dark, he contained no Negro nor Indian blood.

All of the Pennsylvania German frontiersmen were of swarthy complexion, Conrad Weiser, Lewis Wetzel, James Yager, Michael Hite, Peter Pentz, Peter Grove, James Hambright and Daniel Poh were blacker than most Indians. Daniel Boone of English and French ancestry was of light complexion, but the Germans of the wilderness were invariably dark. From reliable sources it would seem that Black Jack was the son of a Spanish sea-captain, who sailed to the port of Philadelphia, and his mother a German lodging-house keeper's daughter. Later the girl married a man of her own race named Swartz, and the baby Jacob, then two or three years of age, was given his step-father's name.

Swartz, the elder, was an adventurous man and moved "up country" to the vicinity of Harris' Ferry on the Susquehanna. Here Black Jack grew up, right on the border of the hostile Indian country. He was a kindly, law abiding youth at first. He eventually married a neighbor's daughter, a girl of Irish stock, and moved with her to his hunting-camp in the wilds.

It was while absent on a hunting trip that Black Jack had his first unfriendly encounter with the redmen. He was captured and cruelly tortured. Though he returned to his people, he became the relentless foe of the Indians. It was for this reason, and not alone because of the subsequent murder of his wife and children, that made him the most bloodthirsty foe the Indians possessed.

After his return from being tortured Black Jack would never go in swimming in the presence of any of his old friends. They soon guessed that he had been horribly mutilated, to be more exact, flayed from the shoulders to the waist.

Black Jack learned to be wily merely by bitter experience. He did not have, in the beginning of his career, the perspicacity of most backwoodsmen. He would often, while on his hunting expeditions, spend nights in frendly Indian camps. He was well treated, and never guessed at treachery. His dark hair and eyes made him fancy that the Indians imagined him to possess their blood; he made no denial when they mentioned the subject to him. Each trip he took, in these young trustful days, made him bolder, less mindful of his own safety. He might have become a white ally of the Indians like Simon Girty had the savages been wise enough to adopt him.

During this time while he was traveling about unmolested, a merciless warfare was going on between the Indians and the Scotch-Irish on the borders. Many white men were murdered or tortured; it seemed peculiar that Black Jack should remain immune.

One night he met a couple of Indians, he declared they were Mingoes, on a trail which led to a popular campground on a bluff overlooking the "big river" at what is now Fisher's Ferry. The Indians were particularly gracious; he had met them before, everything seemed all right.

It was on a stuffy, moonless night in August; Black Jack, man of woods that he was, felt lonely. He liked to spend nights in the Indians' camps, to swap hunting stories, as he knew their dialects, to join in their weird songs. When he reached the cliff and where there was an opening in the deep forest, he saw about twenty braves, under an old chief named Yellow Prongs, seated in a semi-circle about the fire, roasting Heath-Hens, birds now extinct in Pennsylvania, but once very plentiful. When they sat in a full circle it denoted peace; in a semi-circle meant that they were on the war-path. But this did not make Black Jack suspicious; he imagined he was above the feuds between the two races. He was cordially welcomed by the old chief, who handed him his calumet or peace-pipe. He lay down his rifle and sat among the savages. Just as he started to take a good puff at the fragrant tobacco, he was seized from behind, and a gag slipped into his mouth. Unable to cry out, and overcome by superior numbers, he was thrown on his back, and bound hand and foot. He had always thought he could hold his own in a struggle with a dozen Indians, hut he was no match against an attack from the rear. While he lay on the grass, helpless he could see the Indians holding a council of war.

The chief was pointing to a large dead yellow pine which stood on the brink of the cliff. The bark had been worked off by beetles, in the firelight it loomed up like some huge silvery ghost. The Indians soon approached their victim, and dragged him along in the direction of the dead tree. When they got him there, they pushed him to his feet, leaning him against the bare trunk. Then they procured stout leather thongs, and bound him to it. Then they cut off all his clothing. He knew he was to be tortured almost to death, and finally burned "at the stake." He had heard of this horrible fate being meted out to the white men, but never dreamed it would befall him. The gag was taken out of his mouth, and he was asked if he had anything to say before his punishments began. He expressed surprise that he of all white men should be selected for such foul treachery, that he had befriended and saved the lives of many Indians in the past. Apart from the injustice of it all, he had no objections to what they intended doing; he was brave, they could invent no torture that would make him cry out. At this the Indians laughed. They nudged one another's lean sides as much as to say that they had never seen a white man who could remain silent through their entire program. The first step on this occasion was to heat a gun barrel and burn the victim on various parts of his body. Black Jack only laughed; "You are babies in the art of torturing" he bawled out. Then the old chief ordered that he be skinned alive. Narrow strips were torn from his shoulders clear to his waist line. All through this agony the "wild hunter" continued laughing. The gun barrel was heated again, and the raw flesh seared in many places. In doing this the thongs which bound him to the tree were weakened. Black Jack evolved a desperate plan. Amid his laughter he called out to the old chief: "Yellow Prongs, give me that red-hot gun barrel, I can torture myself better than you know how, let me show you." The entire affair had been a failure thus far, as not a single cry of pain had escaped the victim's lips.

The old chief was in a frame of mind to do anything to make the torture more acute. He ordered his torturer to hand Black Jack the sizzling gun barrel. The moment he got it in his strong grasp, he struck the torturer over the head with it, knocking him down. Then he threw the entire weight of his body against the weakened thongs; they gave way. With a leap he ran to the edge of the cliff, and sprang off it. It was a hundred feet to the river below. The startled Indians ran after him, but not one dared to leap off the bluff. All of them, even the old chief, started to climb down the steep ledges, tripping and sprawling in their anxious haste. When they came to the water's edge they made out the head of a dark object swimming in the deep, gloomy current. They shot at it a dozen times and at last heard a weird cry of pain. "Ah," cried old chief Yellow Prongs, "at last we've made Black Jack howl." He ordered his followers to swim after the man, as they had undoubtedly wounded him.

Half a dozen young bucks sprang into the water, and headed for mid-stream with energetic strokes. They could detect a dark object; it was dead, or dying, as it made no effort to get away from them. Nearer and nearer they came to it. The old chief on shore, was howling with delight. When they were beside it, the Indians gave a yell of disgust. They had shot a big white-faced seal. It was gasping its last as they lay hold of it. One of the swimmers returned to the chief to tell him the sad news. The others wisely pursued their way to the opposite bank.

No trace of the missing hunter was to be found. It was too dark to locate any footprints on the soft mud along the banks. Afraid to go back, the pursuers rushed out aimlessly through the forest. After running four or five miles they became discouraged. The thought flashed through their minds that perhaps Black Jack had struck his head on a submerged rock when he leaped from the cliff, and was drowned. Maybe now his dead body was floating down stream. Perhaps the big seal had been disturbed by a corpse floating near his nest by the shore. Perplexed and exhausted, the Indians sank down on the ground, and like children commenced weeping.

Black Jack, whose knowledge of the woods and rivers told him that there was a deep hole at the bottom of the bluff, had no hesitation about the leap. He struck in twenty feet of water, went down, came up again, began swimming. The water was cooling to his burning, blistering body. He was so refreshed by the swim that he felt renewed energy to continue his way when he reached the opposite bank. He was across the river before the first Indian had gotten down the cliff. On the opposite bank he had stepped on the seal, which with a grunt had dragged itself back to the river. It served as an excellent foil, for while the Indians were shooting at it in mid-stream, he was putting miles between himself and his pursuers.

All the time he had kept hold of the gun barrel. He might need some weapon of defense later on. It was lucky that he had been burned after the flaying, as it provided a covering like a huge scab over his raw flesh. But though his sufferings were intense, he made no murmur.

He ran through the forest in a direction opposite to his hunting shack by the Juniata. He knew that would be the way that his foes would go after him. Almost at day-break he came to a stream of water, where beavers had built a dam of considerable proportions. On some high ground above this pond he saw nine Indians asleep around a burned-out campfire. Wrapped in their blankets of red and blue, as the night had been damp, he could not make out their sex at first glance. Going closer, he stealthily lifted the blanket from first one Indian, then another, braining them with his gun-barrel. To his dismay he found one to be a beautiful young squaw. His chivalrous nature would not let him kill her, but he feared to let her live, as she would tell on him. He dropped the blanket back over her face, resolved to run the risk. She might sleep until he had killed his last redman. Unfortunately she awoke with a start, sitting bolt upright, as he crushed the skull of the eighth savage. She immediately sank back in a swoon, more at the uncouth, horrible appearance of the scarred, naked murderer, than at the frightful carnage about her.

His awful task finished, Black Jack seized what provisions he needed, threw a blanket over his burning shoulders, and continued his way. He hid for several days in the Penn's Creek country, living sparingly, while his wounds burned themselves back to convalescence. It was a period of fiendish suffering, but no stoic could have been more calm. At times he regretted the murder of the Indian camp, but he consoled himself by feeling that he had been so crazed by pain and the thought of the Indians' treachery, that he was not his true self.

In a few days he was restored mentally, and this helped his physical condition. But he only returned to his headquarters by easy stages. The whole affair would be a thing of the past by the time he got back. Titanic disasters are forgotten to-day. Indian reprisals lapsed into nothingness in the old days. After nightfall he crept into his cabin, and felt at ease to be amid familiar surroundings once more.

He put on his best suit of buckskin, and apart from his disfigurement, felt as well as ever. He was thankful that his face was un-marred; he could cover the rest. But he always heard that Chief Yellow Prongs never forgot his escape, and the attendant humiliation. It should have made him fearful to leave his wife and children at home, for within a short time after his leap, he took the plunge into happy matrimony. But living as he did, near to other settlers, where no Indians were seen, he imagined his household safe.

One cold night, when he came back from a hunting trip, he discovered his cabin door standing open. He scented trouble, and rushed in. On the earthen floor lay his wife, dead and scalped. The three children had also been tomahawked, and all, down to a three months' old infant in its cradle, scalped. On the mantel was a slip of paper torn from a Bible on which was written "Yellow Prongs." Then and there the outraged pioneer vowed a deeper oath of hatred and vengeance against the Indians. He killed them for the wanton lust of slaughter, though he always spared the women and children. It was his hope that he might some day wear the grey scalp of old Yellow Prongs at his belt, but fate denied him this. The old warrior, worn out from forced marches and fear, lay down and died, and was buried somewhere near the headwaters of Shamokin Creek. "I'd tear him out of his grave if I knew where it was" roared Black Jack, when he heard that his enemy was dead.

The Indians feared the "wild hunter "as they did no one else; they said he was a witch, and had a charmed life. "Hasn't he the Evil One with him" was remarked around many a campfire, "when he could have that seal look just like him for a few minutes, while he was making his escape?"

XI. The Water Witch

(Story of Rattlesnake Run.)

"Of course you have all heard of the Water Witch" said the antiquarian. "If you have not known her in the Pennsylvania mountains, you have come across her in all the literatures of Europe."

"Few in the party had heard of the water witch of Pennsylvania, none had seen her. A few had read of her ancestral type in the literature of foreign lands. "I have seen her" continued the antiquarian, "and only a few weeks ago, but whether she was a dream or a reality I cannot say. Even a dream can be true, it is merely something seen by the spiritual self. The water witch, being the symbol of something ever flowing, travelling, knows exactly the destiny of man. On rare occasions she will reveal the sad story, but in a way which shows her to be completely out of sympathy with humanity.

They say, that is the old mountaineers, that the water witch was an Indian girl who suddenly changed her mind towards her lover. Having influence with the Gods, the deserted one had her made into unchanging water; and in her helpless state, she mocks the petty aspirations of mankind. Womanlike she feels no remorse, and probably longs for a chance to repeat her mischief.

Once a stream in Brush Valley which was loved by the Rain Deity, changed her mind and sought to elude him by running underground. She was never allowed to come up again, and you can hear her mournful wail in her gloomy caverns at all seasons of the year. It is on the Bierly property, Southwest of Rebersburg. The water witch is not altogether unhappy, because she has the power to assume human form; she can come in contact with man, though she is too cold to be loved by him. But endless existence is the greatest pain; her case is an object lesson to those hungering for immortality.

Last autumn, having invited several friends as guests, I started on a hunting trip to the headwaters of Rattlesnake Run. While the weather was fine we would stalk the deer on the wild uplands, if there came a "tracking" snow, we would turn our quest into a bear hunt. Since the cowardly practice of trapping bears was prohibited by law, bruin had become fairly numerous again. Given equal chances, the bear could fight his way with his enemies, it is the sport royal of the Pennsylvania mountains. I started away in deep dejection. Such a beautiful vision had crossed my path but two days before, in such a way that it seemed hopeless to ever see her again. And yet I kept saying over

69

and over again as the train swept along through the brown, sombre valley of the Susquehanna, 'Oh, God, after so many disappointments, please don't let her escape me.' And yet I knew that God has given us the freedom of the will to become the captains or the slaves of our souls. I was not in the frame of mind to fraternize with the jollities of a hunting camp.

All were in good humor at the camp; I felt strangely alone. That is always the case when one has seen someone who could forever destroy that sense of spiritual isolation, but who is lost to us. We feel horribly out of harmony with the world and its ways. The next morning, at daybreak, the gay hunters started off in pairs, it was more sociable. They would ramble for miles together among the ferns, cook their lunches together by some rattling brook, stalk the nimble stags in company. I elected to go alone. Perhaps I felt I was to meet a mystic someone in the wilderness.

It was a cold morning, so much so that the sun seemed loathe to shine. I did not remain long in one place. I heard deer in the distance breaking through the underbrush, but sighted none. I grew hungry early and ate my lunch. While I sat on a moss-wrapped pine log a nut-hatch flew into a birch tree near to me. The nimble little bird watched me with her eager dark eyes. She seemed to wonder why some persons armed with guns would shoot at her, and not like me, let her go about her business.

A little later I met three grouse, while I was strolling down the ravine. They ran from me like leisurely mother hens in a public road. They seemed to divine I was out after bigger game. I was a seeker after the quarry of the spirit. Now and then when I climbed to the top of some ridge I would obtain wonderful views of the surrounding country. It was miles of purple brown mountains, stretching in every direction, their level rows occasionally broken by tall pinnacles or knobs. It was like a stormy sea, as seen from the deck of an ocean liner. I came upon three big does grazing on some late grasses near a spring. They made no effort to depart after eyeing me once or twice. I was in complete harmony this day with wild nature.

I saw a raven perched on a dead pine. He eyed me with the curiosity of the governor of some club, but let me pass. In the early afternoon the sun gained its ascendency, a yellow, bloodless sun, it seemed. But it fought its way, opening the heavens to civilization. Soon the defeated clouds raised to infinite heights, revealing the blue dome. At its apex a hawk was sailing.

I came to a spot noted by huntsmen as the 'play-ground.' It was a favorite haunt for the deer, and justly so. Consisting as it did of an abandoned clearing, fenced in by mammoth uprooted white pine stumps, it was an ideal sporting ground for the nimble creatures as well as an excellent hiding place for nimrods. I surprised four does there, frisking about like overgrown babies. They circled the field several times, but came back to where I had first found them. There were a few wheat sprouts coming up, making tender pickings. Not being anxious to slay anything, I did not hide myself in the blind which other hunters had made behind the pine stumps.

The sun had assumed a deeper tint of gold, it sent some rays of warmth to the slab-like rocks on the hillsides which sloped from the playground down to the headwaters of Rattlesnake Run. I sat down on one of these flat stones, and began watching a solitary original white pine of enormous size on the opposite ridge. A good deal of evergreen timber still stood on that ridge, but the old white pine towered above them all. It was dying at the top, this remnant of the golden age of forestry. It had one branch much longer and thicker than any of the rest, which seemed to be always pointing its menacing feathery tips at the younger trees, with envy, scorn. The wind sighed through the trees in regular cantatas, sometimes in minor, other times in major tone. The Infinite Musician seemed to have selected this as his practice day. At times it seemed as if the long armlike branch of the pine was a conductor's baton leading the sylvan orchestra. Down in the ravine the stream was rushing onward, making mournful music. It seemed to be a hateful task to run so fast over cold stones. The sun did not penetrate down there. The leafless aspens and birches looked wintry contrasted to the sun-kissed pines and hemlocks on the mountain top. A grey cloud descended behind the dying pine, giving it a sombre background in contrast to its sun-illuminated fellows. Now the gaunt finger, or baton waved more threateningly, the music became more weird, more in keeping with the dismal roll of the creek. There was something sad but soothing in Nature's harmonies. I lay out at full length on the smooth rocks. With one eye closed, the other open, I watched the giant, decaying pine conduct his lively young orchestra. Sometimes the wood-wind rose above the creek music but was at other times drowned by the melancholy torrent's roar.

Once I shut both eyes, I was translated to a land of warmth and sunshine. The giant pine, one of many such, was part and parcel of a happy chorus of praise. The stream laughed its way down the dark glen, it was glad to be on its way, yet there were notes of lingering sadness. Instead of attenuated deer, in an open field elk and moose browsed on tender leaf buds in a primeval tangle of monster trees. But the music of the trees, of the creek, were so sweet, why were they not always thus? I could see the stream distinctly below me, it ran in and out among giant hemlocks and beeches, over mossy rocks, it was moving in better society. There was one place where the water, probably from hitting some sharp stones, was ever sending up tufts of spray. At times it would gurgle itself into a mound of water, very much like an old fashioned Bethesda.

And as I dreamed, the fountain increased in volume, in sparkle, in brilliancy. It transcended the banks of the stream, it came rolling, swirling, swishing up the hillside; it was the swish of a woman's skirts. As it drew near to me it took on human form, the very outlines of the beautiful being whom I had seen hut two days before, and who seemed lost to me. But absent were the soft brown locks, the deep blue eyes, into whose depths one could look for a thousand years into the shadowy times when beauty and God were one.

There was the same serious, pouting mouth, it was the mouth of other women I had loved. The nose, retrousse at the tip, hut with good bridge, was just as fascinating in the uncertain lines of sparkling water. Was this the fair image? I must speak to her, and find out.

'I am well aware,' I began, 'that you are not so many hundreds of miles away, but how came you here in form of water, is it that your soul being pure crystal, you came thus?' I heard a mocking laugh, it was not the serious tone of the rare being, was it the swaying pine-music, or the loll of a distant waterfall? No, it came from the shadowy figure before me; I was shocked. When the strange laugh subsided, she spoke out boldly. 'I am not she whom your heart, long-suffering, adores, I have the power to take on the image of each man's best beloved. I am your thought of your love this moment, but am not her in soul or substance.'

'Then you are the Water Witch' I cried out.

'Call me what you will, and no matter what my sad history' she answered, now speaking in gentler tones, like the trickle of a baby brook, 'I am come on an errand of cheer, to tell of future joy, of a wonderful career in store for you. Joy will be attained by all men at some time; usefulness by only a few, you will be one of the favored. In that helpful life love will find a corner; you will see your love again and all will be well between you. I took her form to strengthen your hope. Be of good spirit, glorious, industrious days are before you.'

Comforted as I had never been before, I looked at the fair face of the witch. Surely she had some insight of the universal Plan, and where my humble part lay therein. Why had she come to tell me all these things, I who had never harmed her, but who had passionately loved nature, of which she was a part, unless she meant to encourage me. Many times life, and my place in it, had risen before me like a ghost of discouragement; it was high time to hear a promise of future betterment. I was strangely unconvinced of her past record, that early deception that had made her the water witch.

'I can never begin to tell you how much I owe you for coming to me this afternoon, just when I needed you most. Henceforth I will live on a broader plane, exist on a bigger scale. I will work harder than ever to make myself worthy of my destiny. I will feel that love is not so very far away, it will gild even the most disagreeable tasks with sunlight of smiles. I must forever thank you for coming in the form of her who has won my heart.'

I probably rambled on more, as I am very appreciative by nature, and when people do anything nice for me, I thank them too much, and repay them too liberally. I noticed that the Water Witch said no more, her liquid lips tried to part in a smile, but I heard naught but the distant wood-wind on the ridge. Above it now rose the roar of the stream, perhaps as a signal to the water woman to return to her own. The all-embracing torrent was jealous of her absence. Suddenly the fountainhead dissolved, and flowed down the hill like a mountain rivulet, dancing and leaping over smooth rocks. When it was gone, the rocks were perfectly dry, I could not save a drop of this divine essence.

I reached out one of my arms; my hand touched one of the cold slabs, I awoke. The sun was just about sinking behind the timber line beyond the play-ground. I rose up, there were four does grazing among the sprouts; at the edge of the woods stood a large wide-antlered stag, gazing at me with inquiring eyes. The forest cantata on the opposite ridge had ceased; the wind had fallen with the declining sun. I felt a wild exaltation; I wished for the speedy realization of the joys promised in my vision. As I recovered full consciousness the roar of the run down in the aspen-grown ravine echoed louder in my ears. Its rush and rumble seemed to follow regular beats, to be almost articulate.

In my moment of mental alertness I listened, trying to catch some comforting word. At last I seemed to hear these words: 'I am the water witch, I am at eternal variance with mankind, even with you; I only visited you in your sleep this afternoon to mock you. I know your future, every day of it, down to the smallest crushed hope. You will never see that fair image again, and if you did, only as strangers. You are cast to play a small part in life's drama, your striving will be impotent, footless. Physically you do not live up to your soul. Like my spirit, your name will be written in water. Oh, how I fooled you, how I gave you a taste of a world that can never be yours, your soul must always remain a prisoner.' And from there the voice broke off into a wild weird laugh, cold as the stones over which her liquid lips were running. I stood the laugh as long as I could; I was for answering, and asking the water woman why she added to my load of sorrows. Then I reflected that it would be better to know my limitations now, than to have them thrust upon me by painful experiences. Ever alone, ever a bit discouraged, I must go my way.

The sun had sunk behind the timber line. The afterglow gave a sepulchral yellowness to mountains, trees, and rocks. There was a frost exuding from the hard, stiff clods of the clearing. I tucked my rifle under my arm, and started towards the camp. The dusk, grey and like a pall, was closing in on me fast. As I came to a bend in the trail my downcast eyes raised for a moment, I peered into the forest gloom. Back amid the brushwood I thought I saw the Water Witch, in all the glory of the form of the fair being whom I adored. And despite my limitations, I could not prevent hope from a *resurrection*."

XII. The Lonely Ghost

(Story of Shamokin Mountain.)

Where the bold height of Shamokin Mountain comes to an abrupt end at the river and the railway, there is a narrow carriage road which winds its way along the foot of the ridge, in the direction of Irish Valley. The mountain being of shale formation, the little lane is of the same material, and easy traveling for horses and pedestrians.

On the side of the mountain road only a few stunted Jack pines remain; on the side which slopes down to the culm-blackened waters of Mahanoy Creek, are numerous red birches and a few ancient white-oaks.

Close to the roadside is a jungle of grape-vines, wild honeysuckles, and Solomon's Seal. A few screech owls haunt the solitary dell, there is a grey fox or two still on the mountain, but it is a region singularly barren of wild life. A mile from the river must be traversed before the first house or rather ruin is met with. It was, probably thirty years ago, the home of coal-burners. Charcoal iron losing its vogue, and the cutting of all the available trees, sent the former followers of this humble calling to other localities. To-day the ruin is complete. The roof of split shingles has fallen in, a huge grape-vine which covered the well-box has trailed all over the house; it looks like some beast subjugated by a serpent. The front fence fell down years ago, but someone strung a single strand of now rusty barbed-wire "to keep out the cattle" — but from what? The yard is overgrown with burr-docks, pokes, beggars' lice, and stag-horn sumac.

In the rear of the house lusty young Jack pines are crowding close upon the structure. The stone chimney, partly broken when the roof collapsed, houses several families of swifts. These graceful, eerie birds are most at evidence in the late afternoons, when their circling gives the old ruin a semblance of life. The cellars, and the dilapidated out-buildings are paradises for certain species of rats and mice, bringing the screech owls on the scene, when dusk prevails. After a successful hunt they sit blinking and bulging-eyed on the old mulberry tree above the well. When luck is not good they retire to the oaks and birches along the creek, and sing their lay of blasted hopes. The night wind flaps the broad grape leaves, a ground hog owning comfortable quarters beneath the old out-kitchen sallies forth, burrowing among the half dead plants and weeds in the yard.

Out of an up-stairs room, under the gaping roof, comes an assemblage of particles of spirit, the lonely ghost. Peering first up at the sky, for rain might scatter his particles, or too much moonlight evaporate them, and finding a clear dark night, or one with weird clouds racing across the moon, he emerges. Unable to grasp what death meant, or how to make himself a more vital shade, or how to be annihilated altogether, are some of the burdens of his lament. Tortured with memories of myriad things left undone, of wrongs left un-righted, without the power to help, his plight is a pitiable one. Lonely in every particle, not having held converse with a human being or brother-shade in a quarter of a century, no wonder he sometimes vies with the screech-owls, and the night-wind, in incoherent whining.

Frightening almost out of their wits the few living persons who passed by his isolated haunt at night, he could not tell them how lonely he was, or ask for help. Whenever the thought came to him to pursue people up the road, he would realize it would take him out of his environment, he must suffer annihilation.

Delightful though the state of nothingness might seem, yet something was in his ghostly soul, that he must tell, before he could invite the void. Was it just the story of how lonely he felt, or how unsatisfactory death was, or was it the tale of wrong uppermost in his mind on his death-bed? He was not quite clear as to this — maybe if he met the person who would listen, it would come to him.

What had his life's story been, had he done anything so wrong, that he became an unhappy ghost? Was there any proof that a life of goodness means annihilation, and uprighteousness a life beyond the grave? Was it not the case that good and bad alike survived the grave, for a time? Not having conversed with other shades, he could form no opinions, his spiritual mind reeled like car-sickness whenever he applied himself to the problem. If he had done wrong, and was being punished, like the Good Book taught, he could not particularize upon the wrong.

His mistakes and sins appeared to him no more numerous or worse than those of other men, *even that good friend*. Memories of that good friend set his ghostly imagination into a new channel. Had he ever really harmed him? No, he had not, he had brooded that the good friend wronged him, but in his ghostly state when and how was not clear. The good friend was not better than he ought to be, he probably lied, he knew him to be guilty of sins of the flesh. No, it was nothing he had done against his good friend, except perhaps being jealous of him. Perhaps he was jealous of him, but what of that, wasn't everyone dissatisfied who found himself on the wrong side of the inequalities of life? He had been good to that friend, but he was mighty sure he had been paid for everything he had done, to the last penny. If he hadn't, and his filmy shell curdled with malice, he would haunt that friend's heirs, instead of this lonely shack. Then the ghostly head would reel, he would grow fainter, dawn must be marshalling irresistible forces behind Jack's Mountains to the East.

A chickadee would sing, then all would be still around the ruined house. Despite the open roof, the air was musty and overpowering in the haunted room, no one living could have remained there.

Then would come another night, inky black, with cold desolate winds flapping the flat grape leaves against the house. "A wild night again" would whisper the ghost, and stealthily issue forth. With each succeeding night came fresh impressions of that good friend of the long ago, whom he had hated for many years before his death. It was a horrid thought, to be added to his weight of loneliness and unrest. Perhaps if he had not hated that friend, dissolution might have brought him dreamless sleep.

Life had been full of unpleasant situations, the after-life was disquieting and so lonely. Sometimes vague memories of other friends and relatives churned about in his unstable consciousness. Where were they now, surely this was not the Promised Land where he was to meet them all, at the very house where he had felt the strangle of death. All these images added to his unrest, making him more disquiet and noisy with the advance of years. The ruined coal-burner's shack became known as "the haunted-house." Only those impelled by stern necessity came to travel by it at night. There was a road that followed the middle of the valley, longer to some it proved, but what of it, if it avoided passing the unholy house.

One year, early in June, the creek road was given a thorough overhauling by a new supervisor. He had heard the story of the haunted house, vaguely, as he lived across the valley in the far end of the township. When mending the road directly in front of the old shack, his crew sat by the strand of barbed-wire, under the shade of some vigorous young wild cherry saplings, to eat dinner. Some of the older men, especially those who lived further up the road, complained that the presence of the haunted house hurt the travel on the road. They described the ghost minutely, and whom they thought him to be. The younger men laughed, but none would admit a desire to pass by the shack after nightfall.

The supervisor, who was a middle-aged man, listened attentively. "I wonder if there can be anything in this ghost business, or if it's all make believe?" The older men expressed belief, the young men were doubters.

After the dinner buckets were emptied the entire crew numbering about a dozen entered the house to look about. It was damp and disagreeable on the first floor. Most of the plaster and laths had fallen off the walls and lay about the floor. The stairs were rickety, and some of the steps rotten enough to fall through. The upper rooms were clear and cold, all except one. This one, despite the fact that it had no roof, was hot, and possessed an ugly, sickening odor. "That is the way a ghost room always smells" said the oldest man in the party. "It is the smell of death, of the death that leaves a ghost behind, and fails to liberate the spirit."

"Do you really believe there is a ghost here?" said the supervisor, folding his arms across his long brown beard.

"I surely do," said the oldest man.

"I have a good mind" said the supervisor, "to spend a night here and see for myself."

"You'll have a lot of waiting" chimed in one of the lads, "but you might pass your time shooting groundhogs, there are a dozen making their homes under this old place, I'll bet."

"Well, I cannot stay to-night, I would have to notify the folks, but I'll do it tomorrow if all goes well."

The next morning work was resumed a little further up the road, and amid the toilsome routine old and young thought of the experience in store for the supervisor. He took supper with the oldest man, whose home was a mile above the haunted house, and left his horse and buggy there.

In the evening, which at last came, as June days are reluctant to depart, he walked with his aged friend to the ruined shack.

"Have you got any firearms?" inquired the old man.

"I have my revolver, but I don't expect to use it" said the supervisor. He climbed over the strand of rusted barbed wire, which at places was imbedded deeply in the growing trees, and walked boldly across the yard. He took his seat on the front door-step, peering within, as the door had long since fallen prone in the hall. A gentle breeze rustled the shaggy grapevine; it was now deadly dark, there was no moon. Across the creek a whip-poor-will began its weird appeal. It seemed clearer and more distinct than he had ever heard it. A few crickets chirped in the grass. A night hawk and a bat flitted by him. The thought came to him that all this was very foolish, a strong man like himself absenting himself from his family for a night in order to meet a ghost. Then he recollected that when he was a boy, at the foot of Shade Mountain in old Snyder County, he had heard that ghosts proved troublesome until they delivered their messages. Possibly this one had a sad story; when he heard it, the wraith would depart forever. The lonely road would be rid of its ghost. He would be only adding an extra duty to his task as supervisor. The night grew deeper, and more still. The whip-poor-will and its comrades grieved themselves away into silence, the crickets were lost in the mazes of weeds and grass. The screech owl had complained a while, then lapsed into silence.

The supervisor's vigil bid fair to be a long one. He was on the alert at every sound, even at the flapping of the grapevines against the sides of the ruined house. He did not know where the ghost would appear from, the front door or the side door. He liked the front door step best, he would let the spectre seek him out. But the time was passing apace. The lonely ghost assembled itself in the stuffy upstairs room with the gaping roof, and tremulously crept down the decaying stairs. At the side door he stood irresolute, as all ghosts do, a moment, then emerged. The grape vine, as if to welcome him, flapped ominously against the well-box and the clap-boards. With stealthy tread, the steps of guilt, the ghost stole around the house, and into the open spaces of the yard.

The supervisor, with a grip on his soul, sighted the phantom, recalling his old legendary instructions that a ghost must be allowed to speak first. It took the ghost, with remarkable slowness of apperception, a full half minute to become aware of his human visitor. When he saw him, instead of blood rushing to his face, as in the case of human beings, a weird, white light illuminated his form. As he stood bathed in unearthly aura, the old supervisor had a good look at him. It was a strangely unformed, unfinished face, one not entitled to peace. There was a manifest lack of manliness in the *toute ensemble*. The nose with its pitiable insignificance, the lips receding to disclose the teeth, the restlessness of the eyes, the narrowness of the skull, the flabby chin, the thin neck, as well as the breadth of hips, all were feminine characteristics. They could not be borne by a man capable of great fidelity.

At last the ghost spoke. "I am very glad to see you here, friend, you are the first person who has tried to see me in all the time I have been wandering about, and yet I meant to frighten no one, to do no harm. I have been terribly lonesome, and if at first I tried to follow people, it was for companionship."

The supervisor sat silent for a minute, before answering. He wanted to speak to the point, he might not have a chance to talk long. "Are you sure, stranger, that it was companionship you were seeking, as you could not feel anything in common with living folks, or was it that you had something to tell?"

The ghost smiled, a sickly, unstable smile with his thin lips. "I thought that it was companionship I needed, but I may have had something to tell."

"Then tell it" said the supervisor, bluntly. "I have been very unhappy ever since I entered this state" began the ghost.

"Who did you wrong in life?" broke in the supervisor, "let us have no preambles."

"I had a friend in my youth," resumed the spectre, "when I lived across those mountains to the east, he occupied a different position in life, he was a landowner, and I a farm laborer. I felt unhappy because he owned property and I did not, although his own life in private was tragic in the extreme. I forgot Nature's just balance, imagining he had everything, I nothing. I liked to be with him as he was good-natured and liberal, but away from him I could not restrain myself from abusing him to others. No matter how he suffered I had no sympathy, I inwardly hated him for his material prosperity. And yet I should have felt happy that one like he made so much of me. During a particularly depressing period in his young life, a wonderfully rare girl crossed his path. All his past miseries were forgotten in his love for her. It was as he often said 'the high-tide of his existence.' Persons went to the girl's family and told them of incidents in my friend's life, and they forbade her to see him. An impulse seized me to go to the parents, and explain away the slanders. I could have made things right, I was respected in the community, but as I hated his worldly prosperity, I must see him crossed in love. Later the vile stories were denied by others, and it seemed as if love would triumph.

One bright morning I met my friend riding his horse along the lane which wound around the hills to the fair girl's home. I was wending my way to the fields, with a scythe on my shoulder, it was the time of wheat harvest. I signalled to him to stop, which he did, as he was always glad to see me. There was an expression in his face that told of the inward joy in his soul, the love smile. I told him some things I had heard, mentioning names and places, against the fair girl's good name. I saw he grew deadly pale, and put his arm around the neck of his noble black horse. I drove my awful story home with a wealth of detail and circumstantial evidence. I knew the story to be a lie, though I was so intent on impressing him that I actually believed it at the time. He got on his horse, which he put to a canter, and he was lost to view among the turns in the lane among the oak-grown hills.

"The marriage never took place. The girl married another, the man married another. I never heard what became of her, but my friend's life was wretchedly unhappy. I saw a chance to make a good living as a coal-burner and moved away. When I left I felt sure I had dragged my prosperous friend into the dirt, it was my mental tonic all through the years."

The ghost was prepared to say more, but the supervisor, eyeing him all the while with a cold, penetrating stare, interrupted. "Tell me the name of that man, and I will go to him and right the wrong."

"Too late" moaned the ghost, "he has been dead these many years."

"And the woman?" said the old man, very harshly.

"She, too, is dead, it is all too late."

"Tell me their names, anyhow," said the supervisor. The ghost did as directed. "My heavens" said the old supervisor, "that man was my father, that explains his unhappy marriage, and early death, the tangled state of his affairs." Rising to his feet with angry emphasis he struck at the frail, quavering ghost. With a moan, like a wind among dead leaves, the spectre fell into nothingness.

The old man crossed the yard; at the barbed-wire fence he paused. "This explains the daguerreotype broken in two of a beautiful blonde woman, that we found in father's strongbox, after his death. I can forgive him now for a thousand things I never understood before. I know why he could not give his whole heart to poor mother." There were tears in the rugged old face as he stepped over the fence. "At any rate, I have laid that wretched ghost. If the Good Man takes what is left of his spirit that confession will have made it pure. But the score of people whom he harmed directly and indirectly, no hope for them."

With bowed head he moved along the lane, thinking thoughts deeper than had ever stirred his soul.

His anxious host was sitting up to greet him, on the kitchen porch. "Did you see the ghost?" he called out, when he saw the supervisor coming in the gate.

"Yes, I saw him, and I laid him for good and all" replied the old man with emphasis. And the little lane along the foot of Shamokin Mountain never knew the lonely ghost again; he probably had joined a happier throng.

XIII. The Horse Beater

(Story of the Old River Dam.)

"About the time of the war" said the old grave-digger, "I was very fond of fishing for cat-fish by the new moon's light, above the dam. It seemed as if they bit quicker after night, or when there was some little light from the moon. Early in the evening there were a few other fishermen at my favorite eddy, but along towards midnight I had the whole river front to myself. Even when alone it was not always pleasant; in the spring and fall of the year the banks would be drifted full of barrels of dead wild pigeons, and the stench was unbearable. The hunters killed the birds faster than they could eat or ship them, so when they started to 'go bad' they dumped them barrels and all into the river. I didn't mind when the river was filled with rafts and logs, as I could fish in among them, but the dead pigeons drove me away.

There was an old Yankee stage-driver, he drove the Robertsburg stage, who used to live back on the hill from where I fished. He usually got in from his trips at ten or eleven o'clock, and about midnight he would come down to the river bank to fill a couple of pails of water for his horses. He was a crochety old fellow, and seldom answered me when I wished him good-evening. He was always swearing and muttering to himself; I always suspected he was over-tired when he got back from his long overland journeys, and did not get sleep enough. Often when he went back with the water, I would hear his horses prancing and kicking, and the blows of his cudgel over their heads and backs would drift to me through the night air. Evidently if the horses drank too little, or chafed for more, he would give them a sound drubbing. Before daybreak he would go out again, so he really never had a full night's sleep.

I was of a friendly nature, but try as I might was never able during the two or three years I fished at that eddy, to make any headway with his acquaintance. He was a little, lean man, with a beak nose, and long grey sidewhiskers; he was a type of face and form one could not easily forget.

One rainy autumn he caught a heavy cold, and was forced to take his bed. He grieved for fear he would lose his mail contract, but refused to let anyone else drive his horses. He evidently liked them in some strange, selfish way. While he was ill another hackman in town ran a stage and carried the mail. But he worried so much, that the strain told on him, and he died. As he had run the stage for twenty-five years, ever since the county was established, his faults were instantly forgotten, and there was general lamenting over his demise. A big crowd attended the funeral, his obituaries filled columns in the county papers. He did not live with his wife, and was on unfriendly terms with his sons-in-law, consequently there was no continuance to his business.

The other hackman got the mail contract, and took up the stage-route. The horses were given a good rest for once in their lives, and were being fattened preparatory to sale. They were a husky pair of bays, full brothers, bred in the county, and with a dash of Conestoga blood in them. On their upper lips were tufts of hair like mustaches. Despite eulogies and mourning displays the old stage-driver was forgotten in a few days.

His successor was a big, round-faced, jovial Dutchman, who honestly strove to accommodate. People wondered why they had respected or tolerated the old fellow who died, so long. His peculiarities were thrown into bolder relief in contrast to his genial successor. The pendulum speedily swung the other way, the dead man was roundly execrated.

One night while I was sitting by the hank, I was perched on a big white pine log that had drifted on shore, fishing away, I thought I heard a rustling of leaves in the hazel-bushes which lined the path which led from the hilltop to the river. I looked around but could see nothing. I listened, I heard the sound again. It might be a stray cat, sneaking down to look for dead fish or pigeons. Soon I perceived a human figure emerging from the underbrush. It was stooped and attenuated, and carried two water buckets. It must be some one from the aged stage-driver's home coming down to get water for the horses. It appeared an unearthly time to water horses which weren't doing any work. I looked more carefully; the figure resembled the dead man so closely, I concluded it must be his brother who had come in from Illinois for the funeral. But the brother wore a chin-beard, whereas this man had only side-whiskers. It was surely the stage-driver himself, although he had been dead nearly two weeks. I was too young to know what terror really meant, and gazed with a peculiar fascination at the apparition. He paused not ten feet from where I sat, and stooped over to fill his buckets. I spoke out boldly, 'Good evening, Mister, I am glad to see you here again.' At this the spectre raised up, and glared at me. A few streaks of moonlight, it must have been that, lit up his face, and made it gleam like foxfire. Through the transparent flesh I could see the dark outlines of the skeleton. He glared at me, grinding his teeth, as if I had tried to insult him.

I became a little frightened. 'I meant no harm, sir,' I protested. 'I only said I was glad to see you out again.' This seemed to mollify the ghost, and he stooped down again and filled his two buckets. Then he turned around, took another, and more amiable look at me, and started up the hill. When he was out of sight I realized I had seen a ghost, a particularly horrible one at that. I had heard it said that the baser a man's thoughts or deeds in life, the more distorted looking his spirit after death, and this surely was a case in point. It was the first ghost I had seen; I hoped it would be the last.

But I was a stout-hearted boy in those days and instead of running home and hiding my head under the quilts, I threw my line back into the water, and a minute later landed a big catfish. But I fancied I heard the horses being beaten in the stable.

The next night I was back at the river-bank more out of curiosity to see the old stage-driver's ghost than to catch the fish. I hardly dared hope he would come again, I had a notion, I don't know where I got it, that ghosts only appeared once in the same place. About midnight I heard the hazel-twigs crackling, I knew my weird visitor was at hand. This time he was more sociable, as he wished me good evening, in a tone of voice gentler than he had ever used in life, even to his own family. I was in hopes that he would be more forbearing with the poor horses when he returned to the stable with the water. He lingered around the water's edge, as if he had something on his mind, yet did not have quite the courage or ability to impart it. I know now why he never was able to tell me his story — I had spoken first. A ghost must be allowed to tell his sad story, then human beings can add anything they wish. But the ghost must speak first, else he is forever dumb to explain his sad meaning. Finally the old man, or whatever he was, filled his pails, and scrambled up the steep path.

In ten minutes I heard that awful commotion in the stable. It sounded as if the horses would kick down the flimsy building in their frenzy. It seemed to keep up for half an hour; it must have waked all the households in the neighborhood. The stable stood in the dreary outskirts of the town, but there were a number of houses within half a square.

I left for home after the noise quieted down, considerably mystified by the whole proceeding. The next night the ghost appeared again at the bank, and filled his water buckets. He greeted me gently, but his ugly humor evidently quickly returned, as the racket in the horse-stable was louder than ever. For a week this kept up, and I wondered why the neighbors, God fearing people that they were, permitted it to go on without an investigation.

I did not like to discuss the matter with my parents, who were Church members. If they thought I met a ghost at the river-side they might forbid my nocturnal fishing trips, even though they substantially added to the larder. But I should have done so out of mercy for the poor horses.

On the Sunday night after I had first seen the ghost, I was at my fishing as usual. The ghost appeared, but I noticed he was deep in his ugly humor. He refused to speak to me, and was muttering and swearing to himself, just as he used to do in life. He hung around the water longer than at any other time. He sat on another big log, near to my favorite perch, cursing terribly. I could hear him grit his teeth, although he never turned about to look at me. He kept his back to me most of the time. At last he roused himself, filled his buckets, and clambered up the steep bank. I wondered what was wrong with the old fellow. I was puzzled at the time. I believe he had something to tell, but could not, and realizing his ghostly days were numbered, was wild with chagrin. Soon the rumpus at the barn began again. It was louder than ever. I marvelled it did not rouse the entire town. Horses in our town were generally treated with kindness; though it was before the days of humane societies, there were scores of kindly disposed souls whom I might name, who would have interfered. The noise became so terrific that I hid my lines in the underbrush, and climbed up the bank. I ran to the scene, just in time to see others running in the same direction.

Just as the half dozen men coming from different angles were within a hundred yards of the barn, the doors flew open, and the old stage was backed down the incline, and out into the open lot. No one seemed to be doing it, yet it ran with great celerity. The horses were still prancing about, as if crazed from their beating. Among the men in the crowd alluded to, I recognized two or three. 'Somebody's gone and broken into that barn, and would have stolen horses, stagecoach and all, if we hadn't heard him.' The others chorused assent, but I said nothing, whispering to myself, 'wait and see.'

The men rushed in the barn, hoping to find the thief in the mow or crouched in the feed-chest. None of them had lanterns, but by matches they were able to form a fair idea of the condition of the premises. The doors had been opened, the stage shoved out. That was correct enough. The double harness had been dragged off its pegs, and lay strewn over the barn-floor. This supported the robbery theory. When the horse-stalls were visited, every man was struck for an explanation. The poor beasts were still prancing about, white with foam. Their backs were badly marked with welts where they had been beaten. Some of the skin had been knocked off their muzzles and over their eyes. Back of one of the stalls, in the straw, lay a long oak club with knob on the end of it. That had been the weapon used by the horse-beater, whoever he might be. On the feed-boxes, in front of each horse, sat an untouched bucketful of water. That was why, in my estimation, the ghost pounded the horses, they would not drink for him. The simple men who had been attracted by the noise propounded the theory that the thief had tried to get the team to drink before he harnessed them, and upon their refusal, beat them so unmercifully. At this I literally 'laughed in my sleeve.'

In the midst of the excitement, the two sons-in-law of the deceased stage-driver dashed into the barn, breathless from running. One carried a lantern, the other a shot-gun. Had they not recognized some of us, I believe we would have been shot down as horse-thieves! They could not understand what had happened, except that a thief had been surprised at the crucial moment. While everybody was trying to talk at once, another party put in an appearance. He was an old High German, who lived at the far upper end of town, not very distant from where the new hospital now stands. How he heard the noise that far away I cannot say unless it was louder than I dared to imagine. He stood in a corner of the barn-floor for a couple of minutes, pulling his long pointed beard; an underseized man he was, much like pictures of those gnomes in the story of Rip Van Winkle. Then he leisurely strolled into the horse-stable.

One of the sons-in-law of the stage driver, who knew the old German and myself, followed at a respectful distance. The old fellow went into one of the horse-stalls, seizing the trembling animal resolutely by the bridle. He looked at its countenance carefully, and then came out shaking his shaggy head. He went into the adjoining stall, and examined the other horse's head. When he came out he shook his long bony fore-finger saying: 'Horses with mustaches see things. Those horses have been annoyed by a ghost, and not a horse-thief. I believe that old rascal who owned them has been back, that's all there is to this shindy.'

The dead man's son-in-law scowled at the German, but said nothing because of his advanced age.

We all returned to the barn-floor, where the willing crowd had pulled the stage back into place, and re-arranged and hung the harness on its pegs. The old German recognizing one of the men, said out loudly so everybody could hear: 'This has been a ghost's doings, that old man's ghost; better they sell these horses or it will occur every night.'

'Nonsense, stop such talk,' called out one of the sons-in-law angrily, shaking his fist at the German busybody.

The old man grinned, and turned and walked quietly out of the stable. I followed him and when we reached the walk I ran up beside him and told him I had seen the stage-driver's ghost every night for a week, filling his horse-buckets at the river. The old German laughed heartily. 'I knew that was the case' he said, 'but these smart young fellows think they know more than we old chaps.' But there was every reason to believe that the old German's warning had its effect. That next afternoon the horses were removed to a barn at the other end of town, and a few days later were sold to a farmer from the German Settlement. I fished at midnight a good many times after that. I sometimes heard the hazel-bushes creak, hut I never again caught sight of the ghost of the horse-beating old stage-driver."

XIV. Queen Elizabeth

(Story of Frenchville.)

"From the noise those wolves are making to-night," said old Richard Aubier, opening the door of his comfortable mansion of logs and plaster, lantern in hand, and peering out into the gloom, "I do believe they are going to cross the river and capture the settlement." The loud, raucous yelping of two hundred or more hungry beasts, rose high above the roar of the water-wheel at the sturdy pioneer's sawmill.

The old man's daughter Elizabeth, a tall slim girl of eighteen, with unusual refinement of features, and exquisite blonde coloring, pressed to her father's side, and with him listened to the weird uproar on the mountains across the river at the mouth of Deer. When it would cease for a moment, the roll of the water-wheel, flashing its white spray against the blackness of the night, would become intensified. The old man made a move to go back to the fireside, where his wife and younger children were seated in a huge settle, and Elizabeth slipped the lantern into her own hand. Winding a scarf above her profuse golden hair, of the color that Fragonard would have delighted to paint, she stood on the steps, irresolute for a moment. Then she stepped outside, and swinging the lantern to and fro, leisurely strolled along the boardwalk to the front gate.

The walk was a ponderous swinging contraption, made of cull lumber. Setting the lantern on the grass, she leaned against the gate, listening to the wolfish music, to the eternal splash of the water-wheel. Born as she had been in this primitive French settlement near the Susquehanna headwaters, amid all the struggle for existence and loneliness, she was acutely conscious that she possessed a French soul. With it she saw and felt as no one else about her; she realized a spiritual barrier, even at her early age, which kept her from close association with the other girls in the settlement. She was devout in her religious duties at St. Mary's-on-the-Mountain, she kept up her knowledge of her family's language at the Parochial school under the pines, just by the church. She read whenever she could find the time, even the simplest books made a profound impression on her. She was at this time what would be called "a pure spirit." She was as she had come from the Eternal

Source, no debasing or weakening influences had touched her in this little village of the wilderness.

St. Mary's on the Mountain, Frenchville, PA.

Her father and mother, natives of Picardy, were among the first dozen families to arrive at Frenchville, where they had prospered — the tract of land on which it stood having been originally bought as an asylum for the great Bonaparte. The girl had been born a year after her parents' arrival in the wilds; an older brother had been born in France. This boy Marcelin had been knocked off a raft coming from Cherry-tree the year before; it had cast the first serious aspect over her life; it added to her studious mien, and tendency towards introspection. The entire family had been bowed down by the loss of their only son, so her silence, and abstraction caused no comment among them.

This cold autumn night, as she leaned against the gate, listening to the wolves calling, and the rush and swirl of the big waterwheel, she thought of her sorrow, of the mystery of life, of her personal destiny. She wondered why her parents had left "La Belle France," where they had friends and relatives, and tolerably comfortable social position, for this isolated spot. It was grand no doubt, from a scenic point of view, perhaps more so than the valley of the Allier. On clear mornings from where she lolled tonight, could be seen the three famous knobs of Clearfield County. "Little Alps" the old French people called them, especially when their dark heliotrope crests commingled with the snows. It was a boundless landscape to be sure, an endless sea of pine and hemlock, as wild as in colonial days. The elk were pretty well driven north, which accounted for the added ferocity of the wolves, which fed off the weakly members of the herds, but deer, bears, panthers, wild cats, catamounts and foxes ranged the forests, as bold and plentiful as in the days before the hunters assailed them.

It was a beautiful sight to see the vast flocks of wild pigeons sweeping around the crests of the distant Knobs, like wreaths about the brows of immortal poets.

Elizabeth Aubier was conscious of all this beauty; it gave her a sense of security in the wilderness, and dulled the latent curiosity as to how the beloved France of her parents really looked. The hound-dogs which earlier in the evening had barked themselves hoarse in protest against the wolfish invasion had been still for some time. Suddenly they began again, but in a lower key, a snarling, rasping bark, that someone was nigh. Elizabeth leaning on the heavy gate looked up and down the road, but could discern little in the darkness. She reached over, and picking up the fluttering lantern, placed it on the top of the gate. Its uncertain light danced and eddied on the stony, uneven road, that was little better than a trail.

Despite the lantern, five human figures were almost opposite to her before she noticed them. All five proved to be young men, of good average height, stockily built, and graceful. Their leader stopped when near to her, and saluting her with his rifle, spoke to her in tones of great civility. "Please pardon me, young lady, but does Israel Laverte still keep that canoe at the mouth of Deer?"

Before the girl could answer, one of the other young men interrupted saying: "If he does, we thought we would go down and chase a few of those mountain nightingales back into the tall timber."

Israel Laverte was a young Franco-Pennsylvanian who had gone to school with Elizabeth. "I think the canoe is still there, but he is away lumbering" replied the girl, pleasantly. "We knew he was away" said the boldest young man, "else two hundred wolves would not be howling themselves hoarse directly across the river from his home."

Elizabeth smiled to herself; she had always imagined Israel a great hunter, it was now proved by his being praised by strangers. The dogs were growling and wagging their tails, alternately, but still making quite a noise. Elizabeth heard the side door opening, her father was evidently coming to join in the talk.

The young strangers were clustered close about the gate, confiding and friendly. By the lamplight she could study their faces, she was not surprised to find that they were Indians. She had seen so many redmen in her brief life, they were no novelty. Many of them ran the rafts on the river, or worked in the lumber camps which were becoming more numerous every year in the deep ravines which opened into the river valley. Others bound on hunting trips, passed by the house in the fall and winter. This party of five were an interesting lot of young fellows.

Their leader, the one with the kindly voice who had spoken first, fascinated her particularly. His size and build reminded her of Israel, who was her paragon of manhood, but his features were more finely cut. There was an ascetic droop to his high nose, a melancholy glance in his deep set eyes, a sensitiveness to his mouth, altogether lacking in Israel. The night was cold, but probably from walking far, he felt overheated and removed his cloth cap. The night wind blew a strand of soft, black hair across his broad brow, and sometimes he brushed it back from his eyes. He was in the early twenties, she imagined, as were his comrades.

By this time old Richard Aubier had joined the party at the gate. He shook hands with the leader. "Good evening, Sammy" he said in genial tones. They said a few words about the wolves, and then the Indian cavalcade made ready to move on.

The young leader's eyes met Elizabeth's, there was an answering flash between those orbs of black and grey. Elizabeth rarely opened her eyes fully, but the glance, half-mast, from beneath her long dark lashes, was one never to be forgotten by anyone thus favored.

"Who was that young man, father, he seemed very nice" inquired the girl, as the two, arm in arm, walked towards the house along the boardwalk.

"That's young Sammy Jimmerson, the king of the Senecas, he's grandson of the great chief Red Jacket."

"I thought he was a person of some quality" said the girl, "but where did you meet him?"

"You recall," said the old man, "when I went on that big elk drive at the Flag

Swamps last autumn? Well, we found Sammy, as I call him, camped near the feeding grounds. He joined with us, and not a single elk could escape." Before they re-entered the house they paused a minute on the door-step to hear the wolves. They were howling in concert, like the voice of one huge lion. "Those boys will drive them off," said the old pioneer as he closed the door.

Secretly Elizabeth felt that her Indian acquaintances would not molest the wolves, that the party had stopped because their leader felt a strange admiration for her. Despite her matchless beauty, she was totally unaware of it. She never ascribed motives to mere politeness.

Madame Aubier was coming down stairs, after having put the younger children to bed, as they came in, and Elizabeth told her enthusiastically about meeting the Indian King. The mother took kings, even aboriginal ones, seriously, and said that between her husband and daughter they should have had forethought enough to invite him in. Madame Aubier, like her husband was good-natured, but was less absent-minded and dreamy than he, or Elizabeth, for that matter.

The Indians went their way along the narrow trail beneath the tall lace-tipped pines. They made no effort to molest the wolves, precisely as Elizabeth had surmised. Nocturnal as some wild beasts, they traveled until dawn, when they found a cozy nook beside a gushing spring, and built a fire to cook a breakfast of pine squirrels.

Sammy, or the Seneca King, never spoke a word after he left Elizabeth. Always dreaming, with the hyper-sensitiveness of the white blood in his veins, his heart was touched to the innermost by this, the fairest vision of his life. Young as he was, he had already married after a tribal custom, but it was a temporary alliance, arranged to keep his hot-blood in check until someone of suitable rank could be provided. He thought of Elizabeth as a beautiful vision, almost as a fair unreality, at first. Towards dawn he regarded her in the light of a possible Seneca Queen, a consort with whom to revive the dying magnificence and traditions of his race. Like a royal-blooded Rienzi, he longed to evoke a renaissance among the Northern Indians, not in anyway unfriendly to the whites, but to be the last great personage of his race, before inevitable fate turned them all into vague shadows.

Elizabeth, in her little room under the roof, lay awake until daybreak. There was something about the young Indian that was bizarre, even sublime; he captivated her thoughts. She at once imagined him to possess ideals, and tried to compare him with Israel Laverte.

Israel had been the most sought after youth in the French settlement; yet apart from his unquestioned courage and good looks, was there anything else? She had heard of his being drunk at a speak-easy at the mouth of Moshannon, and even in Clearfield Town. He had tried to kiss her in presence of everybody at a dancing party at the general store; perhaps he had been drinking then, hard cider was plentiful. But Israel was a tangible reality; she could have him, other girls wanted him.

The Seneca King was a passing fancy; in all probabilities she would never see him again. But during the months that ensued, even when she was with Israel, there rose before her the shadowy presentiment of the Indian youth, and that he was thinking about her. She could not exorcise him from her spirit.

She was growing more beautiful all the time; a handsome young aristocrat from Philadelphia, of the proud house of Shippen, who was inspecting the family timberlands, spent a night at the Aubier home. He could speak French beautifully, and charmed one and all. He was smitten with Elizabeth, and she liked him, even though in the background of her soul ever rose the shade of the Seneca King.

As for the King himself, far away, he only thought of the fair Elizabeth, there were wireless messages even in the first quarter of the nineteenth century. With his suite, he had travelled southwesterly to the Allegheny, fishing and hunting just enough to keep the party in provisions. At the Allegheny canoes were in readiness; the real sport began, and they hunted up that historic river clear to Johnnycake. There they went into winter quarters, on the royal island, using their idle moments to tan their elk and panther hides. In work and in idleness, awake or asleep, the Seneca King thought solely of Elizabeth. If he blamed himself once, he did a thousand times, and that meant three or four times a day, for not having gone back, and become better acquainted with the girl. As an Indian King, with a lineage estimated a thousand years at least, and bearing the blood of Mary Jameson, "The Woman of the Genesee," he considered himself the peer of any person.

When he left the royal campgrounds in the early summer, he resolved to see Elizabeth, court her, and if she was willing, make her his queen. He still owned much land in Pennsylvania and New York, besides having tribal rights to vast territory in the West. On the way he happened upon some young Frenchmen who knew his beloved's family well. They mentioned that Richard Aubier was on the committee who were getting up a big picnic of French people, to be held in mid-August on the heights above Keewaydin. The Seneca King felt sure that Elizabeth would be present; he could meet her there. It would be a good place to become better acquainted, when everybody was feeling so happy. He camped, hunted, and fished the weeks away, until the time for the big picnic drew near. Then, with his followers, he travelled one whole night, so that they arrived on the picnic ground at dawn on the famous day.

These picnics are still being held annually, though not always in the same grove, and nearly a century after the first one, are every bit as popular. Fifteen hundred people attended the picnic held in 1912. The grove above Keewaydin had been until lately a feeding ground for elks, and a half century earlier for buffaloes. The grass, long tramped and browsed, resembled a lawn; shade was provided by enormous, slender chestnut trees, and a few original pines. On four sides of the hill were rich springs of water; it was a picturesque and convenient spot in every sense of the word. Most of the French settlers were early to arrive. Some came on horseback, or in wagons, but the majority walked. Baskets and bundles of eatables filled considerable space; a dancing floor of hand-sawed boards adorned a shady nook. There were booths where eatables were sold; one of these was adorned with the tricolor. The big crowd was happy, it was a triumph of this New France. The crowd were well-dressed; orderly but good-natured.

They were a handsome lot, old and young, and among the more youthful participants were about an even number of brunettes and blondes. The young girls liked to adorn their dresses and hair with bright ribbons; some of the boys wore brown velvet coats and flowing red or blue ties. In contrast to these, Elizabeth, who with her family was among the early arrivals, was simply attired. She wore a pale blue silk skirt, and a white waist, made partly from lace her mother had carefully brought from Picardy. Her golden hair was worn coiled about her head, her forehead was covered by little blonde bangs. She wore no jewelry nor ornaments.

Besides the French element, there were other picturesque types represented. The trappers from the wilderness were all on hand, big, dark-bearded fellows, swaggering about with their hands in the pockets of their beaver-skin vests. The rivermen were much in evidence, bearded, tall, and angular, booted, and wearing shirts of blue or scarlet. Then there were short, stout, broad-hatted farmers, from the vicinity of Clearfield Town, taking their pleasures seriously. Of course there were the women and children of these types, as oddly costumed, and individual, as the men.

The Indian coterie, headed by King Jimmerson, wandered among the motley crowd, sometimes casting glances at the pretty girls, but usually travelling with downcast eyes. If they but knew it, they were the sensation of the day. The young King was dressed for the occasion. He wore a red cloth cap, with an osprey's feather in it, a blue coat with red facings and sleevelets, blue trousers, and black knee boots with red tops. A silver medal, a gift from George Washington to one of his ancestors, dangled from a chain of like material around his neck. He wore a cartridge belt well-filled, and carried his long rifle, the stock of which was inlaid with silver, much as the modern country gallant does his buggy-whip, at camp meeting. The other Indians were somewhat less gaily attired. His eagle eye finally rested on the fair Elizabeth, who with several other girls, was watching the unharnessing of the six-horse stage which had brought a goodly crowd from Clearfield Town, twenty miles away. Saluting her with his rifle, he smiled at her with his sad, wistful lips. The young girl's face brightened; she held out her hand; it was like meeting her oldest friend. From that moment until after ten o'clock that night, when the Aubier family started homeward, the handsome young couple were together.

They strolled among the happy throngs all the forenoon, the most admired of all. They ate dinner together at the Aubier spread under a mammoth rock oak; then they wandered off to a secluded nook, where they tarried all afternoon. They made love to the music from the throats of many turtle doves in the tall trees. They ate supper together, with the old folks, and in the evening, though it had the chilliness of a two thousand foot altitude, they sought another glade, where they remained until the enamored King, by the aid of Red Jacket's huge silver watch, saw it was time to rejoin the family party. During the afternoon, and during the evening, he had kissed her, and their love was cemented by a few sincere words. Only once had Israel Laverte's name been mentioned. That was when Elizabeth had asked the young king if he had taken the canoe and crossed the river after the howling wolves. "Of course not," the Indian replied frankly; Elizabeth then confided to him that she had never thought for a moment he would do so. Then they both had a good laugh, and another kiss.

The King spent the night at the Aubier residence, after escorting the girl home. He promised to rejoin his followers at the picnic-ground on the morrow. Madame Aubier was particularly nice to him; he told her freely of his ancient lineage, of his individual hopes to rehabilitate the kingdom of the Senecas. "But," he admitted unhesitatingly, "we are a dying race, my best efforts cannot prolong our glories long."

"It is a wonder," remarked the shrewd French mother, "that a young man of your talents and power has not married."

King Jimmerson did not reply; he could not very well say he had been unofficially married, or that he had not. The next morning he lingered around the hospitable home until nearly noontime. He left telling Elizabeth that he would go home and arrange his affairs, and come back at Christmas time and make her his wife. Meanwhile they would correspond as often as they could get their letters transported. The girl suggested that he ask her mother's consent, but the Indian objected to this. Pressed for a reason, he confessed that he had been married to one of the plain squaws of his tribe, on his eighteenth birthday, but could have the bonds dissolved provided he was marrying some one of equal rank. "That you are, my love," he declared dramatically. "I will have myself freed by the council from my unofficial wife, and return at Christmas time and wed you."

This seemed plausible enough to the love-sick girl, so she bade him goodbye tearfully; and with promises not to tell her mother of his other alliance, they parted. When she told her mother that she was to be married to the young monarch, it pleased the good lady mightily.

A few nights later Etienne Vallechamp, a noted French trader, stopped over night with the Aubiers. He was a great traveller, and carried on a considerable fur business with the Senecas. In the presence of Elizabeth, Madame Aubier told him about the recent visit from young King Jimmerson. "Why he's a married man, and has a couple of children," said the burly trader, bluntly. Then he went on to say that while the young king was a fine example of the old-fashioned redman, morally he was no better than Indians usually were. Elizabeth had already posted one letter to her Indian lover, and with her mother's consent.

Before she went to bed her mother ordered that she write him no further. "If you want a lover, there's Israel Laverte, all the girls in the settlement are crazy over him; he's good stock, and he has got no wife." Elizabeth had ceased to care for Israel, and though she knew he would be home in a few days, it did not quicken her interest. She cried all that night, doubts entering her mind to add to her torment. Perhaps the Indian youth had a real wife; he might be doing an act of injustice to this woman and the children if he discarded them so as to make her his bride.

In three weeks came an answer to the first letter. It was couched in terms of deepest affection. All through it were little sketches of animals, birds, trees, showing that the Seneca King was considerable of an artist. Elizabeth retired to her little room under the roof to read it. She read it half a dozen times before finally tucking it in the bosom of her dress. Madame Aubier had seen the letter arrive, her husband had brought it from the post-office. She forbid Elizabeth to answer it. This aroused a spirit of rebellion in the proud young girl. She could not believe the young King was deceiving her even though he might be doing an unmanly act to put away a wife and children for her. After night, when she retired to bed, she wrote him long and passionately, her little room lit only by the light of a flickering candle. Through the partly opened window she could hear the wolves lamenting on the ridge across the river, at the mouth of Deer, just as on the night of their first meeting. She told her lover just how he had been undermined by the trader Vallechamp, how she still believed in him, that she had been forbidden to write, and was only doing so with the door locked. She finished the letter with these words, "I do love you, forever, and forever, come what may."

In the morning she had errands at the Frenchville store, over two miles away. Old Peter Mignot was the postmaster, and when blushingly she drew the bulky letter from her waist, he put his forefinger against his nose, as was his habit, saying, "Ah, mademoiselle, you have a lover!"

"I may have, but please, monsieur, don't tell a soul," said the girl.

Placing his hand on his heart, with old-time courtesy, he replied, "I promise, upon my word as a gentleman of Picardy." After that Elizabeth had no fear, she could rely on the word of a Frenchman.

But fate was planning her fair bark to drift into different channels. Barely had the letter reached the Indian lover at Johnnycake when Israel Laverte appeared at Frenchville. The lumbermen from Maine, who were cutting square timber at the mouth of Ferney, broke up, and could not pay their hands. Israel, trusted man that he was, became their preferred creditor. They had two rangy red roan horses; these they gave him in settlement for his claim for the wages of his two younger brothers and self. The two younger lads rode the horses, and Israel walked on ahead, up through the valley of the Susquehanna, to Frenchville. At Keating's Store they had to ford the river; it was perilous business with the river running high. One of the boys was unhorsed and almost shared the fate of Elizabeth's older brother.

Getting the horses home in safety, his next thought was to visit Elizabeth. She was not in an unreceptive mood; her mind had been poisoned by doubts of the Seneca King's true marital condition; it was refreshing to meet a really unmarried man. She was glad to accept his invitation to ride one of his horses to a harvest picnic at Beausignor's woods five miles away. The start was made on a clear October morning, with the heliotrope Knobs in full view all the way. Everything seemed big and grand on such a day. It was a more likely day for loving than the calm, lengthy Sunday in August at the big picnic, when the King of the Senecas won the day. Elizabeth loved horses, it was a rare treat to ride the mettlesome roan colt, at the side of its mate, managed so nobly by the catch of the Keewaydin district, Israel Laverte.

The young hunter never looked handsomer. His hair, worn long, was blacker than a raven's wing, as were his small side-whiskers, his eyes, his lashes and brows. His long nose suggested that of the great Bonaparte, an engraving of whom as First Consul, hung above the fireplace in the Aubier residence. Israel was of her own race, a son of Picardy; even if he did drink, he was no wild Indian, no married man and father; he was young, handsome, marriageable. Riding by his side, Elizabeth scrutinized him carefully in profile. He had a stronger face than the Indian lad, it seemed to her. His skin was fairer, his mouth was straighter, oh, she loved him better. Israel must have divined her thoughts, for he asked her that day to marry him. She told him that she had half-promised the Seneca King, hut would give him up gladly.

Israel showed surprise that she knew the Indian. "He is a worthless dog, a married man, a mere savage, a wild man of the woods." Elizabeth bit her lips when she recalled how nicely the Indian had always spoken of Israel. The elder Aubiers, pleased mightily to hear of their daughter's new affection, urged that the young people marry as quickly as possible. This they reasoned out would prevent a possible return of the "wild man."

Elizabeth in due season received an answer to her last letter to her Indian lover. She was too conscience-stricken to read it, and in the presence of her approving mother, threw it unopened into the fireplace.

The marriage took place in November, and after a wedding drive to Clearfield, the happy pair moved into a brand new log-cabin directly across the road from Richard Aubier's watermill. Never was a bride more contented than Elizabeth. All the girls on the heights of Keewaydin, who had wished to win Israel, congratulated her; the priest Pere de la Chau told her she was marrying the finest man she could find in a lifetime. There was not a cloud on the horizon.

It was early in December when a letter came from the Indian King. He could not understand her strange silence. Were her letters lost, or abstracted from the mails? Did she mistrust him, did she fear that he would fail to appear to wed her, freed of previous matrimonial ties, at Christmas time? He asked her for an answer; it would ease his mind before starting. Elizabeth, considerably perplexed, showed the letter to her young husband. He laughed at the Indian's high-flown language, his deep earnestness. He told her not to answer the letter. She said she was afraid the fellow would appear at Christmas time. "Damn him, let him come, I can attend to him," was Israel's laconic reply.

Every day the bridegroom went to work in one of the deep ravines tributary to the river, leaving Elizabeth alone. She had no fear, however, as her parents lived across the road. Old Richard Aubier and his helpers, the three big Coudriet boys could be over in a minute, and drive any wild Indian lover from the premises. Time rolled around; it was the week before Christmas. Elizabeth was busy garlanding the rooms of her cozy home with strings of ground-pine, interspersed with tea-berries. It was about nine o'clock in the morning when she heard a knocking. She got down from her chair, and ran to the door, flinging it open. Before her stood the stalwart form of the Seneca King, decked out in beaver furs, but with a sadder and more pensive look in his cavernous eyes, his sensitive mouth. He took off his beaver cap, he held out his hand. Elizabeth hardly deigned to grasp it.

"You did not answer my letters, but I came anyhow, we must be married."

Elizabeth's drooping lids fell lower, for an instant she feared to tell the truth. "Too late," she faltered, "I am already married. I'm the wife of Israel Laverte."

The Indian stood speechless in the door-way, cap in hand. Finally mustering courage he spoke out. "Could you not have trusted me until I returned; was my word of no value; were your words of love false?"

"No, no," stammered Elizabeth, turning deadly pale, "I loved you, but I was told you were a married man. You know, I felt I was displacing another woman and children. I could not do it."

"Oh, my dear Elizabeth, only woman I have or shall ever love," said the Indian tears starting in the corners of his eyes, "you should have gone through fire and water for the man you loved."

Elizabeth, seeking to end a profitless discussion, became cold, and answered, "I didn't think there was any such man worth the risk of going through fire and water."

The Indian closed his lips tightly, the tears dried, he was captain of his soul. Without another word he reached into his deep coat pocket, taking out a small woolen bag. This he opened, disclosing a band of silver, interwoven with red ribbons. "This was to have been my wedding gift to you, the crown of the Seneca queens. It has been worn by many worthy women for five hundred years. Though you cannot marry me, please take it as a token of my love, of my sincerity. Take it as proof that there will never be another Queen, but you, Queen Elizabeth."

Mechanically she took it, hardly thanking him. The Indian looked at her calmly, with his deep eyes of love. "Goodbye, my only love," he said, as he held out his hand.

"Goodbye, friend, good luck to you," was all she could muster in reply. With head erect, the last King of the mighty Senecas walked out of the yard, and up the centre of the road.

Elizabeth tried on the crown; it was a perfect fit; then she hid it in a cranny in the plaster back of the cupboard. For a moment she felt herself an Indian Queen. Calm as she was, she could not hang any more garlands of ground-pine that morning. When Israel came home in the evening she told him that the visit from the Indian had occurred, that he had been sent on his way. Nothing more was said on the subject; it had been treated with contemptuous jocularity which every satisfied husband gives to unsuccessful efforts to win his wife.

Years passed, the Indian became a hazy tradition. Elizabeth went on living the commonplace physical life, crushing her French soul. She took on flesh, veins stood out on her cheeks, dark puffs further closed her half-shut eyes. Her exquisite arched nose sunk in at the bridge, and thickened at the nostrils. The lips became gray and coarse. Her hair lost its golden tint and became a pasty brown. Her walk became slipshod, she was no longer erect. Children were born, and brought up without ideals, without hopes. She never noticed the heliotrope color of the Knobs. Israel never seemed to get ahead, he drank considerably, and when in his cups was coarse and abusive. At the time of their marriage it had been planned that they would move into a larger house in a couple of years, but they never got it.

When old Richard Aubier died, his widow kept the spacious homestead, and the young daughters when they married moved in with her. When the old lady passed away, one of the girls who had married a steady youth named Andrew Gery bought the house from the estate.

Israel Laverte at the age of sixty passed away, and was buried in the pine-shaded cemetery back of St. Mary's-on-the-Mountain.

Elizabeth grieved over him, but managed to rally from the bereavement. Her family noticed that she became quieter, gentler, more motherly, after he had gone. Once or twice her children observed her sitting by the kitchen window fondling a band of silver, interwoven with faded red ribbons. It must have been a gift from Israel, in the old courting days, they thought. The aged woman lived on until her seventy-eighth year, when she passed away after an illness of several months. On her sickbed she asked her eldest son to bring her the silver band, from its hiding place back of the cupboard. She kept it before her all the time on the counterpane, rubbing it with her knotted, palsied fingers. She expressed a desire that it be buried with her. The children would have granted this request, but in the excitement of the demise, it was left lying on the window sill. After the return from the cemetery it was found. Michael, the eldest son, personally took it and placed it on the grave, where the wayward myrtle soon covered it.

During all these years Sammy Jimmerson, the Indian King, was living quietly on his small farm on the island near Johnny cake. He never re-married, though he became reconciled in later years to his children and grandchildren, the result of his temporary union with the plain-bred squaw. He was especially proud of one of his grandsons, Jimmy Jacobson, who became a great hunter, and killed the last elk in Pennsylvania. In his ninetieth year he expressed a desire to revisit some of the hunting grounds of his youth. His descendants tried to dissuade him, but against his strong will, they were powerless. He started alone, laden only with a little knapsack. In a deep pocket of his black great-coat he carefully packed the crown of Red Jacket, the symbol of authority of five centuries of Senecas. He was a striking looking figure at the time of his last pilgrimage, this last of the line of Red Jacket. His leonine head was covered with snow-white hair, which hung down to his shoulders. He was still erect, and very broad, but he carried an ironwood staff instead of the rifle with the silver inlaid stock of his youth. His deep-set dark eyes glowed sadly as of yore, there was more of the eagle than ever to the bold curve of his nose. His relatives wondered where he was going, as he would not enter into particulars.

He headed for the southeast, travelling by easy stages. Some nights he stopped at hotels, on others in farmhouses or lumber-camps. He seemed well provided with money, paying his bills with gold. He was well received everywhere, and was remembered by many of the older people. In the evenings he regaled his hosts with stories of the days when Indians were supreme, when the Clearfield mountains were a trackless wilderness, abounding with all kinds of game. The little children clustered about the kindly old man; they might never see a real Indian Chief again.

He arrived at Frenchville, dusty and travel worn, late one October afternoon. He put up at the hotel where he inquired about his old friends; all of them were dead. He found he had time enough before supper to visit the cemetery on the hill. It was an impressive sight to watch the grand old Indian, wending his way to God's acre under the pines. He arrived there just at the last moments of the golden hour, when the entire landscape gradually sloping down from the distant Knobs was gilded the color of molten metal. He met the grave-digger coming through the iron-gate, and asked him where Elizabeth Aubier, or Laverte, was buried. The place was pointed out and the old Indian quickly located it, although no stone had as yet been erected. On reaching the spot, the venerable chieftain knelt beside the mound, stroking the heavy growth of myrtle that completely carpeted it. Something smooth and cold touched his fingers, beneath the myrtle. He lay hold of it, and drew it out. To his surprise it was the crown of the Seneca Queens. A happy thrill shot through him; his only love had thought of him in the long intervening years, perhaps had asked to have the crown placed on her grave. Drawing the King's crown from his pocket, he lay the two side by side; at the head of the mound. Then he buried his face in his hands and wept softly.

As he arose, he said half to himself, half to the lofty, listening white pines: "Oh, Elizabeth, Queen of the Senecas the last to assume the title, and the first to hold it forever, in the eternal world of death, after nearly seventy years, we are together again. Our next meeting, which will be soon, will be closer and fonder, in the land of the spirit. Our crowns will rest side by side until I receive my call." Leaning more heavily on his staff than was his wont, the grandson of Red Jacket retraced his way towards the boarding house at the foot of the hill. Just as he was crossing the highroad he met the landlady's daughter, her hands beneath her checked apron, running towards him. "I was just going after you, sir, supper's half over."

"That is all right," said the old man, "I do not need supper, my spirit has been fed for the first time in nearly seventy years." There was a look of glory, of content, in his deep-set eyes.

XV. The Headless Man

(Story of an old River Town.)

"That ghost of the stage-driver who beat his horses wasn't the only spook I've seen," said the old grave-digger. "I have seen dozens of them, so many that it is hard to keep them all in mind. It would be difficult to tell which was the queerest one, they were all so strange." The old man's big brown eyes kindled with reminiscent fire, as he sat down on a marble slab marking all that was mortal of some Scotch-Irish celebrity, prepared to relate another marvellous experience. It was a bright November morning, with the earth browning after the white frost of the night before. Except for being in an ancient cemetery, it seemed hardly the time of day to relate a ghostly experience.

"When I was a young lad," began the old man, "I used to be out pretty late at night, courting the girls or playing cards. It wasn't anything for me to get home at two or three o'clock in the morning, midnight was early. There were three sisters, triplets, who lived near the dam who were quite popular in town. They were North Irish girls, and had only moved into our community recently. Their father was a camp boss at a big job near the mouth of Hyner Run. With two other young fellows, I spent many an evening in their society. They were good natured and witty, so the time passed rapidly. However when the clock struck twelve, their mother would come to the head of the stairs and call to them that it was time to go to bed. That would have made some young men angry, but we liked the girls too much to care about such a trifle. We merely picked up our caps and said goodnight. Poor girls, they are all dead now; I dug the grave for the last one at Highland last April. Well that is a long time ago since we did our courting, it was the last year of the war!

One night in February, it was real cold; twelve o 'clock sent us out into the street as usual. Two of the boys lived in the upper end of town, so they followed River Street, in that direction. I lived over near the lower railroad bridge, so cut across town, in the direction of the tracks. It was about ten minutes past twelve when I reached the crossing, which was situated about half a square below where the Pennsylvania station now stands. There was no moon, everything looked one sombre mass of black, there was no dividing line between the mountains and the sky.

When I got on the centre of the cross-over I noticed a lantern flickering; it seemed to be a hundred yards further down the track. It must be in the hands of a track walker, I thought. Being in no great hurry I waited to have a word with the fellow, who appeared to be moving in my direction. I always liked to talk with people whom I met at night, in the darkness. There seemed then to be picturesqueness to the dullest personalities. He seemed to be moving rapidly, and was beside me in an incredibly short space of time. I turned to wish him good evening, when to my horror, I saw the figure was headless. Where the head had been severed close to the shoulders was an ugly red gash; I could see it plainly by the lantern-light. To my further dismay I noticed that the creature carried the severed head under his left arm; with the right he was swinging the lantern. I was about to call out 'stop your fooling,' for I had recently seen the Rogers statuette of Ichabod Crane and the Headless Horseman, where the latter carried a pumpkin with eyes, nose and mouth cut in it, under one arm, when the being, or whatever it was, edged up close beside me.

I had pretty strong nerves, for I had seen the stage-driver's ghost, and a couple of others, so I tried to hold my ground. The figure, which I might add was that of a big, powerful man, threw such a lot of strength into his task that I almost tumbled over on the rails. I wanted to cry out that I wished to go to my home down the track, but I recollected that if this should happen to be a ghost, I would spoil everything by speaking first. Evidently the headless one wanted me to go up the tracks for some reason. While I was not particularly anxious to get home, I hated to be forced to do something against my will. I was not in a mood to fight, so I concluded to appease the figure by going in the direction he desired. So I turned about and started to stroll up the tracks towards the station. My pace did not seem to please the figure. He edged up beside me again, urging me to walk faster and faster.

"The railroad ran through the centre of the sleeping town. I noticed that there was not a single light in any of the houses. Most of them were two story frame structures, with doors opening on the level with the railroad and the street. I had often seen people on the loneliest highways at midnight; here not a soul was stirring this night. I did not even see a stray cat. As we neared the station I saw a dim light burning in one of the windows. It was the telegrapher and agent, who kept open until after the arrival of the twelve-forty Philadelphia Express. When we came abreast of the lighted window I wanted to stop, to get away from my tormentor. I peered through the window, but the operator was temporarily absent from his desk. In my moment of indecision the thought flashed through my mind that perhaps this headless spectre had something he wanted to show me, a spread rail, or a burned-out tie further up the track. If so, there would be no time to hunt the operator. My watch said it was fifteen minutes of train time. It would do no good anyway, as there wasn't an office open nearer than Rattlesnake. The trouble might even be a mile up track. I struck a more lively gait, which seemed to please

98

the ghost tremendously. Divining that at last I understood him, was in sympathy with him, he forged on ahead; I had to walk lively to keep up to him.

The Great Island

"My guess was right, I walked nearly a mile before I found why I was wanted. The time was running dangerously close to the train's schedule; several times I looked at my watch by the rays of the ghost's lantern. Every step I took I carefully scrutinized the rails, the condition of the ties, the state of the road-bed. I was not a railroader, but I lived near enough to the tracks to know the kind of defects which caused bad accidents.

"For over half a mile our way led through the outskirts of the town, or along the river bank. There was a steep bank rising fifty feet above the track, on the side furthest from the river. Finally we came to a bend in the line, where we entered a deep cut; the bank on the side nearest the river was at least thirty feet in height. It was so far from the shore that it would not have paid to excavate it away. It was a melancholy, lonely spot, and darker here than anywhere we had traversed.

"When we came to the blackest part of the cut, the spectre raised his lantern and swung it wildly. It seemed to be a signal for me to be on the alert, to meet a possible emergency. I looked ahead; by the lamplight I could see a huge pile of old ties on the track. There were at least forty of them. A dastardly attempt had been made to wreck the express. It was at a point too, where the train still traveled at a high rate of speed, before it began to slow down for the station. I knew now what the ghost wanted; it would be a big task, I figured. Just then I heard the faint echo of the train whistle; it was probably at the crossing half a mile above Quinn's Run, and a mile and a half from where the ties were piled. It was a horrible moment of suspense, but I set to work with a will. When I started to roll the ties away, I found to my horror that they had been spiked together; they formed a compact mass, that a Hercules could not budge without an axe and a spike-mall. There was no use wasting time trying to do the impossible; I carried no implement bigger than a Barlow, and rocks could not hammer the impediment loose.

Meanwhile the ghost was standing by, holding aloft his lantern, so I could comprehend my job. I threw myself against the solid structure, then shook my head. I pointed up the track; I made a signal as if he must stop the train. For a moment it seemed that he failed to understand me, so I seized the lantern, and ran in the direction of the on-coming express. I did not look back to see what became of the ghost. The train whistled again, this time for the river bridge, half a mile above, in a minute more it would be stopped or cause one of the worst wrecks in the history of the road. I thought of the poor souls asleep in the coaches, who would be hurled into eternity, of the conductors and trainmen, of all the stricken families; I must stop the train at any cost.

"I had another reason, a somewhat selfish one, for my intense vigilance. The cut was a long and deep one, I could not get out of it before the train hit the awful barrier; if I was found half way up the bank, or up or down the track by any possible survivors, I would be accused of the foul deed. I *must* stop it or gladly die in the attempt.

"I could hear the train slow down a trifle as the long line of coaches rumbled over the old wooden bridge, one of the few bridges, by the way, which later survived the Flood of 1865. Then it seemed to increase speed again, and came bounding towards me through the night. I ran as fast as I could, tripping now and then on the ties, but determined to get as far as possible from the tie-pile before beginning my flagging operations. I ran until I was breathless. Then I planted myself in the centre of the track, and began waving my lantern. Soon the giant headlight, and the big bulbous smokestack, belching grey smoke and sparks, hove in sight. It seemed as big as a mountain; as impossible to stop as a mountain landslide. It was a cold night; I could hardly expect to see the engineman's head leaning out of the cab-window. I kept on waving, waving, waving. To my gesticulations, I added terrific shouts; I had a powerful voice, but all sound was lost in the roar of the oncoming express. I could not detect that my lantern was seen, and I had to jump off the track to avoid being run down.

"There was only a single track, I had barely room to lay flat against the smooth earth of the bank, and avoid being sucked under the heavy black mail-cars and coaches. I hardly dared look down the track as the long line of cars swept past me. As the last one lurched by, I felt that some motion of the hand-brakes was in effect; it rocked unsteadily, though I saw nothing of any brakeman. I heard a second afterwards a hideous rasping and squeaking, and wailing, like we hear on logging-cars to-day when the brakes are thrown on at a trestle on some narrow-gauge; the train almost left the track in its sudden halting; I knew all were saved.

"For half a minute I lay on the ground, unable to get up, or speak. I was crawling to my feet when I saw the conductor, with face white as a sheet, carrying a lantern, and accompanied by several passengers running in my direction. I was standing up, but shaking like a quaking-asp, when the parties reached me. They held out their hands, congratulating me, and calling me a brave man. Other passengers and trainmen poured from the cars and I was soon surrounded by a shouting crowd. Some of the men slapped me on the back so many times it added to the nausea I felt after my long run. One of the passengers offered me a twenty dollar gold piece. I wanted it badly, but I knew I was entitled to no credit for what I had done; it was the ghost's doing, so I refused it.

"'Tell me your name, son, and we'll make up a purse of gold and send it to your mother' said the same passenger, undaunted by my refusal. There was a chorus of 'yes, yes, he's saved our lives' and so on. I deliberately gave them a wrong name and address in town. Several of them wrote it in their note books. I felt sorry a moment later, as someone in the throng might recognize me, especially as I knew quite a few trainmen. But all faces appeared strange to me, I could make my escape. If credit was due, it was to the headless ghost, but this I could not very well explain.

"I could not get away very fast, as everyone wanted to know how I found the tie-pile, and how soon before the train appeared. I explained everything in detail, with becoming modesty. No one could understand my modesty, especially when I seemed so indifferent to rewards.

"In the excitement everyone had forgotten about removing the obstruction. They were amazed when I told them that the ties were spiked together. It took the engineman and fireman, the brakeman and passengers half an hour to get it off the track. They worked with axes, saws, with picks and pokers, gathered from the emergency kits in the coaches and from the engine. Everyone from the engineman down insisted on shaking hands with me before the train started. The engineman, a queer fat old fellow, scratched his head saying: 'It was the closest running I ever made after I saw you, it was my quickest stop.'

'Say, pop,' said the young fireman, just as they were climbing into the cab, 'did you notice a man down by the tie-pile, he seemed to duck back of it just as we stopped.'

'No, I did not,' said the old man with surprise.

'Could he have been the wrecker?' I believe it was the headless man.

"There was no time for further talk, the train was now nearly an hour late, so all hands got on board. I even declined to ride on the train as far as town. It is a wonder my actions did not arouse some suspicion. But everyone was too excited. I waited until the red tail lights were out of sight, and then leisurely wended my way down the tracks towards home. At the first crossing I left the ties, and struck across town in the direction of the mountains. I was home and in bed by three-thirty.

"The next day all the town was agog with the story of the dastardly attempt to wreck the Philadelphia express. Everyone wanted to find the stranger who prevented a horrible catastrophe so nobly. I said to myself: 'If there is any glory or rewards, they go to the headless man, not me, I will keep out of it.' It was a seven days wonder; like events of even greater magnitude, in due season it was forgotten.

"I used to like to talk to the railroaders, especially after the wreck. One of the section hands, quite an old man, told me about a brother of his, the first trackwalker on the section after the road was built, several years before, who had been beheaded by the Philadelphia express, the night of its first run. 'That was a couple of years back, you mind it,' he said. In a moment it flashed through my mind, the headless man was the spirit of that trackwalker; it was he who had saved the train, the night when I figured as an unwilling hero. Yet I hated to tell the old man I had seen his brother's ghost. Doubtless the spectre had haunted the railroad during these years, watching jealously the safety of others. The ghost had conquered my reluctance, and had brought me to the scene, in the nick of time. I had known at least one ghostly hero. If such deeds are of consequence in the land of shades, this track-walker has earned a blessed immortality."

XVI. His Rival's Ghost

(Story of Buffalo Creek.)

The shadows of the long autumn afternoon, vivifying in its crispness, were deepening among the hemlocks and laurel as Ambrose Gailly drew near the Forest House. The ride through the Narrows, which seemed so interminable to those who do not know nature, was on this occasion unbelievably short. Perhaps in those days it did seem shorter, even to the most prosaic travelers.

Most of the original timber, pine, hemlock and beech, was standing, completely arching the moist, narrow trail. Under these forest monarchs grew tall masses of rhododendron, and branching laurel, interspersed with young maples now tinting gold and scarlet in the frosty nights of early autumn. Sweet springs gushed from among the moss-grown rocks at intervals of every mile or so, making little rivulets along the road, through which the horse's hoofs splashed audibly. Late summer flowers peeped here and there, and once a belated orchid, green striped with red, was met with. Wild life was plentiful in this twelve mile glade.

Lewis Dorman, on the previous Christmas eve, had slain the nine foot panther, famed in song and story, on Shreiner, not so far away, and had brought the carcass to the Forest House. Its mate, and several lusty cubs were said to still prowl about on the heights of Jack's and Shade, whining vendetta.

Wolves and foxes, wildcats and catamounts, as well as numerous bears, even a brown bear or two, felt at ease in the forest depths. Ambrose Gailly saw more than one set of bear tracks in the mucky road. Grouse frequently flew up from their covers at his approach. Once a covey of quail trotted in single file in front of the horse. The "spray of bell-like notes" of the wood-robin echoed and re-echoed among the hemlock tangles; high up, among the yellow pines on the summits came the mournful yet sweet "a-coo, coo, coo" of the turtle dove.

Once he saw a big yellow porcupine, which seemed to take no heed of him. All this was the joy of the forest primitive. There was somewhat of a clearing on the brow of a hill, the last he must cross, before reaching the old hotel. The choicest pines had been removed, the rest had been girdled and left to die, along with the hemlocks which could not endure separation from their lifelong companions, the pines. There was an old saying among the backwoodsmen, "when you cut the pines, the hemlocks will cry themselves to death." This was true, but the real reason was that the roots of hemlocks grow along the surface of the ground, and when the pines are cut the sunlight falls heavily on the tender fibres, killing the grand old trees. It is even said that all who walk through a hemlock forest, except those who are moccasined will kill trees in their stroll.

Around the dead trees and stumps of this clearing, grew a sparse crop of buckwheat, the settlers' delight. Above it a few wild pigeons fluttered. Some of the mammoth pine stumps fired days before were still smouldering, but the buckwheat seemed to thrive on the constantly falling ashes of these miniature volcanoes. In the distance the Red Hills were apparent, now lavender tinted, in the fading light. Beyond the clearing the trail led again into the dense original forest. Ambrose Gailly heard a roaring sound, to a townsman it would indicate proximity to some great railway, with an express train thundering past but he recognized it as wild pigeons returning to their roost. He looked aloft, but the timber met in an arch above the road, he felt as if he was crossing under a railroad bridge, so deep was the intonation above his head. Straight upward, out of a mass of pine boughs, flew a pigeon hawk, piercing the heavy canopy with unerring instinct, bound to retrieve by nightfall, a few of the laggards or invalids of the pigeon myriads.

Through a quarter of a mile of forest darkness, and then the road emerged into another and larger clearing, with the Forest House and the tumbling run standing in bold relief, triply distinct in the last phases of the golden hour. Several men armed with shot-guns were running across the clearing, pointing in the direction from whence the rider had come. He turned in his saddle, and could see the pigeons in their majestic flight above the forest. Stretching across the broad valley from mountain to mountain, in a purple-black cordon, possibly a mile wide, they darkened what was left of the sun. There would be a pigeon supper at the Forest House.

In front of the hotel was the tavern sign, on a tall pole, a large circular plaque decorated by a golden, many antlered stag, painted on a black background, with "Forest House, 1856" lettered below. Landlord, helpers and hostlers were too busy acting as provenders of pigeon pot-pie to care much about a traveler's arrival. Ambrose Gailly sat on his horse for several minutes before anyone appeared. When the door opened, it disclosed Mabelle Banks, the Yankee landlord's fair-haired daughter. Wiping her pretty hands on her apron, she began to laugh. "Oh, 'Brose Gailly" she said, "if you had not known us so well, I wouldn't have blamed you if you had ridden on, with such a reception. The whole household has gone crazy about those wild pigeons. Sometimes when they go off on a rampage like that they don't get back until after dark."

"Well," replied the horseman good naturedly, "even if I had been a stranger, I would have hesitated about riding past. It's a good ten miles to the next public house, and it will be dark in less than an hour." The stalwart young man swung out of his old post-boy saddle, and after shaking hands with the pretty girl, led his big brown horse to the cozy, old-fashioned barn. He knew every stall in this old place, so much like a stable in one of Morland's pictures; he had stabled there time and again in his calling as a drover. As he walked towards the barn, he began to hum an old tune, "Billy Grimes, the drover." When he was upset, or downcast, he invariably hummed it, though he doubtless saw no connection between the ridiculous personage in the song and himself.

The sight of Mabelle Banks had sent his mind into an unpleasant train of thought. He had known this girl before he had met his bride; both girls had been barmaids in mountain taverns. Why he married Reba Stoneman in preference to Mabelle Banks was a question he could never answer when he saw the latter. Side by side, Reba was the prettier, and a couple of years the youngest but there were other controlling reasons which weighted the scales in the opposite direction. Yet these he had refused to consider during the melting pot of passion called the courtship. He had loved Reba with a flame more intense and jealous than he had any other girl during his checkered and eventful career. It sufficed to win the girl, but it left its scars afterwards. He never felt easy when he was away from her; despite her oft-repeated lovestory, her apparent devotion, he mistrusted her. He felt certain he could have trusted Mabelle, and now when passion's fires were calming, knew he loved her as much as he ever did the girl whom he had married.

Despite their cordial greetings, both Gailly and Mabelle felt self-conscious in each other's presence. It was always that way since his marriage. He knew why he felt thus, it was because he loved her, and though he refused to admit it, his soul told him he had wed the wrong girl. He wondered if Mabelle's embarrassment arose from the fact that she still loved him; it would be better if they never met, if such were the case.

In the old barn, with its sweet odors of hay and fodder, he soon had his faithful horse feeding away, and bedded for the night. When he returned to the open air, dusk was falling fast, ashes of roses were replaced by steel grey, as the prevailing tone. He paused a moment, to admire the tavern sign, the golden stag - which after all these years still hangs before the Forest House - for even a drover or a traveling man can be sentimental, an admirer of the beautiful. Then he unswung the old-fashioned latch, and entered the lobby. Several tallow-dips illuminated the big low-ceilinged room. There was one on the table, and two on one of the broad window-sills. A cheerful beechwood fire was blazing in the huge fireplace with a deep-seated chair, as if placed there recently, before it. Although stoves were in general use in the mountains, even in 1869, the Forest House still clung to its open fireplaces, still had the crane hanging. Patronized by lumbermen, drovers and hunters, the blazing logs promoted sociability, at least such was the opinion of landlord Azariah Banks, late of Vermont, an innkeeper of forty years experience. He had conducted the Forest House since its opening nearly fourteen years before, it had never been the scene of quarreling or disorder, in a business way it was a pronounced success.

Banks had come to Central Pennsylvania to look for a missing relative, a young riverman, and becoming impressed with the possibilities of the new country, bought the recently constructed Forest House, and prospered. Its walls had echoed many jollities, when rivermen, with well-filled purses homeward bound, stopped there for the night, when Civil War soldiers, nearing their homes and loved ones in the valleys, spent a night to break the journey, when hunters came there to rest on their homeward way, and display the trophies of the chase.

The biggest jollification was when Lewis Dorman had brought in his panther on the last Christmas morning, and a swarm of mountaineers attracted to the scene, induced him to remain all night and fiddle for an impromptu dance, for Dorman was as great a fiddler as he was a nimrod. With the panther propped up in a lifelike position on the mantel-shelf, his maw held open by a skewer, and plenty of lights and garlands of ground pine, with cider and punch, and good things generally, the merry crowd of mountain boys and girls, some of the boys wearing their old soldier suits, danced from eight in the evening until eight the next morning.

Ambrose Gailly had happened to be there that night; he spent most of the time in the kitchen with Mabelle. Neither had cared to dance much, they were deeply in love. When the young man rode away that brisk morning, behind his drove of sixty Brush Valley steers, he imagined he was going to marry Mabelle. Yet he had left the words unsaid, until the next time. But is there a "next time" for anything we really want to do now? Experience, the bitterest experience, teaches us "no."

As he seated himself in the comfortable chair, and gazed into the translucent beechwood blaze, pictures of that eventful night, of but nine months before rose up vividly, torturing him. He could not trust his wife, he knew not why. He knew he loved her, that she was younger, more beautiful, more bewitching than Mabelle Banks, yet he was not satisfied. Folding his arms, he began reviewing his courtship with the woman he had married, and how Mabelle's influence had grown less. The night was very still, until he heard the landlord's dog barking outside. Reba Stoneman was an orphan, he had pitied her for that. She had to work for her living in the tavern at Antes Gap, tending bar, an ignoble calling for one of her rare beauty. Before her character had fully formed, she had been betrayed by an older man, and this evil reputation had made her the target for all manner of unscrupulous attacks. She had thrown off her early influences, developed a beautiful spirit, she needed pure, honorable love to reward her conscientious up-building. Ambrose had always admired her beauty, there was much of the distressed Magdalen in the drooping corners of her rather thin mouth, in the big soulful rock-blue eyes that most persons thought were brown, because the long lashes were that color, in the lachrymal wave of her ash-brown hair, the deadly pallor of her countenance. He had talked hours at a stretch with her, and knew her well, long before he felt sure he loved her. Love must have grown out of pity, for he found it full-grown in his heart one day. He was miles off at the time, in the Young Woman's Creek country, but he traveled to Antes tavern, and told it to his beloved, on the little balcony that overlooked the sunset bathed Alleghanies, rising in castellated peaks to the north and west. She had placed her pale hand in his, and then her cheek against his, then sat on his lap, and in a perfect rapture, they had felt themselves one. She told him how she had loved him ever since the first time she saw him, three years previously, how he had always appealed to her as different from any man she had ever met, and so beautiful. She declared she could not marry him, as he knew her past, that she could be no man's bride, let alone his. He had pled, but in vain. He had gone away down-hearted, thinking only of her, that he must marry her. It was during those melancholy days that he entirely forgot the existence of Mabelle Banks. Eventually he induced Reba to marry him, had installed her in a comfortable brick cottage in Jersey Shore, on a street which overlooked the bend in the river, where it was shaded by spreading elm and willow trees. It had been an ideallic existence, on the wedding trip to Harrisburg, and in the home; he had never been so happy in his life.

Alas when he went away on his first business expedition, he felt the presence of the other man, he mistrusted his bride. He fought the foul fancy night and day, it was like a canker on his passion, he found no antidote. All he could see was the great, vicious, bloated form of the horse-dealer who had ruined his wife, when she was sixteen, and little more than a child. One offense might have been condoned, but the fact that the relations had continued for a couple of years at least seemed unforgivable in his feverish mental state. The man might come back, in the girl's heart might lurk a spark of regard, capable of revival, for wasn't he her first love? No woman ever ceases loving the man she loves first, whether the love be spiritual or carnal. In some cases carnal love lasts longest. If there is doubt as to this let every man ask his heart. Ambrose Gailly's business trips became hell on earth. Reba noticed his altered appearance, but he told her he was expanding his business, was naturally fatigued. All these things flung themselves through his mind this autumn evening, as he sat before the fire, at the Forest House. His face was set like a vise, his eyes rigid, when Mabelle opened the door to tell him supper was ready.

"Just to think, those crazy hunters haven't returned yet," she said to put him in good humor. The girl knew he was unhappy, and guessed the cause. All through supper she waited on him, he quite forgot his ills. After the meal they sat together by the fire, until the hunters came in. They had killed so many pigeons, they said, they would have to go after them with the spring-wagon next morning. "We've got them in a pile so high" said Azariah Banks, indicating the height of the mantel-shelf. They had brought some pigeons with them, slim, slate-colored squabs, and they insisted on roasting some of these before bed-time. There was a royal feast, which did not break up until half an hour before midnight. It took time to pick and clean the birds, to cook them right.

Mabelle, always assiduous, lighted Ambrose up the stairs. She even went in his room, his favorite little room under the roof, to see that the candle was burning properly. The young man felt like taking her in his arms, he knew she would not mind. Yet she was his ideal, he would do nothing with her to lower his self-respect.

He had ridden that day all the way from Early sburg, with many side trips on the way to see farmers about cattle, so it was not long before he fell asleep. The last sounds he heard were the disconcerted katy-dids, frost was making a panic in their orchestra. But he was not to sleep long. He rose up in bed, half awake, to count the old New England clock on the stairs chime twelve. Then he heard footsteps in the room. It was pitchy dark outside, so no light came through the shutters. He called out "whose there?" He got a gruff reply: "It's me, Jake Bendel." To his horror he was in the room with the brutal horse trader who had wronged his wife. How came this fellow here? He had not registered at the hotel up to bed-time. There were some matches on the little table-stand by the bed, he clutched at them, lighted one. By the flickering bluish light he beheld his rival, more bloated, hideous, and red-bearded than ever. Springing out of bed with a horrible string of oaths, though he was usually not profane, he rushed at the huge, soggy figure. Grabbing at the throat, he administered a terrific kick, as though to throw him through the door and down-stairs. To his horror and pain, he did not kick Jake Bendel, but drove his bare foot clear through the panel of the heavy walnut door. Crazed with suffering, mental and physical, he sank back on the bed, where he lay for half an hour.

Then he lit his candle. His foot was terribly mashed and bleeding, the floor and the bed were stained with blood. Tying up his wounds as best he could, he lay awake until daybreak, cursing himself. He had not seen Jake Bendel at all, it was a dream, conjured up from his senseless distrust of his loving, beautiful, young wife. He had made a laughing stock of himself; he must get away. Putting on his stocking and shoe with much effort, he crept down-stairs. He left his lodging money on the lobby table, getting outdoors unnoticed. He went to the stable, finding his horse rested, and ready to sally forth. He watered him, he saddled him, he started down the trail towards Youngmanstown in the misty light. He was utterly ashamed of himself, and blamed it all on admiring Mabelle Banks too much, and through her to think too many unfavorable ideas concerning his wife. It was best he did not see her again, she was perhaps an evil genius. He did not let her enter his mind all day, even what she would say when she found him gone, or the insane condition of his bedroom. That night he sat up late in the cheery publichouse at Youngmanstown. He was not afraid to go to bed, but he preferred jolly company to the solitude of a cold upstairs room. It was nearly midnight when a belated traveler appeared. Like many of those already present in the bar-room, he was a stockman. "Heard the news?" he said almost with his first breath, "Jake Bendel died suddenly last night at the Eagle Hotel in Watsonburg. Some say he took a dose of rat poison. He was an evil cuss and suffered remorse at times, but I doubt it that he would suicide, guess he just played out."

Ambrose Gailly, man of the world, man of facts, turned pale. He placed his hand for support against the hot pipe of the stove, and jumped away in pain.

"Give me some ice water, Benny," he said to the bartender, "I guess I'll go to bed." "Those stockmen hang together pretty close," drawled an old farmer, after the young man had gone upstairs. "Gailly seemed to take old Jake's death powerful hard."

XVII. Canoe Place

(Story of the Cherry Tree.)

History seems to be strangely reticent about the canoe trip made by William Penn to the headwaters of the West Branch of the Susquehanna, and his promise, given at this time to the Indian girl, Rose-Marie, not to continue his province further westward. Undoubtedly the time will come when the subject of this momentous trip will be carefully investigated and given to the public. Meanwhile it must slumber and grow less authoritative. The legendary part of it, however, is just as fresh and replete with details, as the day the trip began, and can supplement any missing links which the historians may require. In addition to giving the historical narrative, the legend furnishes us with an accurate pen picture of the famous Quaker, his manners and general characteristics. For this we could search in vain in written history, as the truckling historians of the time preferred to paint him perennially as he appeared at the age of twenty-two in _____'s portrait, which is familiar to all.

At that time he was Penn the courtier, the gilded youth; he had not had his religious awakening, he had not languished for months in an Irish jail, from which even his influential father had difficulty in rescuing him. Penn, in the legend of the canoe trip to Cherry Tree, appears as a very human and likable personage; as such we prefer to remember him, we who are human, and like heroes pretty much like ourselves. Despite the age of the tradition, it comes to us in "apostolic succession," through earlier Indians to Sammy Jimmerson, the redoubtable Seneca King, who when revisiting his boyhood scenes in Central Pennsylvania over half a century ago, told the story to one of the old pioneers, whom he had known in his youth. It was from this splendid old gentleman of Scotch-Irish descent who recently passed away on the eve of his ninetieth birthday, that the present chronicler heard the story.

It seems that from the time Penn first set foot on soil of the domain which was to bear his name, he evinced a desire to explore the interior. In this he was often dissuaded, as the inconveniences and uncertainties of travel in the wilderness were much exaggerated to him by his luxury loving advisers. But in 1696, during his second visit to the province, affairs had taken a different turn. The population had increased with marvelous rapidity, it was becoming difficult to confine them in the then acknowledged boundaries. Technically speaking, Penn was owner of all the territory now included in Pennsylvania, and more besides, but that had only the authority of royal grant. The Indians must yet be reckoned with. They had always acted in a friendly manner, and shown even anxiety to please the Quaker newcomers. A large white population had suddenly encamped in their midst, but they uttered no word of protest. The elm tree at Shackamaxon had played its part, soon it was to have a western prototype, a cherry tree.

It seems a pity that these two trees do not appear on the arms of the present commonwealth. They were the timber from which budded most of its greatness. They would be more appropriate than two horses rampant. In order to allow his settlers room to spread out, Penn made a number of local purchases. These were filled before the Indian quit-claims were prepared, he must acquire land on a larger scale. The valley of the Susquehanna, praised to the skies by explorers and hunters, was the logical line of expansion. By a council with the chiefs, he was able to arrange for the purchase of a "right-of-way" for his colonists "through the Susquehanah to unexplored countries." At first glance this carried little except the privilege to pass up-stream unmolested in canoes. But it was to be broadened by certain rights along the banks, but these extra privileges were to continue "only so far as a canoe could navigate."

A trip was arranged to the point where the canoe could go no further. Indian chiefs and trusted surveyors, with French guides were to compose the party. The journey had an irresistible fascination to Penn; he decided to go along, partly incognito. That is while acknowledged as the great Penn, he would be treated merely as a private citizen en route. He would see the country and the aborigines at close range, without the pomp and pretense of an official progress. Even the words of sycophantic interpreters could not be strictly relied upon as translating the true attitude of the redmen towards the proprietary government.

Penn, although about forty years of age, inclined towards corpulence and good living, was as enthusiastic as a boy over the trip. Although he had come to Pennsylvania accompanied by his special steward to provide him with properly cooked renditions of his favorite dishes, his several valets, he was willing to leave this all at Sedgley and face the hardships of the wilderness. That he would start off on such a lengthy and hazardous outing was viewed with concern by some of his councilors. There was no stopping him, however, but lest the matter of his going arouse some impious plot to harm him on his way, or his government while absent, he agreed that the trip be kept a secret. He would be merely resting at his country seat, that would explain his absence from Philadelphia. But some of the same timorous councilors sent emissaries ahead to inform certain influential chiefs that Penn himself was to be a member of the purchasing and surveying party, and to see that he got all delicacies in the way of game, fruits and vegetables that the season might provide. But the local historians were left in the cold; when some Indians wandered into Manayunk and said that they had met Penn at the mouth of Conewago, the historians clamored, but all they got was the official statement that a mistake must have been made, Penn was resting at Sedgley.

In All Its Majesty

Thus in the days before shrewd reporters and telephones, was history woven, just to suit those who were the most influential actors in it. And it may be made to suit certain parties to-day; it is said a true history of the Spanish-

American War would make startling and humiliating reading. How much more so a history of a wild region, peopled with ignorant settlers, savage men, and beasts.

Penn, in order not to be recognized, was driven in a coach as far as the mouth of Conewago, where the embarkation was made. As the Indians had never been hostile, a large armed force was unnecessary. Penn, his secretary, two Indian interpreters, two surveyors, two map-drawers, two cooks, a valet, and four French guides made up the party. The identity of the guides is fortunately preserved for us. They were Provencal Reattu, Paul Torney, Denis Coursant and Ernest Larrey. The last named did not return from Central Pennsylvania, and Larry's Creek, in Lycoming Country, is named for him, or his son. It is said that Penn was in fine spirits on the entire trip, and his geniality increased as he penetrated further and further into the forest. He accepted bad weather cheerfully, being drenched to the skin in several sudden showers which came up on the river. His cooks knew how to please him, and that they intimated to the Indians and guides was the cause of the "great white father's" excellent demeanor. But he was also democratic, which is a deeper trait than mere courtesy; the Penn who had wandered and preached in Ireland, Holland and Germany, who had slept and fraternized with peasants, came to the surface again. There was not a single member of the party but who genuinely liked him, and who would have laid down their lives for him, long before the site of Harris' Ferry was reached.

The attitude of Penn towards the Indians was carefully studied by the French guides, who before the start were not slow to admit that they doubted the sincerity of his protestations. One by one they were convinced; above motives of self-interest Penn loved the Indians; he was a lover of all peoples, a humanitarian. Aristocrat though he had been born, this early self seemed to have died, and a broad, gentle, tolerant spirit taken possession of his frame.

Personally he looked different to his observing companions than the flattering portrait-artists portrayed him. To the guides in the woods he appeared a man of goodly height, true enough. But he was very stout, so much so that he walked with difficulty. As the trip progressed his muscles hardened, and his weight reduced, still he was what might be called a fat man. His hair, which was growing thin at the temples, was of a medium shade of brown, and very thick at the back part of the head. His big nose was retrousse, and had full nostrils, much as he appeared in the early engraving by Chopman. He had large, deep-set dark blue eyes, clear and mild of expression, the eyes of a genius and a thinker. A recent writer has pointed out that most of the really great men have had blue eyes and medium brown hair; it is the type denoting intense mental acumen.

Napoleon, Wagner, Cromwell, Luther, Shakespeare, Victor Hugo, Grant, Poe, Roosevelt, John Singer Sargent and Robert Louis Stevenson are a few of the great men whose eyes were blue, whose hair was brown. His voice was particularly pleasing, anyone to whom he addressed a word was captivated instantly. This engaging mode of speech took the place of the smile. Penn smiled very seldom, when he did it was with the lips, never with the eyes. The descriptions of great men may sound like those of individuals of ordinary calibre, but there is a psychic difference, which is felt by those who have come in contact with the leaders of human endeavor. That Penn was an inspired man, a master mind, was acknowledged by all who met him, and especially by the Indians, who claimed he was the only white man they ever truly liked or could trust. With such a personality, with such sincere and lofty motives, his founding of a great colony, without any bloodshed during his lifetime, seems perfectly comprehensible.

As the trip progressed Penn was delighted at what he saw. The grand forests, the high mountains, the multiplicity of beautiful streams running into them, the well-tilled Indian farms, the abundance of game animals and birds, the lovely climate, all made him feel he was passing through an earthly paradise — all his own. Indian canoes and pirogues manned by chiefs or wise men often paddled out to meet the party, urging them to stop and partake of sumptuous feasts. At first Penn liked the idea, but after awhile he suspected that advance news of his coming had caused such rash hospitality, and he tried to avoid unnecessary stops, saying he wanted to make time. But he was invariably polite and gentle, especially to the squaws, who almost acclaimed him a divinity. They all liked his blue eyes, so sad and serious, just as the men were won by his voice.

Penn's trip, incognito, or almost so, was a huge success. Good time was made, as he would not delay for the weather, and when tired he was slow to admit it. On the way several French trading posts were passed. One, magnificently fortified with high earth works, was near the site of the present town of Muncy. These would have to move out when the Penn title was confirmed, but the great Quaker made no threats, he even went out of his way to pleasantly greet the Frenchmen.

A notable stop was made at the most extensive of these posts, which stood where later a fort was erected by the British during the French and Indian War, nameless it was then, but during the Revolutionary days when rebuilt by the patriots, was known as Fort Horn. Penn took a great liking to a very young Frenchman who was in charge. His name was Beauchamp or Bushong. He was amazed to learn from him of the vast amount of business done annually at the fort; the number of furs, precious stones and bars of silver collected. He confided to his secretary that in due season this would all be superseded by an English company. For some reason, he made no effort to effect this change upon his return to Philadelphia, and the French post remained undisturbed until through a quarrel with the Indians, it was attacked and burned. In the melee, Beauchamp lost his life.

A great flight of paroquets occurred while Penn was sojourning at this post. He was amazed to see the mass of green and yellow colored chattering birds. He said that in his boyhood his mother had had a favorite parrot brought from the Indies; he had always wanted to see them in a wild state. He refused to allow any to be shot, saying that the wild birds and animals, unless of value commercially should be allowed to live as they added much interest to the scenery.

That night a pack of wolves assembled on the nearby Round Top and serenaded the distinguished visitor. "They are one of our chief sources of wealth" said Beauchamp.

"In some way they should be protected except when they bear the winter coats" replied Penn. He added that he had once heard wolves barking in Savoy, and it had made a lasting impression. He took great delight in inspecting the hides of the beavers, fishers, wolverines, catamounts, wild cats, silver foxes, and martens, which formed the chief articles of purchase in the line of furs. The hides of panthers, brown and black bears, also elks and buffaloes, and even deer were bought, but they were too plentiful to have more than a nominal value. The existence of silver ore made Penn realize that his province contained vast mineral wealth. Though the silver supply petered out, other minerals created the wealth of the state.

After leaving the trading post, the Penn party encountered few further signs of civilization. On the Sinnemahoning Creek, beyond its confluence with the Susquehanna, was another French post but as Penn followed the main river, he did not meet with it. The scenery from the "meeting of the waters" became romantic in the extreme. Penn went into ecstacies, and proved himself a veritable nature lover. The river became very narrow, and the giant trees almost met overhead. He was particularly pleased by the seven round tops which reared their swarthy heads near the mouth of Moshannon.

Every mile or so bands of Indians waved friendly signals from the shore, or paddled out to shake the hand of the "great white father." Many of them brought gifts, such as gaily colored beads, bright feathers, skins, or bits of gold or silver ore. Under such pleasant circumstances the voyage progressed rapidly.

The stream became so narrow that in places not more than two canoes could go abreast. It grew so winding that it required considerable skill to "cut the corners." But the water course ran deep, so the frail boats had no trouble to keep afloat. It was at the last moments of the golden hour, and the sun had already begun to sink behind the western mountains when the flotilla bid fair to reach a point where further progress was impossible. With huge gnarled roots, which seemed to arch the stream as an impassable barrier, grew a gigantic cherry tree. In diameter it must have been as much as twelve feet, its straight brown trunk rose a hundred feet in the air without a limb. There it joined the moss-green verdant canopy of pines and hemlocks.

Nearby grew a beech of almost similar proportions, the cherry and it were the two biggest trees in sight, and on its smooth silvery bark was boldly cut the initials and date "E. B. 1615." Penn was so engrossed by this legible signature in the wilderness, that he scarcely noticed that a troop of Indians had come out to meet him, or that the canoes could navigate no further without a "carry." Even on the other side of the bridgelike roots progress would be unsatisfactory as the bed of the stream was full of jagged rocks, and there were wildfalls innumerable. "We can go no further" shouted Ernest Larrey, the premier guide, and Penn realized his journey's end had come.

A large number of Indians, men and women, appeared out of the forest, and waved a glad welcome to the voyagers. Among them were fully a dozen chiefs, magnificently attired with beaded suits and feathered head-dresses. Those who did not take leading parts in the welcome, the squaws and young bucks, some of whom had black wolves used for hunting, in leash, leaned in picturesque attitudes against the tall trees. Penn's calm eyes scanned the assemblage. He was favorably impressed by the appearance and bearing of the Indians, by the beauty of their women.

There was one young squaw, upon whom he cast a second and third glance. She was easily the flower of the flock. She was enveloped in a dark green blanket, with yellow fringes, which she kept drawing tightly about her, showing off to advantage the wonderful lines of her supple back, her hips, her legs. Her hair was dark, and her eyes, which were what are called "flat eyes," were very black; she had a short yet aquiline nose, a tawny complexion. Her lips were colored by Vermillion, according to the custom of the time. In her hair was stuck a single red feather, a dyed eagle's plume no doubt. She kept eyeing Penn and his party with cold curiosity, punctuating each glance by tightening her grip on her blanket. The French guides bowed to her obsequiously, which led Penn to believe her to be an Indian girl of quality. When out of hearing he asked Larrey who she might be. "Why that's Rose-Marie" he replied. "She is the adopted daughter of old Chief Kinhochkus, the daughter of his second wife by an earlier marriage. She was an Algonquin from north of Lake Ontario. Her first husband was a great warrior. Rose-Marie was educated by the Jesuits, and is so level-headed and wise that her step-father confers with her about matters of state. She says if she ever marries, her husband will be a white man, so she's a prize for some one."

Just then the old chief himself stepped forward to help the hefty Penn out of his canoe. After the first cordial greetings, the great Quaker inquired what the letters "E. B." and the date "1615" carved on the giant beech tree signified.

"They were cut there many years ago by one Etienne Brule, the first white man ever seen by the Indians in this section of the country. With his long red beard and pale eyes he scared all our people terribly. He was not prepossessing like yourself."

At this essay at flattery Penn was compelled to smile. "You are very kind to compare me favorably with such a great pioneer." During the impromptu reception held on the bank, Penn's eyes reverted again to the fair Indian girl, who continued her classic poses, beneath the shade of the giant beech. He did not look at her with eyes of conquest, for he had no such thoughts; it was with the eyes of a man of the world, who understands and appreciates beautiful women. He regretted that the fair sex was held in such low esteem among the Indians, as surely this girl with her Jesuit education, would have made a better interpreter than Ernest Larrey.

Penn knew a little of the language of the Lenni-Lenape, yet preferred a trained interpreter to carry on the conversation, lest some slip of the tongue spoil everything. He was anxious to finish his important land purchase without even the shadow of friction. Above all he desired a title that would survive the years. With all his witnesses present, the business matter was brought up — and by the chiefs themselves — within ten minutes after he was assisted out of his canoe. Penn was glad of this, as it was a big transaction, full of intricacies and diplomatic questions, and the sooner accomplished the better. The Indians, he heard, were great at changing their minds. Like all of his dealings with the Indians, he avoided red-tape, and preambles, and went right to the gist of the matter. By the time the hospitable chiefs announced that supper was ready, Penn was master of the Susquehanna as far as the Cherry Tree.

During the repast, which consisted of various kinds of game and vegetables, the Indian women remained standing. Rose-Marie, stoical like her race, had never left the tree against which she lolled, although when the party was seated, she was directly opposite, and not ten feet from Penn. Like all intellectual men, he had a strongly developed appreciation of women, and looked forward to the finish of the long meal, when freed from responsibility, he might act as the gallant with her for a few minutes. Despite her serious face, she smiled sometimes when Indian children ran up to her and gave her cakes. Penn became impressed with the idea she wished to talk with him, for some reason. Perhaps he calculated, she wanted to know about the condition of English women, or if he was pleased with his new country and the beauties of the region.

The meal was well served, and Penn partook freely. He said jokingly that his English steward could learn considerable from these native cooks. One of the chiefs could speak some French, and with him the great Quaker carried on a friendly conversation. During the meal darkness fell rapidly, and big fires of rich pine were lighted in the open spaces of the forest, giving a rare red coloring to the scene. Penn remarked that it reminded him of some of the pictures by his favorite artist, Godfried Schalken, the master of candle and lamp-light effects.

After the meal, Penn strolled over to where the patient Rose-Marie was standing, and bowed to her in his most courtly manner. She spoke to him in excellent French, to which Penn replied in a delighted manner. "I have been wanting to see you for a long time" she said. "Your coming to the redman's country, your peaceable association with us, your kindness and justice have appealed to me greatly."

The Quaker was noticeably pleased at these words of appreciation.

"I was a little disappointed," she went on, looking him straight in the eyes, "at your decision to purchase more land, to bring settlers as far west as the Cherry Tree. I had hoped that by leaving our people the land that remained to us that both races could spread out, there would be room for all. Now the white men are to encroach on our choicest hunting grounds; a few more purchases like these, and your boundaries will join those of the French; it means annihilation for the redmen, — squeezed in between."

"But all the sales were cheerfully made by the Indians, among them by your good and wise father," broke in Penn, still smiling.

"That is all very true" replied the girl, firmly, "but if we had refused to sell, we would have been forced to go to war, and where would we be, poor unarmed savages, against the guns of the white men!"

"We have always had the most brotherly feelings for your race" said Penn.

"I know" said Rose-Marie, "but a change could come. Now will you do this for me, I am sure you are fair minded, a great soul?"

"I will do anything" replied Penn, "you need have no doubts of my sincerity."

"Then will you agree to limit your territorial additions to where you stand to-night, to go no further west; I know it is all yours by the grant of a King across the big water, but it is not actual possession. Will you agree?"

Penn smiled, answering promptly: "I will be glad to make such a promise. This trip was made by me to personally view the furthest west of my possessions. I will probably never get here again. While I was granted the territory west to the great rivers, I do not want it for settlement, it can remain as a happy hunting ground for your race. It will be neutral ground between my lands and those of the French. Apart from motives of fairness, it will be to our advantage, as it will ensure the permanent support and alliance of all the Indians dwelling there." He held out his hand to seal the bargain, and Rose-Marie gave it a hearty shake.

As the conversation was drawing to a close several of the chiefs drew near. Penn turned to them smilingly, and said: "I have had a most delightful talk with this charming young princess; she has made me many valuable suggestions. In your presence friends, I will say that all I discussed with her will be carried out."

The girl bowed graciously, and withdrew into the forest. Penn spent the balance of the evening with the chiefs and his staff, engaged in friendly conversations. The next morning he started for the east, pleased with every detail of his trip. Rose-Marie was on hand to wave him good-bye. On the way he told his secretary that the Cherry Tree was to be the western boundary of actual settlement; he requested him to make full record of this decision. For all the French guides and Indian interpreters understood, there was no question about the matter. It was a wise move, and would have made the redmen permanent allies.

The return trip was uneventful, except for Indian entertainments, and before long Penn was safely back at Sedgley. Later he went to England, and died thereabout twenty years later. After his death settlers began moving west of the Cherry Tree, though the Indians made immediate protest. Penn had said their settlements would end there. Their objections were unheeded, and gradually the good feeling between the two races subsided and bloody warfare ensued. Down to the time of Teedyuscung, the Indians complained of broken promises, of shattered faith, but deaf was the ear of authority to Penn's promise to Rose-Marie.

XVIII. Golden Hour in the Camp

(Story of Young Woman's Creek.)

The Golden Hour had settled in the Camp. The cloudless sky was of that delicate tint which the French call "bleu-ciel," toward the horizon it was shading into pale gold. Across the hollow, every leaf of the tall hemlocks and beeches was clear cut as a diamond in the soft light. The smooth trunks of the trees had assumed tones of lavender. Here and there crickets chirping in the grass punctuated the evening stillness; high in the evergreen boughs somnolent turtle doves were sweetly cooing. Supper over, we had all taken seats outside the shanties to absorb the dreamy beauty of the scene. Rough woodsmen though they might be, there was not one but felt the charm of atmospheric content. Old Nicholas, the Indian cook, was saying that he liked the Golden Hour the best of any part of the day, that he had never seen an evening more beautiful than this. "I have seen *one* more beautiful" said old man Connelly, the forrester, "it was in the Mohawk Valley, I was traveling through there in the train."

"That was because you were going to visit your best girl," said Nicholas, "I know you well." Gradually long dark shadows, like streamers, fell from the tallest trees, and lay across the clearing, giving a black color to the creek, as it wound its way around rocks and slabs. Speckled kildeers, perched on partly submerged rotting logs, were drinking daintily at the water's edge. Once or twice came the tinkle of a distant cow bell or a crisp breeze from the heart of the hemlocks. A small flock of wild pigeons, flying high, swept across the blue canopy. "They used to nest here by the millions," said old Nicholas. "When they cut the last hemlock, you'll see the last of the pigeons, nature sent them to destroy the hemlock beetles." Some of the men smoked, and dropping off the benches - lolled in the grass. One big lad was softly humming "Nellie Gray." Memories, sweet bright memories, were in every breast, fairer memories than those which haunt us by the firelight. And the tint of lavender gradually overspread the shades of sky blue and gold. The sound of voices came upon our ears.

Two of the boys were talking loudly as they approached, the rich, jerky intonation of the lumber woods, now heard no more. Soon we saw them, they carried on their shoulders a huge chunk of beech-wood, probably four feet long. One end was jagged, showing it had been broken, the other had been sawed through by a crosscut. "Bringing in a choice piece of firewood, buddies" called out old Nicholas, jocularly, "thought we needed it, mor'n you did your supper."

"Wait till you see what we've got" answered the lads in chorus. When they got to where we were seated, they lifted the chunk from their shoulders, and carefully laid it on the grass. Then they took off their caps, mopping their perspiring brows with red handkerchiefs. They did not have to show us the reason for fetching the beech-log. On the smooth bark, deftly cut, was a profile fourteen inches long, doubtless an Indian face. Evidently it had been carved there many years, as the lines were softened, and in some corners almost indiscernable, by the development of the bark. It had the soft sketchy, indeterminate atmosphere of an etching. Below were some hieroglyphics, which might once have been a name. At the first glimpse, Nicholas had gotten up from his bench, and dropped down on his knees beside the carving. "Boys, oh, boys, where did you get that?" he demanded.

"It's poor Tschinque's face to be sure." "It wasn't on our job" replied one of the boys. "We were headed back here for supper, taking a short cut through Deloy's slashing. About a hundred yards from the Otter Spring we saw this slab lying among the tops and logs. Some big hemlock in falling, probably this morning, had broken off the top of the beech, and the crew never noticed the curiosity. There was a crosscut handy, so we sawed off the upper part where the branches began, and carried the chunk along with us."

"That's too bad," said Nicholas, "I had forgotten all about that tree, we called it when I was a boy 'Tschinque's beech.' If I had thought I'd have told Deloy to spare it. He'd have done it for me. Too bad, too bad." We all asked the old Indian to tell us the story; he smiled sadly, saying that he would, if we would promise not to forget it.

"As long as that tree stood poor Tschinque had a good chance of being remembered, but now, unless we who are here tonight keep the story alive, his sad romance will end in oblivion." We promised never to forget, and besides we liked to please old Nicholas. The old man resumed his seat on the bench, and leaning his back against the rough logs of the cabin, began his story.

"Tschinque lived considerably over a hundred years ago, as near as I can judge. He was before my father's or my grandfather's time, it was an old story to them. In his early youth he was the greatest hunter in this country. Before he was twenty he had killed more panthers and brown bears, buffaloes and elks, wolves and catamounts, than anybody in the tribe. The chief's son was jealous of his prowess and planned his murder. By keeping in the wilderness, he escaped with his life. A slow fever carried off his royal rival, some said from a broken heart, so he moved about with freedom after that. He became by common consent the official hunter of the tribe. Whenever fierce animals harassed the camps, he was allowed to go out to slay them in single combat. And he never came back defeated. Many Indians said they would rather have his good looks and courage than royal blood. He was without a parallel in hurling the spear, or drawing the bow. Women of all degrees loved him, and he managed to carry on many affairs at the same time. He was unscrupulous, and boastful of his conquests, like are all ill-bred men, white as well as red.

But at length he fell in love with one girl, Gilkissin by name, of about his own caste, whom he loved more than all the rest. While she encouraged him, there was no woman living who could do otherwise, she did not yield herself to him, she kept him at a respectful distance. She was beautiful, intelligent, was pure and clean. Though she adored the great hunter, she was not anxious to marry him immediately; she feared that once he had conquered her, he would go in search of other prey. She must know him better. If there was a good side to his nature, he showed it to Gilkissin. But she was not satisfied in her soul, though she dearly loved him for his physical beauty. When she did consent to a marriage, she set a date three months ahead, a long time according to the customs of those primitive Indians.

"During this final period of probation, Tschinque desired to augment to his reputation as a hunter. He choked a monster seal to death in the river near Peter's Steps. This was an achievement even in those days, as they were never plentiful. He killed a mammoth moose, the last one seen in this region. He allowed a pack of fierce black wolves to chase him to the edge of the camp, and killed them all by deft spear thrusts in the presence of the frightened population, and before they had time to touch a single soul. He killed a family of six ferocious fishers in seven minutes. He killed a herd of a hundred buffaloes in a single day. Even for him that was an exhausting task.

At night he returned to his hunting camp, flushed with triumph at his great achievement. He ordered his followers to depart immediately for the scene of the butchery, and bring in the hundred tongues, lest birds of prey or wolves spoil any of them before morning. A great bonfire had been lighted to commemorate the event far and wide. The flames rose at least a hundred feet in the air. Utterly worn out, though he would not admit it, the hunter sat on a log, at the edge of the fire, leaning on his spear. His followers had departed by his orders, there was no one by him. He gradually fell asleep, still leaning on his stout spear. The flames running in the grass and chips had crept close to where he rested. They licked about the handle of the spear, they coiled up it like tiny serpents. The stout hickory began to burn, it charred clear through, it broke asunder. Sleeping soundly, Tschinque no longer upheld by his support, tumbled into the hot fire among the grass and chips. Lying there on his right side, the flames wrought sad havoc with his arm, the side of his face, burning out one of his eyes. He would probably have been burned to a cinder had not a rain arose, which even quenched the triumphal bonfire. When his followers returned at dawn, they feared to lift him from the charred earth, lest his flesh come away with the soil. When he awakened, of his own accord, he quickly realized his predicament. Proud to the heart's core of his personal appearance, he waited for three days until the earth dried, then he lifted himself up with safety. But even then, he arose a caricature, a ludicrous travesty on his former beautiful self. His right eye was gone, his face burnt in patches clear in to the skull. Nothing remained of his right arm except the bones, which he broke off in horror and disgust. Though his physical sufferings must have been hideous, he suffered more from mortification than from his hurts. No longer was he the handsomest youth of his generation, no more the greatest of nimrods. Half blind, and one armed, he could never hurl the javelin or draw the bow. Perhaps he might learn to use the spear left-handed, but with poor eyesight the game would have the advantage. He stood, with tears rolling down his cheeks, gazing at the hundred buffalo tongues, which his faithful henchmen piled up before him to assuage his grief.

"The chief to whom he sent the hundred tongues, despatched an embassy of condolence. His sweetheart swooned when she heard the news, then hurried to his side. When her eyes rested on the horrible human mockery, she burst into tears. Alas, they were not tears of sympathy, but came from a realization that she loved Tschinque the beauty, the nimrod, nothing else. He had no character to adore, no gifts which might atone for his vanished charms. Something gave way within her, she felt no more for her stricken lover than one would for a broken piece of china-ware. It pained her to feel, that with all her high ideals, she had loved mere clay; her love penetrated no deeper than others of her sex. Her worship had been founded on physical beauty alone; as it is in most cases. Instead of throwing her arms around her stricken favorite, she shuddered with repulsion, and like a startled doe, ran off into the forest. But a short time before she had gloated because she had gotten this handsome man away from a host of fair aspirants.

"'Some other woman will love him' she repeated to herself again and again, as she ran and ran — through the silent forest depths. But no other woman now loved him. The many who had striven for his hand, or yielded to his caresses, kept aloof; they loved the handsome beau ideal, the gallant nimrod, they wanted none of a dull, weird monstrosity.

"Tschinque realized his altered position, he was like a bull dehorned and gelded turned back into the pasture that once he ruled. Like a wounded or a sickly animal is deserted by its kind, the Indians cruelly shunned the mutilated hunter. Food was thrown to him gingerly, as to a dog; all who secretly envied him before, emphasized their revenge. He found that with one arm he could climb trees, and carrying his sharp scalping knife in his teeth he scaled the hemlocks and beeches in search of pigeons' nests. He lived off squabs and eggs, he who formerly would eat nothing less than a buffalo's or antelope's heart. The squirrels, black, grey and red, seemed to divine he was different from other men, they mocked and chaffed him, as did the scornful redheaded paroquets.

The Hand of Man

Photo by W. T. Clarke, Conrad, Pa.

"One afternoon he climbed a huge beech, that contained a veritable harvest of pigeons' eggs. He feasted for several hours, sometimes eating shells and all, in his greedy triumph. Loneliness and chagrin had touched his head, though many Indians declared he had always been a trifle queer. When he had eaten the last egg, and had yawned in satisfaction, he leaned against the fork of the tree, and began to meditate. Unfortunately thoughts of his former high estate descended upon him, of the women who once ran after him, of his present lowly condition. His mind became strangely normal, all the awful truth of his tragic downfall rose clearly to his vision. He was hated and despised, why should he continue such a loathsome existence? There was no earthly reason. Accustomed as he had been to the worship of women, public approbation, popularity, neglect and opprobrium cut him like knife thrusts. As far as women went, he would never feel their interest again. If his powers as a hunter had been snatched from him and he could have retained his looks, he felt sure everything would have been the same. But deprived of glamor and looks, he was useless in his old world. Women had loved him for his physical beauty, he had no other charm. He realized how impossible it had been for the chief's son, who died of a broken heart, to outshine him with all his power of royal birth. This youth had not been handsome, and he lost out in every love tilt. Nature demands the mating of the physically desirable, and will break down the thickest walls of caste to attain her purposes. It is only when a man of the commoner sort who is handicapped by homeliness finds it impossible to grasp a prize above him.

"As the afternoon advanced into the Golden Hour, the wretched Indian resolved to die. Yet he hated to skulk out of the world, unremembered, unrecognized. If he could have some enduring memorial, he would go gladly. He ran his left hand over the smooth bark of beech, and over the sharp blade of his hunting knife, which he gripped in his teeth. He looked about him; where he sat was too full of branches, too deeply hidden in foliage to suit. Even in winter leaves cling tenaciously to the beech. Below the fork the trunk of the tree ran straight and smooth to the earth for eighty feet. He cut his buckskin jacket into ribbons, and fashioned a swing by which he could let himself down half a dozen feet, to where he wished to work.

"When he had adjusted his device, tieing the knots with his teeth, he lowered himself, and began his task. He had never suspected he possessed artistic abilities, perhaps they had developed suddenly in the intensity of his despair. With his keen blade he carved on the soft bark a profile, resembling the good side of his face. He knew it well, had admired its reflection in a hundred pools. He laid especial stress on the noble arch of his high nose, the deep eyesocket, the leanness of the cheek. For an untrained hand, it was surely a masterpiece. When finished he gazed at it in open-mouthed admiration. No wonder that all women loved him. But he was not done. Beneath the portrait he cut his name, and the words 'beloved by all women, master slayer of fierce beasts.' That handsome face, with the record of his achievements, would attract attention to his personality for years to come. The beech tree, loved by the Storm God, would escape the lightning; no human hands would care to fell it with its curious inscription. It was too high in the air to be mutilated by vandals. When he had gazed on the likeness and inscription to his satisfaction, he cut the ropes which held him, and dropped. He turned several somersaults in the air, and struck earth head first; death was instantaneous.

"That night the skulking black wolves that he had oft times harassed made merry with his mangled corpse. They tore it to pieces, yelping and romping with fiendish joy. They seemed to divine the identity of their feast. It is said that to animals each human being has a distinctive scent. By morning there was not a bone nor scrap of hair to serve as a physical memento of Tschinque, once greatest of hunters.

"The lynx-eyed Indians passing through the forest were not long in discovering the face and inscription on the beech, even though it was so high above the ground. They made certain signs to ward off devils as they passed. 'Cursed is he who seeks to make his own immortality.' Some of the more serious-minded detested the phrase 'beloved by all women,' but none cared to climb the tree to erase the words. 'Time will wipe it out soon enough' said the wisemen. A century or more came and went, the legend below the profile became indecipherable, nature was its own eraser. But the stern face remained, time softening a little the bitterness of its lines. Oh, had I realized the nearness of Deloy's operations I would have asked him to have care taken not to injure the beech. But I guess nature wanted the tree, and all record of Tschinque to go; my tongue was tied." We looked up, the strange story was finished. A crimson sunset overspread the horizon, gone like Tschinque was the Golden Hour.

XIX. The Weathervanes

(Story of the Old River Bridge.)

When he was younger, it was much harder for Matthew Annot, the bridge-tender, to pass the time, than latterly. Had it not been that he was shot in the leg in the Civil War, while serving in Hawkins' Zouaves, he would have chosen a more active occupation. Kind friends had the position at the bridge offered to him, he was always glad he accepted. Even the slight exertion of getting up from his arm-chair to count out change and hand over tickets hurt his leg, especially in bad weather. At first he thought he might maintain a room at the lockkeeper's cottage, several hundred yards away, but his infirmities made it impossible. He fitted up a couch in the toll-house, hung his favorite pictures above it, including the little daguerreotype which was taken when as a boy in France, he first became a sailor. How he drifted from the quarter-deck of a French coasting-vessel to the wilds of Central Pennsylvania, even serving in the Union army during the war, was one of the romances of destiny. Now his friends in this adopted land had provided for his welfare by making him bridge-tender. In addition he drew a pittance from the government called a "pension."

His father had been a clever wood-carver in Bordeaux, his specialty being the figure-heads for the old-time sailing ships, and Matthew inherited something of this gift. During his idle moments he was always whittling something. During his first months at the toll-house he carved many mantel-shelves, wall-brackets and what-nots. These he gave to the kind friends who had helped him when crippled he came back to the village where he had only lived a year before enlisting. He was a silent man, he could not express his gratitude in words; by small gifts he sought to show how appreciative he was for such spontaneous goodness.

The second period in his wood-carving was that of making weathervanes. He cut out of the soft white pine little fishes, dogs, horses, deer chased by hounds, birds, men and women. These he painted prettily, and also gave them away. All the boys and girls in the village became his friends, they wanted the little vanes to put on smoke-houses and wood-sheds in their shady cottage yards. It was a gay sight to see them spinning about briskly when the Keewaydin or home-wind blew.

Then came a period when the bridge-tender carved no more figures, but sat moodily reading and re-reading a letter which at all times lay before him on his shelf at the toll-window. Those who knew him well suspected that it related to some old love-affair, the cause probably of his taking up his abode in the wilds of Pennsylvania. It was during this time that he let his black beard grow, and shaved the upper lip, like the custom of old-time sailor men. To a few, it was suspected he contemplated returning to sea. But little use would be a crippled seaman.

He kept a light burning all night in the tiny shanty, and the shade drawn up; belated travelers often peered in to see the ponderous form sleeping heavily on his bench, an old-fashioned pistol lying beneath his folded hands. But during this period of soul-struggle, he was uniformly gentle and courteous, people pitied rather than blamed him. Then he shook off his lethargy, put the letter aside, and became the blithe spirit of old.

He carved a weathervane for his own use. It was the sprightliest one of all. It represented a sailor-maid, and a sailor-man, standing at either end of the arrow. The figures were not more than six inches high, but were exquisitely done. The girl's face was truly beautiful, rosy cheeked, black haired; he must have had a living model in his soul. She was attired in a blue blouse and skirt, with white collar and cap. The painting was excellent, and glistened like enameling. The tiny sailor-man was similar. He wore a blue blouse and trousers, and with collar and cap. The sailor's black beard and red cheeks were noticeable features; all the boys and girls said it was a model of Annot himself. When some of his young friends put the new vane, and the graceful arrow, which was gilded, on the roof of the shanty, it presented a brave appearance, swinging and rattling in the breeze. Carters, lumbermen, fishermen, tramps, women and children all stopped to admire. Ten years passed and it had not ceased to be a novelty.

Meanwhile the bridge-tender's life moved on uneventfully. Sometimes he was very busy, as lumbering operations on the high mountains sent a constant stream of wagons across the bridge. There were slack times, when he moved his bench out in the sunlight, and watched the blue, rippling river. He sometimes fished for shad, and was accounted a good fisherman. He had a pet at this time, a strange one it seemed. Some idle boy had shot and wounded a Great Blue Heron. The poor bird, broken winged and panic-stricken, had dropped on the bridge approach, in front of the toll-house. The old man hobbled over to it, and seized it, despite its flapping of wings and frantic efforts to spear him with its strong bill. He tied it by one leg until he could build a pen for it; a dish of minnows and a little kindness, and it became very docile. Outside the shanty he constructed the pen out of rough boards with slats on one side; it was a roomy and comfortable place. The heron and the bridge-tender became fast friends. Ultimately he let the bird have its freedom, but it always returned at night.

One sunshiny morning in the early spring, Annot was fishing for shad, with the heron perched beside him. He always fed it on the heads, tails and entrails of the fish. But sometimes it would fly up stream, especially when it saw others of its kind. On this morning, having fed plentifully, it started out to try its wings, disappearing among the red birches and buttonwoods which lined the shore. There was a loud report of a shot-gun, and soon the heart-broken bridge-tender saw a stranger running towards him, dragging the big heron by its bill, shouting: "See what a monster bird I killed."

"What did you do that for, buddy, you have shot my pet heron" said Annot, his voice trembling with emotion.

"You can have it" said the stranger unfeelingly.

"I don't want it *now*," replied the bridge-tender. "I always hated stuffed birds." The loss of the heron sent the old man back into the train of melancholy thoughts that had possessed him when he had received the letter ten years before. To rouse himself, he began carving another weathervane. This one was his most ambitious effort. It was an acrobat, apparently, dressed in white, with white cap, short white trousers, and black stockings. In each hand it held an Indian Club, which were to swing around in opposite directions from the figure as it revolved in the wind. A new generation of boys and girls crowded about the window to watch the old man work on his masterpiece. "It's a good thing he lost that gandersnipe if it sets him to work carving" said one thoughtless woman of the neighborhood. He worked for nearly a month on the figure before he considered it perfected enough to adorn the shanty roof. The friendly boys, who had watched the new device grow from a block of pine to a little figure correct in every detail, mounted on a gilded arrow, put it in place on the roof. For some reason they placed it on the same

126

end as the sailor-girl and the sailor-man, and not very far from them. Despite having faced the elements for ten years, they were in prime condition. Every year they had been repainted, so that they looked as fresh as the time when they were first carved from the pine.

The new vane was an added attraction to the toll-house. A big prop-timber job had opened on the lofty mountain. The heavy teams were constantly crossing the bridge as the props were shipped by canal to the coal-regions. The drivers lingered longer than necessary at the shanty, to watch the winds sway the little figures. "Haint they the derndest things you ever seen" was the general comment of the teamsters.

As the summer wore on folks noticed that the sailor-maid had exercised a powerful attraction over the acrobat. He was leaning towards her, almost touching her. The ruddy face on the sailor-man had grown paler, the summer heat was fading him quicker this year than usual. This was noticed by the teamsters for a long time, yet they disliked to mention the matter to the old Frenchman. But the boys and girls were not so circumspect. "Mister Annot" one of them said, "your acrobat is getting bent over by the wind, we're afraid he'll soon bump into the sailor-girl, and both vanes'll get broken."

"I suspected something was wrong" said the old man quietly; "they made an uncommon racket at night, it sounded as if one of them was crying; wonder could the sailor-man been getting jealous?" The children did not answer, but looked at one another. The biggest of the boys climbed on the shanty roof, and straightened the acrobat. It was less than a week before it bent over towards the sailor-maid again. Before anyone had a chance to report it, the old man had noticed it. "Boys" he said, "won't you please straighten that little acrobat? It seems he can't keep away from the sailor-girl; it makes my little sailor that unhappy I can't sleep nights."

The acrobat was set right, but in a single night he was bending towards the pretty sailor-maid. "Please take down that acrobat" said old Annot, "and I'll make a new base for him, so he *can't* bend."

The figure was taken down, and fitted on a new pivot, made from a larger and more solid piece of wood. But despite this, it again leaned towards the sailor-maid. "I wouldn't mind," remarked the old man, "only there is such an infernal noise at night, I can't sleep." But he gave no further orders to straighten the offending manikin. "The old man's going daffy over those figures" was the way in which the young folks dismissed the matter from their minds. It was during this time that the old man received another letter. The post-mistress, a soldier's widow, said in all the years she handled the mail, this was only the second he had ever received, except of course some patent medicine advertisements and notices of reunions from his old regiment.

Like the first letter, the second bore a foreign post-mark and stamp. The old man was always reading it, spread out on the shelf before him, and his face wore a troubled and weary look. But he never forgot to be gentle and civil with those who crossed the bridge. His abstraction over the receipt of the letter was ascribed by the busybodies in the little community as the reason he paid no attention to the acrobat's awry position on the roof. But one bright morning, after a heavy windstorm, those who crossed the bridge noticed that the acrobat was no longer to be seen, though the sailor-maid and sailorman still rattled about in the morning breeze. It was a cool morning, but the old man was sitting outside the toll-house on his bench. There was a smile on his face, a buoyancy to his manner, that was quite unusual. "I see that tornado ripped off the little acrobat" ventured one of the teamsters.

"Yes, and I'm glad of it," replied the old man, grinning from ear to ear. "He couldn't behave himself, was always leaning towards the sailor-maid, and making my little sailor-man so jealous, I couldn't sleep nights." Then both teamster and bridge-keeper laughed, and the conversation turned to other channels.

Everyone, from teamsters to school-children noticed the absence of the little acrobat. They commented on it, and it always set the old Frenchman to laughing. To some he said: "It's an ill wind that blows nobody good."

A week later, the body of a man, middle-aged, dressed in acrobat's costume, was found pounding against the jetties of the dam a mile below. Evidently he had belonged to some strolling circus, and had either fallen or been pushed into the river. His head and body were covered with bruises, but whether these had come before or after he got into the water, was an open question. It was impossible to tell where he had fallen in, but the body looked as if it had been in the river at least a week. The county coroner could not solve the mystery, and the corpse was buried in the myrtle-carpeted graveyard on the hill. "It's a bad month for acrobats" said the old bridge-tender rather cheerfully, when the story was told to him. "It's an ill wind that blows nobody good." A traveling pony circus was found at Hummel's Wharf, and all hands detained, but no connection could be proved between them and the body taken from the river, forty miles below. That closed the incident as far as the law went.

A month and a half later another letter was received by the old Frenchman. He actually forgot his limp, for he walked all the way to the post-office to personally drop the reply into the letter-box, two hours later. His spirits became very high, he laughed like a school-boy. A week afterwards he announced that he had worked long enough, twenty years in one place was a good service, let a younger man have the job. He had saved up enough he said and with his pension he could be comfortable. Besides he was going back to France, to be married, he saw his way clear now. It was with regret that the bridge-owners let him go, he was as efficient as popular and picturesque. But they could not detain him, so off he went. "It's an ill wind that blows nobody good," he said as he boarded the train for Harrisburg.

XX. Elphe Soden

(Story of Two River Towns.)

There was a great crowd in Patriot Square watching the election returns. They represented all classes of humanity, almost all colors. They were good-natured, alert, watchful, and above all, patient. The important news was a long time coming, and in the intervals stereopticon pictures of well-known statesmen were thrown on the big sheet. Every few minutes a clanging trolley car, brilliantly lighted, would plough its way through the throng, the surging mass of humanity falling back like dark furrows. Often automobiles, filled with merrymakers, and decked with flags and streamers, would attempt the tactics of the trolleys, but it would take much tooting of horns, and good natured raillery to force a passage.

On the four corners of the square, beneath the glow of the street lamps stood many parents, holding aloft infants. They feared to risk the precious burdens to the middle of the thoroughfare. The tiny folks took little notice of the bright lights or magic-lantern views; sometimes they pricked up their ears when the band on the steps of the newspaper office struck up a lively air. But most of all they were interested in the gay young figures flitting about in a dancing school in the fourth story of a building across the way. The shades were up, and sometimes between dances the young people would throw open the windows, leaning out to watch the crowds in the square below. It was a scene full of life and animation, one to destroy the *ennui* that comes to very youthful dwellers in interior towns. It was the false gaiety that many misinterpret as the joy of living.

Once when an impromptu marching club of lads shouting gaily, none of whom were old enough to vote, cut a swath through the assemblage, the figure of an unusually pretty young girl was disclosed. She could not have been over sixteen years of age, she had the willowy lines of the first blossoming period, and she clung tightly to the arm of a girl friend, perhaps two years older, more fully developed, and almost as pretty. The very young girl was a star of the first magnitude as far as beauty went; any eye, skilled or unskilled, could tell that at first glance. She was one of those rare master-works that are turned out now and again by the halfhearted potters in the celestial workshop. Like most of the fascinating women of every age and clime, she was a blonde; her fairness was of the golden order, and not the pale flaxen, which possesses no charms at all. She was above the middle height, as graceful as she was slender. She wore a small blue velvet bonnet, all the world like a baby cap, with the velvet ribbons tied under her chin. From the corners of the cap tufts of her frizzy gold hair were flying out. Her rosy face was round like a baby's, as were her big blue eyes. Her arched nose turned up just a trifle at the end, her sensitive lips, inclined to fullness, were very red. She wore a tight-fitting blue cloth jacket and skirt. Over her shoulders was a large lace collar or Bertha, which further accentuated the baby-like appearance. She had carried the sweetness and innocence of the cradle into her teens. She possessed a sense of humor, and laughed at everything that happened; the night was a merry one to her. Strictly brought up, and closely watched at home, because of her rare beauty, she was glad to be out this one night, to feel perfectly free. Her name, Elphe Soden, was as bizarre and attractive as her appearance; hers was a personality bound for a voyage through pictur-esque channels.

Her friend, Marie Neff, eighteen years old, just out of high school, and more or less experienced in the ways of men, was an inch shorter in stature, in col-oring her eyes were hazel, her hair dark brown. She had the same type of nose as Elphe, which always indicates extreme powers of fascination. While her influence on the younger girl could not be bad, the watchful parents feared that Marie would prove of a jealous nature. Already she had been crossed in love; they knew that if she saw her young friend running into realms of perfect bliss, she would rebel, and try to thwart her plans.

In the crowd was a dashing young traveling man, or "drummer," who was watching the fair Elphe intently. He had not seen her until the marching club parted the throng, although for probably half an hour she had stood within a few feet of him. He had become weary sitting at the window of the hotel lob-by, with his feet on the sill, and had strolled out to mingle with the election night merrymakers. He was of the type that is always successful with women. The scientists say that such a man closely approaches "the type of the race," and women subconsciously are striving for the ideal. Such men generally cross a woman's path once in a lifetime, they are scarce, and once seen, haunt her memory to the grave. She measures other men on this pattern, and of course they fall short, and she cannot feel completely happy with anyone. The traveling man knew his powers, and once he saw the fair young girl, edged nearer to her, so she could see him. He was flashily dressed; he knew that would always charm, especially in an inland town, where the social posi-tion of strangers is often measured by the width of trousers, the padding of shoulders. His face was round, indicating good food and gratified passions, there was a dimple in his full chin. His eyes were blue, and never at rest, al-ways glancing from one thing to another, the unstable eyes that women think are worth trying to conquer. His short nose was lacking in bridge, but the clear blue eyes, and the white even teeth which he displayed on every possi-ble occasion more than remedied this defect. He had fine dark lashes and brows, and his full head of hair was curly and black. He often took off his nar-row-brimmed brown derby, to show off his abundant locks. He had good healthy color, and despite a tendency to stoutness, was well made. His brown suit was cut college style, making him a sure winner with the girls. His age was probably twenty-eight, though he was as experienced as most men of fifty. Hardened by the advances of a thousand attractive women, he was in-different to most of the sex.

Yet when he saw Elphe Soden he instantly admitted to himself that she was the most beautiful girl he had ever seen. He wanted to know her at once, he who boasted that he would not walk around the corner to meet the most beautiful woman living. His name was Clyde Bauchle, he traveled for a leading cigar company, and while he had lived in many states, had been born near Allentown. It is from the "Pennsylvania German Capital" that spring many of the most winning figures in the worlds of stage, circus, turf, and gay life generally. Clyde Bauchle was a shining example of a Pennsylvania German high-roller, or man of the world.

Elphe was not long in spying him, she nudged her friend, and both looked long and admiringly at the jaunty Adonis. They tried to catch his eye, but could not, his glance was too furtive, too restive. This piqued them, could it be that this attractive stranger saw nothing in them worthy of notice. But Clyde was only playing his game well, aided by his unstable, soulless eyes. They were eyes with surface, but without depth. The returns were slow at coming in, the faces of the same statesmen had been projected on the big sheet time and time again. The girls became restless, partly at the lack of news, partly because of their proximity to the handsome stranger. Elphe whispered to her friend that it was time to be moving homeward, and holding tighter to one another, they elbowed their way through the crowd.

They passed close by the traveling man, who caught Elphe's eye and smiled. The battle was won, although Marie felt chagrined that the greeting went to Elphe and not to her. The traveling man took off his hat, and began the conversation as if he had known the girls all his life. It was charming how neatly he went about it. Not a person in the crowd could have suspected that he was anything but an old family friend. He walked with the girls to Elphe's home, as Marie had pretended she must see her young friend indoors first. He lingered quite a while on the steps, getting her permission to call and to write to her before he left. He only walked with Marie as far as the corner of the street where she lived, he wished her the most frigid of good nights. Marie knew she was a pretty girl, that many men admired her. She roiled inwardly at such marked favoritism. It only made her like the showy stranger the more for his indifference. Towards Elphe arose in her a sense of jealous hatred, a desire to wreak on her a soul-crushing revenge. It scorched her pride to feel that twice when walking in the direction of her home she had asked him to call on her, but he had not deigned to reply.

Two weeks later he returned to the town, and spent a long evening with Elphe. The fair girl, on her guard as all women must be, did not tell her friend of his expected visit, but the next morning, bright and early, though she was feeling wretchedly tired, hurried to break the joyous news. Marie tried to look unconcerned, but despite her efforts, could not refrain from asking if he had inquired after her. Perhaps Elphe should have fibbed and said "yes," but the desire for sole triumph was too great in her, so she said he had never mentioned her name. Revengeful feelings became stronger in Marie than ever, though she was usually a mild girl. She was impotent to think of anything definite however.

Clyde began making special weekly visits to town to see Elphe, shortly after this. She always told about them to her friend the mornings afterwards, which stimulated her deep-seated hate. Apart from the subject of the handsome traveling man, Marie truly loved the young chum and otherwise would not have harmed her. She could not understand why he preferred Elphe to her, and was so brutal in showing it. It takes years' experience, and study to understand and overlook the seeming injustices of life. Clyde's visits consumed over a year of Elphe's life, yet he made no move to propose marriage. The young girl, who was still attending high school, gave up all her boy friends, neglected her girl friends, was insolent and undutiful to her parents.

Marie still clung to her, as she expected Clyde to tire of her suddenly and drop her; she wanted to be on hand to gloat over her ignominious downfall.

But the night after Christmas, the traveling man spoke the long expected words. Elphe and he were together in the cozy front parlor, on their favorite upholstered Morris chair; she was on his lap of course, with her beautiful arms around his flabby, rather thin, neck. The single gas jet was turned low, but a score of tiny lights twinkled in the dark foliage of the Christmas tree. The hard-coal fire had burned low in the open grate; outside the sleet beat incessantly against the window panes. Elphe had hardly expected such joy as came to her. Out of a conversation most commonplace had arisen the words of love. He asked her to marry him, in a month if possible. All the startled girl could reply was "Yes, yes, I love you very much." Then she smothered his beefy smooth face with kisses. It was arranged that he return in the morning to ask her parents' consent; he must come early before her father left for the big department store where he was the head accountant.

The parents were surprised, but took the matter philosophically. They had been afraid that Clyde's intentions were not serious; Marie and other friends had hinted this to them. They feared if he deserted her it would send the girl into a decline. Now that he had asked for her hand, it was best to give their consent, though the girl lacked six months of being eighteen.

The consent given, Clyde hurried to catch a train for York, while Elphe flew over the icy pavements to tell the news to Marie. The girl was dumbfounded, but forced a smile and gave her congratulations. Clyde was devoted during the period before the wedding. He was at his fiancee's home at least twice a week, he made all kinds of promises for the future. He would take an apartment in Philadelphia. This was the best piece of news of all. Elphe had envied only one class of people; they were the ones who went to live in the great city. It was as much of Heaven as she could grasp, merely to live there. She told about going to live in Philadelphia on all sides; she dug up discarded acquaintances just to impart this choice bit of joy. Never had she looked so beautiful as this month of expectancy before the wedding; a thousand hopes made a crown of loveliness around her fair young face. No bride-to-be ever looked into the future so confident of happiness. She knew she was to marry a handsome man, he would take her to Philadelphia to live, that was enough.

The wedding was a quiet affair, attended by Elphe's relatives and close friends. Marie was the only person present who noticed that the bridegroom brought no one with him. Even the Methodist preacher who tied the knot was the Sodens' family pastor. A wedding trip to such delectable spots as Atlantic City and New York was taken. Then the young couple moved into their apartment in Philadelphia, and for a time were supposedly happy. Perhaps all did go well at first. But if it hadn't, Elphe would have never told. When at Easter time she came home for a visit alone, with a basket containing a red azalea in one hand, she was full of enthusiastic accounts of the theatres and shops, the gay life of the Quaker metropolis. But she was somewhat reticent concerning Clyde. He only wrote to her once while she was home, and this caused her much anxiety. She wrote him daily, and when she did not get a second letter, sent him three or four telegrams. She tried to get him on the long distance telephone repeatedly, but was unsuccessful. Fearing he was ill, she cut short her visit and started for Philadelphia. What happened upon her return there will never be known, but in forty-eight hours she was back with her parents, this time for good. Marie said she confided to her that she found a well-known show girl installed in the apartment, and had offered Clyde the choice between the two, and that he had selected the actress. Further than that she hinted that she discovered he had only married her to make the show girl jealous, as she had taken up with the son of a noted millionaire.

At any rate, Elphe's brief romance was ended, much to the grief of her devoted parents, and to the ill-concealed joy of Marie Neff. Elphe was loathe to tell the true story to her parents, and was always blaming herself for not having forgiven Clyde. But after a year, when he showed no signs of coming hack, she reluctantly gave information to the family lawyer which enabled him to get her a speedy divorce. But divorce did not bring her happiness, she was lonelier and more melancholy than ever.

Family friends tried to entertain her, they invited her to camping parties on the river, and during August to Cape May. Most of these invitations were refused, but she consented to go to the shore. She liked the sea-coast, part of her honeymoon had been spent on it.

The house-party at Cape May was given by one of her mother's old friends, a woman happily married, who had several grown-up sons; one of whom was a recent bridegroom. The guests included the three sons, and girl friends of the young bride.

There was a young man named Walton Cresson stopping at a nearby hotel. He had gone to school at Mercersburg with the young men at whose home Elphe was stopping. He was a prosperous young business man in a town not quite a hundred miles up the river from the fair girl's home. He saw Elphe, and like most men, was smitten by her charms. He obtained an introduction, and soon showed himself to be deeply in love. He was good-looking, gentlemanly and generous, so Elphe could not treat him as rudely as she had most men she met since the night she first fell in with Clyde, the despoiler of her young life. But she surely gave him no encouragement as a lover. He was with her constantly all through her visit at the shore. He got up picnics, dances and sailing parties, took her driving, and showed not only Elphe, but her friends, a splendid time. He asked permission to come to see her after she returned home; the privilege was reluctantly given. Perhaps she had hoped to see no more of him when she left the resort.

For over a year or about as long as Clyde Bauchle was attentive, Walton Cresson pressed his suit. The only difference was Cresson proposed marriage after a week's acquaintance, it took Clyde over a year. Elphe refused the young business man bluntly, but he was undaunted. She confided this to her friend Marie, who advised her to accept him. In the jealous girl's mind arose the thought that if her chum was married to another man, perhaps she might meet Clyde in town, and get him to call on her, and by writing it to Elphe, make her miserably unhappy. She was actuated by no desire to see her close friend obtain happiness in life.

Finally Elphe did accept the persistent suitor, and was quietly married to him. There was a marked difference in this ceremony. Elphe's face was serious throughout; a score of Cresson's good friends were present.

After a wedding trip to Washington and Old Point Comfort, the young couple settled in a handsome mansion in a shady street overlooking the river, in the old town where the bridegroom had spent all his life. Marie was invited to visit the couple. She saw evidences of comfort and refinement, of Elphe's popularity with her husband's large circle of friends, of the young man's great love for his beautiful bride. But none of these things made her jealous. The reason for this was that as soon as she arrived Elphe had foolishly confided to her that while she liked her husband, and her new home, she still loved Clyde Bauchle, and would never forgive herself for leaving him.

It pained Marie to realize that Elphe had found two husbands, while she, a girl almost as pretty, could not get any. Perhaps she loved Clyde too much to make herself agreeable to eligible men. But Elphe confessed to the same thing, yet was married to an attractive man. The young people gave parties for her, tried to get her interested in well-known young men of the town, but could not make any headway on either side. Loveless though she was, Marie went back to her home in a happy frame of mind, because she knew that Elphe was unhappy. That seemed to be her greatest joy in life, she was a human mistletoe.

One afternoon a couple of months after her return she was walking across Patriot Square on her way to a tea given by members of her old high school sorority. She saw a jaunty figure, "a symphony in brown" coming towards her. It was Clyde Bauchle. Dressed from head to foot in what he still considered his most becoming color, and carrying a small bamboo cane, he was calculated to make any unsophisticated feminine heart stand still. That very morning a girl in the railway station had said so he could hear: "I love my husband, but oh, you!" And he was always hearing nice things like that. The girls just wouldn't keep away. When he saw Marie, instead of being distant like in the past, he smiled showing off his pearly white teeth, and holding out his immaculately gloved hand. He spoke pleasantly for a few minutes, but made no reference to Elphe or the past. Marie forgot her own desires, revenge now might be at hand. "I've just come from a visit to your former wife, Elphe. She's still dead in love with you; she's terribly unhappy with her new husband." At this Clyde straightened himself up, and showed his fox-like white teeth from ear to ear. "Why don't you go to see her some time when you're passing through her burg, she'd go crazy to see you." Clyde continued to show his teeth, but made no answer. He accompanied Marie to the steps of the house where the tea was held, paying her compliments, and asking if he might call.

When she got indoors among her friends they all crowded around her, asking the name of the handsome man with whom she was walking, for they had been peeping through the curtains. "He's a dream in brown," said one dark girl, rolling her eyes upward.

But Clyde did not call on Marie, nor had he any intention of so doing. He merely used her to get the information he desired about his former wife. He knew she still loved him, he would show this to her new husband very shortly. He kept smiling and showing his gleaming teeth like a fox in a well-filled hen-roost. He would take his time about visiting his former wife. He would let Marie send a letter as she surely would, telling her of the meeting, by making her wait it would cause her desire to see him to reach the boiling point. He had often been in the town where she lived, he knew her husband and his habits, by repute, very well.

While Marie expected him to upset the connubial bliss, she never dreamed the scheme that evolved itself in his head. Six weeks passed, he waited to make his move like the human fox that he was. Every day he tarried the more sweeping his success would be.

At length the day arrived, and he dropped off the train in Elphe's town about one o'clock in the afternoon. He sauntered down the main street, looking boldly into the windows of the big emporium with the sign "Cresson and Son" above the door — the concern which the unsuspecting bridegroom inherited from his father, and which he now conducted with such marked ability. Every woman who passed turned around and looked after him; he was surely a ladies' man *par excellence*.

He turned into the shady street which led along the river bank. Birds were singing in the old elms and maples, the air was sweet with the scent of newly-cut grass and old-fashioned flowers. Old colored gardeners were working in some of the ample yards. The river sparkled in the afternoon sunlight; beyond the rolling fields on the opposite shore, the dim lines of the White Deer Mountains loomed like mediaeval battlements against the horizon. All was so peaceful, so still, so serene, so sweet, not like the field for a sordid episode by any means. He reached the comfortable brick mansion. A fountain was playing in the yard, there were many beds of hyderangias about the well-kept lawn. Old maples and lindens along the sidewalks drooped heavy shade over the premises.

On the piazza, in a red hammock lay Elphe, attired in a sky blue filmy gown, fanning herself, and reading a novel. She heard the front gate open, she looked up, beholding the idol of her dreams. With a pretty twist of her dainty skirts, a quick motion to adjust her tangled hair, she was on her feet, and came running forward to meet him. Clyde took off his inevitable derby hat, and shook her by the hand, smirking and showing his glistening teeth with all the effusiveness inherent to ill-bred men. He did not mince words. "I have come to take you away with me," he began. "You cannot be happy with anyone but me. I am sorry I let you go that time in Philadelphia."

Elphe, who looked just as beautiful and young, and like a baby-doll, as she did the eventful meeting-night in Patriot Square, beamed into his eyes saying: "Yes, yes, I knew you would come for me. First love is the only love that lasts." He made a move as if to clasp her in his arms, but she motioned to him to come up the steps, indoors. They sprang up the steps, and were inside in a jiffy. The heavy ground-glass door shut with a bang, they were together in the dark hall. Elphe, crazed with delight, threw her arms around the traveling man's neck, he was not a tall man; holding on to him with a grip of iron, she rained kisses on his eyes, cheeks, forehead, mouth indiscriminately.

Clyde showing his teeth, and with unstable eyes ablaze with passion, was trying to talk. At length he stammered: "Get your things at once and board the first trolley that passes the door for Derrstown. I'll follow on the next car and meet you there. We can get a team and cross the river in time to get the four-forty express east from Sunbury. When that husband of yours comes home from the store, he will find he has the nest all to himself."

Elphe kissed and kissed him again, and whispered: "I don't want to carry anything except my money and jewelry, which will fit easily in my vanity bag." She ran upstairs, flung on a long automobile coat, jammed on her pretty head a small bonnet very like the baby-cap of Patriot Square days, collected her jewelry and money, and rushed down again. With a parting caress and kiss, she ran out the door, down the tar-pebble path, just in time to board the car. Twenty minutes later Clyde was on another car bound in the same direction. As it jolted along he began to do some thinking. "I'll only keep her a week, and then I'll skip; she can go back to her folks. I only want to show that guy she married who's the *whole show*."

At six-fifteen Walton Cresson reached his home. The German servant girl who had been taking a nap all afternoon knew nothing of her mistress' whereabouts. A novel, "Anna Karenina," a box of chocolates, and a fan were found by the red hammock on the porch. Upstairs the bureau drawers were in a state of disarray; all the jewelry was gone. But the grief-stricken husband did not suspect that she had gone off with Clyde Bauchle, her former husband. She might be at Lewis' Lake with friends resting from domestic cares.

It was only when six days later he received a telegram from her from New York saying she was stranded there and penniless that the truth began to dawn on him. Kind and just that he was, the affair struck him with horror and disgust. When he composed a reply, it read: "Can do nothing for you. Have communicated with your parents; they may send for you."

XXI. The White Deer

(Story of Kettle Creek.)

It was the first day of "trout season" at the Ox Bow. The weather was decidedly disagreeable with gusts of bitter wind and cold rain. The skeleton arms of the dead hemlocks along the creek rattled in the icy blasts. Probably because of the near approach of dinner-hour half a dozen rubber-coated fishermen had gathered in the bar-room of Jim Hamersley's hotel. Most of them were liberal, convivial fellows from Williamsport and Sunbury. They were lavish with the treats they bestowed upon the "natives" who were idling about the place. The news seemed to spread in some mysterious manner, as a steady stream of mountaineers flocked down from the high peaks, to share in the largess. At the last "round" before dinner was announced, thirty-three men by actual count lined up at the bar. But the genial railroader who footed the bill never winced.

Outside on the porch-bench sat old Jakey Van Alen, a wooden-bucket, with a burlap tied over it at his feet. The bucket was filled with magnificent trout, which he had caught before daylight; these he might present to some unfortunate angler, for a gift in return.

The frequenters of the desolate backwoods hotel were easy to get acquainted with, and all were eager to tell their hard luck stories. Summed up their plaints were pretty much the same. They all related to the passing of the lumbering industry in the narrow valley, which left them stranded with homes or farms which they could not dispose of. They were mostly middle-aged men, of many different races, New Englanders, New Yorkers, Irishmen, Germans, Pennsylvanians, as they lived in what would be called a "new country." But at any rate all the natural resources of this "new country" had vanished in a third of a century or less.

Old Lew Phoenix was loudest in his complaint. "We could have lumbered in these mountains for a hundred years if it hadn't been for the Goodyears. We did it slowly, and while we marketed one crop of logs, another was growing. Now those big millionaires put narrow gauges into every hollow, and on every mountain top, and skinned out every stick of timber in ten years. Then the fires went through and we had trouble even to save our homes. Some of us did lose our barns and crops. After the fires there wasn't even an animal left to trap; why you can travel a day and never see a chipmunk."

The younger men had deserted the lonely valley, for the most part going to work on the railroads, but the old folks were stranded in the desert with their real estate. But these same men had gladly welcomed the "big lumbermen" if they would be frank enough to admit it; they were all given work, occupation for their teams, market for their hay and produce at good prices — for a time. When the last log was whisked away, they found themselves stranded like whales on a beach. No wonder they would walk miles to imbibe a little conviviality and a chance to unload their burden of sorrows.

The gaunt bartender kept piling wood into the huge whitewashed stove, but even at that the atmosphere was damp and penetrating. After the dinner the fishermen hated to go back to the frigid creek; a couple of them were already conversing in undertones with Jakey Van Alen.

Back of the stove during all this busy scene sat an old man with a long blonde beard turning white. He was of handsome appearance, despite his incessant tobacco chewing. He sat rigid as a statue with hands folded across his knees, watching the gay kaleidoscope. He always refused to line up at the bar, but once accepted with evident gratitude, a paper of tobacco. He had clear blue eyes, high cheek bones, an aquiline nose, his might have been the face of a painter or a poet. It seems a pity when men do not live up to their faces, for a noble countenance has the possibilities of world power. A man with an ignoble face, a short nose, try as he may, can never be any greater than the salary he draws — except in his own estimation. Here Nature sometimes lowers a rosy curtain and he sees himself pictured among the great.

One of the fishermen evidently accepted Jakey's liberality, for he got in the stage, plus a basket full of fine trout, and started for the railroad. The others returned to the Creek. The idlers separated in groups of two or three. A dozen of them walked over the bridge to where another of their kind with much misdirected *superfluous* energy was chopping down a superb white pine which stood across the road from the little white church. The few idlers who still lingered about the bar fell to discussing deer hunting, how under the present laws these animals were rapidly increasing in their region. "It's too bad," remarked one, "that they're getting so much smaller. In the old days the stags were twice the size, had much bigger antlers, were wilder and gamer. Now and then we'd run across a white deer; it always took a silver bullet to lay him out. By spring the hide would turn grey; that was why we were sure that white deer were linked with the devil himself."

We asked if any of those present had seen a white deer; they all had, and one or two had shot them. "They weren't much satisfaction after you killed them; their meat went bad in a night, their hides would turn grey." This interesting information caused one of the fishermen, who had re-entered the bar-room, to order another round of drinks.

After that, as the afternoon was getting late, all left the room except the bartender, who began to doze against the sideboard, and the old patriarch back of the stove. We sat beside him, and asked him if he had done much hunting. He answered slowly, with a decided German accent; evidently he was a foreigner. "Yes, I've hunted a good deal" he said. "I got here when the wild pigeons were so plentiful that their flights darkened the sun. I was here before the last elk was killed by Jimmy Jacobson, when there were still wolves, panthers, otters, fishers, and wolverines. I never killed an elk, but I've brought in most everything else. Now if there's an otter on the whole length of the creek I don't know of him; there may be a fox or two, a few raccoons and groundhogs. The forest fires and the bounties wiped out all the wild life; a few got what belonged to all our citizens. I had a queer experience with a white deer, soon after I came into this wilderness forty years ago. All the big timber was standing then, but I cut a little hole in it, and there I lived happily for a while. All kinds of game was so numerous it was looked upon as a nuisance. I didn't feel that way, as I was born in the old country, in Bohemia, where we were taught to value it. Late one afternoon in Spring - I know it was early in the season for the skunk cabbages had just come out - I was in my little garden, pulling up old roots, and setting things to rights generally for the planting. Something caused me to look up from my work, and I saw, standing on the far side of my log fence, a beautiful white fawn. It was a doe, and had soft brown eyes like a gazelle, though most of our old hunters in this valley say a white deer must have pink eyes. It kept looking at me and wasn't a bit shy, so I decided it wanted to be fed. I went in the house and brought out a piece of bread, some sugar and a few nice cabbage leaves. The white fawn stretched its neck across the fence and ate as if it was hungry; then to my surprise, it licked my hands. I stroked its pretty head, then it trotted off into the forest. I decided not to say anything about it to my friends, as they would only try to shoot it; even though they knew no one could eat a white deer's flesh. By keeping my own counsel, I had no trouble at all. The deer returned every afternoon at the same time, becoming a great pet. It could not be coaxed across the fence, but I was satisfied to see as much of it as I did.

I kept a couple of cross wolf-dogs at that time, but for some reason they took to the fawn, and would not tongue at its approach. If a Canada lynx was within half a mile of my cabin they would set up a terrific howl, there was no holding them when a wolf was nigh. But they wagged their tails, and frisked around the garden like puppies at sight of my deer. The deer had no fear of them; it seemed like a regular "happy family." Even my six-toed cat, which I kept for good luck, became friendly with the deer.

Where it came from, and why it had no companions was always a source of surprise to me; I devoted much thought to the subject. It always came at the same hour, and towards the last of summer this happened to be at dusk. It made a pretty picture coming so white and pure out of the gloomy pinewood. Under kind treatment and plenty of food it seemed to grow; I believe it

Susquehanna River and Indian Island, near Lock Haven, PA.
Photo by H. W. Swope

was twice as big in September as it had been the day it first appeared to me. On account of my interest in that deer the summer passed rapidly; despite my hard work, I had felt lonely ever since I left the old country, now I was contented. I felt happier just to feed it than to spend my evenings down at the post office for there was no hotel in those days. I was beginning to feel that a pioneer's life wasn't so bad after all.

One afternoon I was busy getting in my potatoes, heavy frost had been predicted, but I kept an eye out for my deer. At her coming I would drop everything for a few minutes; she always gave me more strength to finish my day's work than if I hadn't seen her. At about the regular time that afternoon I looked up. To my bewilderment, instead of the white deer, there stood on the opposite side of the fence, my old sweetheart, Berthe Kersteins, whom I had left in Bohemia, with her hands stretched out to me. I dropped my hoe, and bounded to the fence, for I was a lively young chap in those days. The figure of the young girl had not stirred, but her lips were moving as if she was trying to say something. I stopped a moment to listen, I could not catch a word, so I started to climb the fence. There was a sweet smile in the girl's lovely brown eyes, evidently she was glad to see me, but her lips kept moving pitifully. Just as my hands clasped hers — they felt like real flesh and blood — she faded away into nothing. I sank down on the fence, heartbroken and exhausted. The sudden realization came over me that my loneliness had been for her, that the presence of the white deer had made my situation tolerable. As soon as my head felt better I clambered off the fence, and ran headlong into the forest, in the direction I imagined she must have vanished. I don't know how far I ran, but it was pitch dark when breathless, I was compelled to halt. I lay down in a heap, and could not get up until daybreak. When I did arise, I dragged myself, a shadow of my former self, back to my shanty. My mind was flooded with an awful tide of retribution and remorse. I saw everything clearly now.

Fifteen years before I had left my native village, full of high hopes as to what I was to accomplish in the new world, the land of the free. I had promised my sweetheart that as soon as I provided a little home, I would send for her, and we would be married. All the way across the ocean I danced and sang, I was so full of life, so sure I would win my way. The first sight of New York chilled my dreams. It looked as old and weary and heartless as anything I had left behind. I found vested interests, class distinctions, injustice, poverty, just as in the old world. I even had a difficult time to get employment. It was hard to exist, let alone to think of providing a home. I heard life was easier in Philadelphia, so I tramped there, but found the inevitable struggle. To Pittsburg I next beat my way, and I wasted my best years in the blast furnaces.

My letters to Berthe had been fewer and less hopeful; hers were always full of love and confidence. She did not know.

After ten years of misery, including several accidents, and discouragement, I learned of the wilderness in Northern Pennsylvania. There land could be had almost for the asking, there were no classes, no taskmasters, there was a living for all. When I left Pittsburg I resolved to cut myself off from my sweetheart, at least until I would find if what I heard was true, I could provide a home. When I reached the wilderness I found it just as promised, hut the task was a terrible one to clear enough ground on which to erect a shack. I now decided not to write until I had the ground cleared and planted, the house erected. For a year I lived in a lean-to of hemlock boughs, subsisting mostly off the animals and birds I killed, wild fruits and berries. When I did put up my shanty I surveyed it with disgust. Was this the best I could do after twelve years' toil in the new world, the land of the free!

I postponed writing until I got a better house, but as time wore on I became selfish and indifferent. I decided not to write at all; Berthe had doubtless forgotten me during my two or three years' silence, had most likely married some one else. I cut her out of my mind and heart, yet I was frightfully lonely. Thus it is that the struggle for existence dulls our loftiest instincts. I had never identified her as the cause of my loneliness until I saw her vision standing outside my garden fence that autumn evening.

When I returned to my shanty with much difficulty I unearthed some writing paper — I had not written a letter to a soul in five years. The last letter I wrote was to a poor girl in Pittsburg, returning five dollars she had loaned me, when I was in distress. In my letter to my beloved Berthe I poured out my heart, explained my disappointments and poverty; I begged her forgiveness; I stated I would enclose an order to pay her passage to America. When she reached New York she should write me and I would go there and accompany her to my mountain home. As a postscript I told her of my vision, could she have been thinking of me at that time?

I tramped down the mountain path to the little post office — Leidy — named probably for the famous Pennsylvania scientist, and asked my good friend, Abner Brooks, the postmaster, to get me a money order the next time he went to the county town. I left the letter and the money with him. I returned to my clearing just at dusk. I looked in vain for the vision of Berthe, or even the white deer. On the next evening I watched, but saw nothing, and so on for many weary evenings. Winter came on, I was lonelier than ever, yet when I thought I should be getting a reply to my letter, that would cheer my most dejected moments.

I often visited the post-office, and one evening a letter was handed me. It was from Bohemia, but it wasn't Berthe's handwriting. I opened it in the office, I was so excited, I couldn't wait. To my sorrow the unused money order fell out on the floor. "Dear friend" it read, "We are sorry to inform you that Berthe is dead. She died of a broken heart only last September 30, she could wait for you no longer. We are glad you have prospered. Karl and Lena." These were the names of my sweetheart's parents. The poor girl had probably died the afternoon when she appeared to me in the forest; the white deer was her fading spirit.

Like one struck on the head I staggered from the office. I saw no more of the white deer; but I made myself an old man slaving in the lumber camps."

Appendix A.

"A Frontiersman's Diary" is of course an imaginary composition, although it has a basis of fact. It is putting into diary form the story of the signing of the historic Pine Creek Declaration of Independence as told to the writer by the late Jacob Quiggle, Esquire (1821-1911) of Pine Station, Clinton County, Pennsylvania, whose grandfather, Philip Quiggle (1745-1800), was one of the signers. While most of those whose names were affixed to the document resided near the mouth of Pine Creek, the scene of the actual signing was within the palisade of Fort Horn, on the opposite side of the River, on the banks of Curts' Run so it should be really called the Fort Horn, or even the Curts' Run Declaration of Independence. The story of the burying of the signed document inside the stockade is undoubtedly correct, and with diligent investigation might be unearthed. Philip Quiggle, the relator of these incidents, was a native of Cumberland County, but settled in what is now Clinton County as early as 1773. The land which he obtained by right of conquest from the Indians, is still in the possession of his descendants. He revisited Cumberland County in 1777, and being an ardent patriot, enlisted in the army of the Colonists, eventually serving as Ensign in Capt. John Hamilton's Company, Col. Samuel Lyon's Regiment, Cumberland County Associators.